Havers & Blethers

An Anthology
by
The Red Book Writers

Contact: redbookproductions@hotmail.co.uk

Published by

Cauliay Publishing & Distribution
PO Box 12076
Aberdeen
AB16 9AL
www.cauliaybooks.com

First Edition
Edited by Sharon Hawthorne

ISBN 978-0-9558992-9-4
Copyright © The Red Book Writers
Cover design. Ian Beattie
Illustrations. Amy McMillan

A CIP catalogue record for this book is available from the British Library.

For Graeme

Cheers!

Contributors

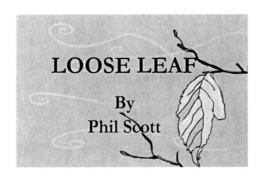

LOOSE LEAF

By
Phil Scott

There was still quarter of an hour before the train was due to arrive – then depart. Grasping his holdall tightly, Rob left the agreeable warmth and disagreeable company of the crowded waiting room to make his way to the furthest bench on the platform.

There were a few people standing under the main body of the station but the strengthening autumn wind would carry the tell-tale smell from his grass joint in the opposite direction. Placing the holdall between his feet, Rob turned his back for the shelter, eventually managing to get the joint lit. The smoke collected in his mouth before he quickly forced it down into his lungs, held it and then exhaled, the exhalation turned into a cough and he spat a glob of phlegm into the dry leaves that rattled along the grey concrete.

The BING BONG preceding a tannoy announcement startled him. It was hard to make out exactly what the voice said but Rob gathered that it didn't concern his travel arrangements. He settled back into the unaccommodating bench, pulling on the joint. The wind funnelled through the station blowing ash and smoke into his eyes, causing them to water.

Rubbing his eyes with the heel of his hand, Rob's vision cleared. A false ceiling of badly bruised cloud hove down on the city skyline. Lowering his gaze, he focused on the tree standing opposite outwith the station wall.

The wind buffeted the tree. Its branches yielding then returned. Random leaves were torn from twigs, carried and then dropped, scattering out of sight. Taking another hungry draw, Rob selected an individual leaf and watched.

Despite the wind's insistence, the leaf seemed determined to cling on, fluttering and flapping like a ragged flag. Yet this determination might have been part of the leaf's struggle to free itself, rather than remain. Perhaps it was the tree that retained its grip, keeping the connection from trunk to branch to twig to leaf. Either way, the wind would not be denied. With a final ripping tug it achieved its aim. Rob's leaf left. There was a slight pause at the moment of separation as if, at the very moment when it was too late, the leaf had changed its mind.

Whatever the reason for the pause, it didn't matter. It had gone. Rob finished the joint, flicked the roche onto the track and stood up, his holdall in his hand. His train was due and it was time to go.

LORD ASKUM OF STRATHBOOGLE
by
Jennifer Shand

"Jeeves, Jeeves, where are you man? Can't you see that I need you to pour my cream onto my porridge? Oh, you're not Jeeves, where is he? Who are you?"

"Your Lordship, he left at the weekend. I'm your new butler. Your wife hired me yesterday."

"Oh, I suppose you will have to do. Now, let's get this straight I always call my staff by their surnames. I've never liked this habit of over familiarity. What's your name then?"

"James Darling, Sir."

"Ah, James, pour me my cream then, and pass me the brown sugar too. Once I have eaten breakfast, I want you to inform the groom that I will be going out for a ride on Black Bess, and to get her saddled up."

"Yes, my Lord."

I'm not sure if I have made the right move here. Yes I needed a job quickly, but it always worries me when staff suddenly leave with no real explanation. The agency just told me that I was needed at Boogle House in Strathboogle. I'd never heard of the place and had to Google Strathboogle. Lady Askum was very convincing when she said that Jeeves had left as his mother was very ill. I suppose once I get talking to the other staff things might become clearer.

"James! Where are you? I need you in the dining room to clear away the dishes, and then I need you to switch on the shower and get me my riding clothes."

"Yes, my Lord."

"Ah, very well my man, get on with it."

I can get a cup of coffee and some toast too, now that the Laird has gone for his ride. Hopefully I'll meet more of the staff as well. I only met the cook yesterday briefly before she finished for the night. I must thank her for leaving me the most wonderful game pie and clootie dumpling for tea. Maybe with the right questions I can find out why Jeeves left. Somehow I don't think his mother is ill.

"Good morning James, did you manage to get a good night's sleep?"

"Oh hello cook, yes I did, and thank you for the most wonderful supper."

"Not a problem James; let me introduce you to the rest of the staff. I'm Mrs Bridges; everyone calls me Annie, except the Laird. I'm obviously head of the household and I don't like being crossed. John Baird the Chauffeur-cum-handy man forever known as Logie and Rose Marie the housemaid. She's very quick on her feet and needs to be when the Laird is about. He's a bit too keen on the ladies. Richard the Groom is out with the Laird, probably galloping along the river, hoping that the Laird will fall in. The garden is looked after by Harry and Donald Smith, sons of our retired gardener Bert Smith and very loyal to the Laird. No doubt they may see the error of their ways yet!"

"Hello, nice to meet you all. I'm James Darling the new butler, but you probably all know that already. What I want to know is what the Laird is really like. And more to the point why did Jeeves leave in such a hurry?"

"Well James, nice to meet you too. As Annie said in the introductions I'm Logie. To be honest we were surprised that Jeeves lasted as long as he did. Eight months, that's the record so far. You do realise you are Butler number four in the past year? The Laird is a law unto himself and he can be very demanding. What do I mean by can? No, he is always demanding. "Baird, take me to the shops," and halfway there it's: "No I meant the Garden Centre," which is in the opposite direction. He always goes to the Café for a tea and cream scone. For a month or so Annie was getting worried for her job as she thought that her cooking wasn't good enough. After a while I figured it out, and was able to tell cook that it wasn't the cream teas that enticed him there, it was the scone maker, Mrs. Smith."

"I was relieved about that, but was worried that Lady Askum would find out."

"It's ok Annie, the way he chases me around the house, I'm sure that her Ladyship knows what he's like."

"You're probably right Rose Marie, but I don't want to be the one to tell her."

"What have I let myself in for? It looks like we have a randy old git as a boss, his wife knows and puts up with his strange and annoying ways and will continue to pretend that she and we do not know what is being played out in front of us. Well I'm here now, so I'd better get on with it."

"I suppose its ok for us as we get paid to be here, she doesn't."

"Very charitable of you Rose Marie, but every time Lady Askum comes into the kitchen for our weekly menu planning session I want to ask her why she is still here with the old trout."

"Can't bring yourself to call him a git can you?"

"Oh hello Richard, if you're back it means the Laird must be."

"Yes he is, but he's spending some time with his dogs at the stables before coming back into the house. You must be the new butler. Have we started taking bets yet as to how long he will stay Annie? I'm Richard Headly the groom. So what's your name?"

"James Darling and if that's the Laird back I need to pour a bath for him now. I suppose that will be me busy till lunchtime."

"The Laird likes his lunch at 12 noon prompt. Staff lunch is at 1pm, give or take whenever the Laird finishes his dessert. Lady Askum is out today with her mother Lady Amile Hesky and won't be back until dinner."

I'd better get this bath run; luckily I had presence of mind to lay out his day clothes after he went for his ride. But why he has four tweed suits in the same check I'll never understand. It must be a landed gentry's thing as they all seem to do it. The longer I'm here the quicker I understand why Jeeves left. He must have put up with a lot of grief before it became too much. Now I'm the fourth butler in a year, oh dear this is not looking good at all. Lady

Askum seems nice enough, but no doubt puts up with a lot more than she should.

"James, James, where are you? Why have you put green bubble bath in when it's blue on a Monday? Tuesday is green, Wednesday is red, Thursday is purple, Friday is white, Saturday is pink and Sunday is a Butter Ball Bath Bomb. Don't you know anything?"

"Sorry my Lord, I will pour another bath."

"No it's too late now and the old boiler won't allow another one today, but I'll be confused for the rest of the week you know, I will have to manage I suppose."

Argh, it's not going to be easy. If he keeps coming up with stuff like that I will either kill him or myself, I'm not sure which yet. Note to self, place bubble bath in order of the day of the week, and write it down somewhere, just in case Rose Marie moves anything.

Oh this is going to be so much fun. I'm not sure if I will add myself to the betting list as to how long I'm going to stay. Better see what the odds are!

"James, bring me my towel, the blue one for a Monday. Um, no, bring me the green one since you put the wrong colour bubble bath in. It had better be warm; none of this cold and not ironed stuff."

"Yes, Lord Askum"

It's going to be a long day, I just know it. I'd better check with Rose Marie as to where I find the colour coded laundry. It was so much easier working for Lord and Lady Heskwith, they may have been old school but at least they weren't barking mad. I wonder if they would take me back? Perhaps not, as I believe they got a new butler when they moved from Blair Drummer to Havant in England. Anyway, I didn't particularly want to go that far south, a couple of miles to Hayling Island and then you're off the end of England and into the sea.

I digress, back to my situation now.

"James, where are my black shoes?"

"At the end of your bed."

"Ah yes, there they are. Where are my glasses?"

"On the top of your head."

"So they are. Tell my wife I'm going to the shops and tell Logie we're going to the garden centre."

"Logie, the Laird wants to go to the garden centre, but if you see his wife you're taking him to the shops."

"Ok James, I don't like lying to Lady Askum but it should be alright as Annie said that Lady Askum was away to her mother's for the day and she left after breakfast. We are usually half an hour at the centre, that will give you time to set the table for lunch, although he's never very hungry after a visit to see Mrs. Smith, and he always comes back to the car looking flushed. Make of that what you will."

"Oh I get your drift Logie, how long has that been going on? Is that the same Smith as the two gardeners?"

"It's been going on for at least 19 years, and yes the twins are Mrs. Smith's sons. They celebrated their eighteenth birthday last week."

"The penny is dropping very loudly here, are you sure Lady Askum and more to the point Mr. Smith don't know?"

"I'm not sure, but if they know they've kept it quiet. The boys certainly don't know that old Lord Askum is dearest daddy. They are not the brightest light bulbs in the chandelier, but they are excellent gardeners and lovely people."

I've yet to meet these two boys, I wonder what they will be like? Will they look like Askum himself or not. I wonder if I will be able to keep quiet? I think I may just take a wander over to the garden to get some fresh flowers for the vases.

"Hello, hello, is there anybody here?"

"Over here in the cabbage patch."

"Oh you must be the new butler? I'm Harry, and this is my brother Donald. Welcome to Strathboogle. Planning on staying long, then?"

"Yes, I'm the new butler, James Darling. What is it with this place that the butlers don't stay long? Mind you, I'm beginning to figure it out. I won't be leaving yet as I've just arrived and anyway I like a challenge."

"Aye, Lord Askum could be called a challenge, amongst other things."

"Now Donald, that's not a nice impression of the Laird you're giving to Mr. Darling."

"Harry, that wasn't an impression, you know I can't do impressions. Jokes, yes; James, what do you call a Frenchman in sandals? Philippe Fillope."

"Very good Donald, but can you gents tell me which flowers I need to pick for Lady Askum, and where they are?"

"Ah, anything from the greenhouse. Lady Askum likes everything we grow, but the Laird doesn't pay too much attention to what's on the table unless it's food. If her ladyship walked in to the Dining room naked, apart from some strategically placed flowers, he wouldn't notice, but if she lay on the table covered in fruit, he'd be asking for the cream!"

"Thanks Harry, I'll head over to the greenhouse and get organised with the flowers. See you later Donald."

Oh dear, why did I compliment Donald on his joke telling, I'm now setting myself up for all his future attempts at humour. Jings, is that the time? I had better get a move on, or the Laird will be home, and the table's not set yet. I'm still not convinced that I've made the right move, but needs must and all that jazz.

"James, Logie has just called to say that they are leaving the garden centre, which means they'll be here in 10 minutes."

"Thanks Annie, I'll only need to get a fresh jug of water for the table and I'm done. Does Logie call you every time?"

"Yes he does, which helps greatly. The Laird is always impressed that meals are on the table as soon as he arrives back, he thinks I'm psychic. Far be it from me to explain to him about mobile phones. Any which way, it is Scotch Broth and mince and tatties. For pudding it's jelly, fruit and ice cream. Our lunch is the same today."

"Sounds good to me and I'm looking forward to it."

"Lord Askum, lunch is served."

"Where is my wife James, will she be joining me?"

"No Sir, she is away for the day with Lady Hesky."

"Oh, she never seems to be here anymore. Ah well, more of Mrs. Bridges' wonderful cooking for me. After lunch I will have a nap in the Library and I want you to wake me at 2pm as I want to walk the dogs around the grounds."

"Yes my Lord."

At last I can get some lunch and some peace and quiet away from the Laird's incessant demands. Hello Annie, hello Richard. Ooh the broth smells nice. I will certainly be having some of that.

"James, James, did you hear about the two aerials that fell in love and got married. The ceremony was rubbish, but the reception was wonderful."

"Hello Donald, do you ever stop telling jokes?"

"Only when I'm with my girlfriend, she's not too keen on them, she is a twin as well. I'm meeting her tonight to go to the pictures."

"So is it twins going out with twins?"

"Funnily enough, yes."

"Donald, do they ever play jokes on you and Harry, like pretending to be each other."

"No James, we would know as they are not identical. Jilly has long blond hair and Josh has a beard."

Oh boy, talk about putting your foot in it. But then again, how was I supposed to know, no wonder Annie and Richard were smiling so much. It's almost 2pm I had better go and wake the Laird. I don't suppose he will be any less grumpy.

"Lord Askum, it's 2pm, you asked me to wake you."

"Humph, well then have you got the dogs ready? And why haven't you changed into your outdoor clothes?"

"Your Lordship, I wasn't aware that I had to. I can speak to the groom to arrange for the dogs to be brought to you, but why do I need to come with you on this walk? Wouldn't your Factor be a better person to go with you to check on all your land and buildings?"

"Probably; but, it's his day off and I want you to be with me for company so I can show you around my domain. Plus I employ you, and you will do as I say."

"I will get changed Sir, but I am doing this under duress as this does not come under my duties as a butler."

I think tonight I will be packing my bag and leaving, it's a shame as I really like Lady Askum and all the staff, even Donald's dodgy jokes. But how anyone can put up with his behaviour is beyond me. After the Port has been poured and he's settled down with his beloved dogs, I can quietly leave out the back door. I'll speak to Richard to see if he can give me a lift to the station, and ask him for discretion. I must leave a note for Annie and for Lady Askum that's only fair. Four hours to go, I can manage that.

"Lord Askum, your wife will not be joining you for dinner as she has decided to stay overnight at her mother's, she will be returning tomorrow in time for lunch. Would you care to come to the dining room now as dinner is served?"

"I'm on my way James, have you remembered the English mustard for the table? None of this French foreign stuff."

"Yes."

"Thank you James, please tell cook that the steak was magnificent and that I am ready for my pudding. James why have you brought the cheese knife before the pudding has been eaten? Have you forgotten all your training?"

"It's too late your Lordship; I've had enough of your demands. Different coloured bubble baths and corresponding towels on different days, expecting me to do duties which do not come under my remit as a butler. Your indifference towards me and the other staff is appalling. Is it any wonder I'm the fourth butler in a year? Before I kill you, please pick up the sponge and start eating it. Do remember that this knife is very sharp."

"James, not my late grandmother's Ivory handled cheese knife!"

"Be quiet. Now pour the custard over your head, the mixed fruit salad too. Don't forget the cream. Keep eating that sponge"

"James, are you mad? Don't you walk away from me, come back into this room at once. You know I won't be trifled with!"

GHOUL BUSTERS
by
Amanda Gilmour

The white paint, dusted with grime and splattered with mud should have been unobtrusive, incognito, but as it drove through the village it was noticed by every person who laid eyes on it.

In a village this small, where everyone's families had grown up together since its founding, that was to be expected. Everyone knew everyone else's business, in the nicest way possible, for though they were short on gossip they had a true respect and love for their fellow man (unlike in bigger towns).

The white van crew came here expecting to be seen. Their reconnaissance on both basic and hacker levels had come up with almost nothing. As far as Google maps were concerned this village didn't exist.

The van drove onto the pavement outside a small but obviously still used chapel and came to a halt. A stocky man with black hair shaved in a military cut jumped out, immediately lighting a cigarette and taking a few draws as the side door slid open.

"No friggin' car park," the smoker muttered. "Why the hell is there no car park?"

"I think you'll find everything's walking distance from here, genius," a woman said as she got out the back. She nodded at the cemetery crawling out the side of the church, ancient grey headstones fading to terracotta to black a few metres away from them. "And no cussin' in front of the dead."

She swept her long black hair up and wrapped it round her hand and into a bun-like creation at the back of her head in seconds.

Two men now got out the van, one from the passenger seat, the other the same way to woman had. The two men looked like polar opposites. The one from the back appeared to be the youngest of the lot – an illusion created by his loose jeans, converse hi-top trainers and messy hair. You would never tell by looking that he was the resident techno whiz. Even the glasses didn't give it away. As he jumped out he was working with what looked like a hybrid between an iPhone and a Blackberry.

The man from the front seat walked round the van, his black boots silent on the pavement, trench coat swirling softly behind him. He stopped in the middle of the group, eyeing the church's door, windows and a sign announcing the theme for the service two weeks ago along with a community bulletin. "The church doubles up as town hall."

"Convenient," the girl smiled. "Good job we're not the demonic ones around here or we'd be screwed."

"Quit the wise-assing Kealey. Time to meet whoever's in charge of here."

"You said it boss, but I think we're underdressed, it is Sunday after all."

Ignoring her now, the group walked up the small gravel path. Bright pansies and timid snowdrops lined the earth along the concrete slab walkway.

The olive green door opened before the group and a short round man came to meet them. He was wearing an expensive looking suit and huge gold necklace across his shoulders. It was ornately designed with black stones in all the pieces. "Mayor Adams. So grateful you could come. Mrs Fogg called and said you were parking outside, which isn't a problem of course. Come in, come in Mr Smith."

"David will be fine Mayor Adams. Allow me to introduce my team," their leader said when they had finally maneuvered into the Mayor's office, which for some reason seemed to be the only room without a mass of animals in it. "Gus, tactical expert," Gus nodded once and went back to looking around the room. "Ferb, recon and tech."

"Did you know Mayor that as far as Satellites are concerned this town doesn't exist?"

"Yes, young man. It's the way we like it."

"Kealey's getting the teas in. She's our mythological expert."

"Mythological?"

"Yes. Did you have another explanation for why you would need us and not the regular police channels?" David asked.

"I...we..." Mayor Adams suddenly found the floor very interesting as he pulled and fiddled with his tie. "I..." A sigh. "We tried the police. They were..."

"Inexperienced?" Ferb piped up.

"Useless! Completely and totally useless! Wanted to interview *'all the known troublemakers,'* the town has a population barely over fifty people, we don't *have* any troublemakers! But they thought I was defending the culprits, so they poked around – in all the wrong places I would imagine – and set up some CCTV surveillance which showed nothing. Then they said they had bigger crimes to solve and I've been trying to get hold of them since!"

By the time he had finished the rant he was holding a cup, steam rising with elegant curls. "Thank you dear... excellent. One of the older boys had heard of you and said he would find out how to contact you. He gave me the number."

"That's all right Mayor," Kealey said, using a tone you normally would with a scared child. "This is going to be fine now. Getting rid of what the police can't is our job. You did the right thing. Now, tell us from the beginning..."

"Well?" David asked Kealey a few hours later. They were in the main hall, looking at cows that had been stuck in this room when they had arrived but were now milling around in the field outside. A border collie was trotting around on the outskirts of them. There were no calves and as a result the cows were ignoring the dog.

"They keep all the farm animals in here overnight, letting them go out in the close fields during the day for a few hours with two people watching each herd. Then they round them up and bring them all back in. The folks round here are keeping their cats on harnesses in the back garden so they don't wander off after dark....Cats. On harnesses....Mental."

"Actually I meant 'well, what did the Mayor say.' But what you said was...interesting."

Kealey smiled. "I would say he's telling the truth. Problem is he doesn't know much. A couple of people went missing a fortnight or so ago. Everyone noticed straight away because, you know...*no one lives here.* They did a search, found nothing, then the farmers realised some of the livestock was missing as well. The police came in, blamed kids killing the animals, the missing people running away; maybe forgetting to tell anyone about the holiday they're now on, the usual.

"The problem with what the Mayor has told me is it really doesn't help us figure out what the thing is. We think CCTV won't pick it up but that's about it. Some people have had a look at it but we just can't trust witness reports as hard evidence until we get a good a look at the thing ourselves. But as far as we know it hasn't fed in a week or so...that's why the animals are in here. And the cats are harnessed in gardens..."

"Can you get off the cats?"

"I'm trying to David.... I think firstly we need to get some thermal imaging on the streets for this evening. If this thing isn't coming up on video, a la Dracula, we might get some sort of heat signature from it.

"And while we're on the subject, why am I once again the tea and chat girl? I hate doing the comforting bit, you know that."

19

"Thermal imaging? Good thinking, I'll get Ferb on it. And there's no way anyone else is doing the comforting bit."

Thermal imaging is a type of infra-red imaging science. Also known as infrared thermography, thermo graphic imaging or thermal video, it uses the black body radiation law to detect and show temperatures of all objects and shows them on a thermograph camera. Due to the fact it shows the heat spectrum instead of the light spectrum, these cameras can be used where it would be too dark to use a regular camcorder. Incidentally, they can also detect certain creatures that for whatever reason are not detected by cameras, regardless of how bright it is. In English, it is a camera that picks up body temperatures and can work in the dark.

The rest of the afternoon was used setting up these cameras around the village, a task made a lot easier by its size. In the end they were finished with a few hours to spare before sundown. Kealey walked into the office, stopping behind Ferb. She watched him plugging cables into a handheld monitor for a minute before speaking.

"Almost done?"

"Yuuuuuup. It's looking good so far." He flicked some stray stands of hair out his face.

"I was wondering if you wanna go get some noms with me before dusk."

"Yeah, sure. What's going on over there?" Ferb motioned out the door where they could see the main hall. A couple of cows were milling about.

"Ahhh....Here be what is commonly known as a round-up. All the cows were put out to pasture and they now need to be brought back in. By going on a food run we will be conveniently out of the way while all this goes on."

"I see," Ferb put the monitor down on the Mayor's table. "Best be off then."

*

The monitors were a dull haze of blues, purples and blacks with the occasional cylinder of bright white indicating street lamps. The office stank of grease and vinegar. Nothing of interest was showing up as the four sat round different screens eating cooling chips.

Kealey leaned back on her chair, stared at the ceiling and prodded her chips with the little wooden fork.

"Focus people," David said, eyes never leaving his screen.

"Sorry boss," Kealey mumbled. "It's just hard looking at the same thing over and – WHAT THE! Sorry, branches just moved into shot."

Ferb sniggered into his coke before taking a gulp. His gaze wandered to the master TV which showed all the cameras at once.

"I have a question," Gus asked from his corner of the room. His monitor was also showing a series of purple to blue shapes with varying hazy sections. When no-one looked up or protested he continued.

"How do we know if this thing isn't showing up because the cameras aren't picking it up or because it hasn't come out to play?"

"Shit!" Kealey almost spat a mouthful of chips on her screen.

"Kealey?" David asked.

"FUCK!" A shrill ringing interrupted them. Kealey jumped, her swivel chair wobbling slightly. They all looked at the Mayor's phone, sitting in its rightful place, as always, waiting to be spoken to.

Before Ferb could finish saying, "No, don't pick it up yet." Kealey had it resting on her neck and shoulder, still watching her screen at an angle.

"Hello? Hello. No, it's not, I'm afraid he is indisposed at the moment. Yes. Kealey. Kee-Lee. Yes. I see." Kealey's eyes lit up in the dull room. "That's great! Sorry, I didn't mean it that way. We are working on it right now. Thanks. Thank you very much. Goodnight."

Kealey slammed the receiver down and wheeled her chair to her station, watching the other screens intently. She grabbed Ferb's arm to stop herself in front of her monitor.

The guys all watched her.

"That was Mrs Fogg. Gentlemen, we are about to find the answer to Gus' remarkably intelligent question."

There is a feeling you get when you watch something in silence that is unnerving. Films, TV and radio shows all use music to effect, creating in you the mood they want to portray. It is a subconscious reaction on your part, but once you are told about it you begin to realise how true it is. When watching a bad film you will be very aware of the pop music highs, melancholy orchestral lows, the lack of routine used in horror films, the dreary dull elevator music. When watching a good film, these very things are done in such a way that they pull you in, make you feel the way the character is feeling to the point where you forget to pay attention to the music. You are submerged completely and utterly in the piece.

To watch something and hear nothing in the background is almost unheard of in the world now. Vehicle traffic, chattering, birds chirping in the morning, even your house creaks from time to time when it's heating up or cooling down.

Even in the middle of nowhere there is noise in your peripheral.

Complete silence gives you the impression of an alien environment you have no control over.

For the four ghoul-busters to sit, eyes glued to their screens and hear nothing made them all uneasy. Anticipation of the reason they were in this tiny town made them all tense; the unknown about to be made known. If all was to go well.

"There," David said, nodding at his screen. Kealey jumped again and they all looked at the one screen.

It was showing up in hues of green with very slight tinges of yellow. It moved fluidly, like it wasn't touching the ground.

"It's not human," Kealey whispered, glancing quickly at all the monitors for anything else alive that might get in its way. There was nothing.

"'Figured that when it didn't come up on CCTV,'" Gus muttered under his breath.

"There was always the possibility it was a human who knew to avoid cameras. You know, like *ducking under them*. With these temp readings its core is far too cold. A human would be freezing to death. Humanoids come up orange to red. Ooh!" She leapt up out her chair and peered out the window. "It's coming up our street!"

Everyone but David joined her at the window, peering into the inky dark, illuminated at various spots by orange street lights.

A thud made David look up. A stack of papers was now in front of him.

"All the witness reports, they are in order of most to least helpful information for us to use. I made Gus help me, was I heck doing this on my own...Anyway, the reports all back up what we saw last night. Short, thin, creature, wearing full length clothing. Male. Long...hair." Kealey made a motion towards her head.

David had been the only one that hadn't seen the creature first hand. Its crown had waves of waist length hair that had been whipping around behind it like a cape. When it had walked past the church they had seen how straggly and unkempt it was, matted and clumped with dirt. Kealey glanced out at the main hall. "But still...there's something not right about all this. I can't place it."

"Don't worry; just keep doing what you're doing. We're on the clock now but the fact we got something last night is good."

"Yeah..."

"As long as they see us making progress it should be a relatively stress free removal."

"Yeah..."

"And it didn't get anyone else last night."

"Yeah...David, hold on," Kealey walked over to the main hall, where all the animals were out grazing again. A small girl was sitting in the middle of the room. Her brown hair was up in pigtails, tied back with pink bobbles that had plastic pictures on them. Cross-legged, she was in front of a turquoise and purple plastic machine that had drawers full of bits and pieces in it. The girl was thudding her doll into the floor.

"Hello," Kealey crouched down on the balls of her feet. "My name is Kealey."

The little girl looked up at her and smiled. "I'm Isla."

"Isla? That's a really pretty name. I like your bobbles."

"Thanks," Isla smiled and blushed. "They're Mitchie from Camp Rock. She's my favourite."

"Cool. Isla, honey, can I ask you a question?" Isla seemed to think about it for a minute, then, nodded her head. "Why were you hitting your doll on the ground?"

"Because," Isla looked nervous, far too nervous for a little girl. "Because she saw something that she didn't want to and I want it to go away."

"Isla, will you look at me please?" Kealey took her hands and smiled at her. "Me and my friends, we're here to make everything right again. I promise. I'm not going to force you to talk to me, but do you want to speak about it?"

This time the thud was a folder and the whole team was there to look up.

"I've got it guys. I know what we're dealing with," Kealey interlaced her fingers and stretched her hands out, pulled them above her head. They all looked at her.

"Have you done something to your hair?" Ferb asked her.

"Yeah," Kealey ran her hand through her hair, showing the streaks of pink. "Isla and I did them to each other. She's a cool kid. Because of her I figured this out."

"And?" Gus asked.

"Cailleach Bheur, both Irish and Scottish, is a 'divine hag.' Legend has it that she made the hills and mountains, with varying reports as to how she did it. She is seasonal, ruling from Samhuinn to Bealltainn. In Scotland she is also known Beira, Queen of Winter."

A lot of the supernatural can be linked to season, tides and the equinoxes so for this creature to be linked to the winter months was no surprise to the group.

"She rules from November 1st to March 1st?" Ferb asked. Kealey nodded. "Wait a minute…*She?*" Another nod. "But it's a male creature. All the reports said it's male. Hell, we all said it was male."

"That's true Ferb, with the shape of her body and the way she was moving everyone wrongly assumed she was male. Looking at those reports this morning something was bugging me but I couldn't figure it out until I noticed Isla outside. When I was speaking to her it clicked.

"Beira is also the mother of all gods and goddesses – can you imagine the power she would have wielded in the past? When all of this was just marshes and crofts, how much would she have done for all the Scots if they were willing to pay her price? I wouldn't want to piss her off and say she was ugly, would you? And the image of beauty has changed so much over the ages – robes, corsets, miniskirts it's always been changing. Maybe when Beira first crossed the world she was the ideal of beauty."

"Fair point," David nodded. "So how do we kill her?"

"That's the thing. I'm not sure if we can. It's not easy to kill a god, let alone the creator of gods. We're talking power off the scale of anything we've seen before. If Beira is at full power she will be bigger and stronger than everything we've killed put together. We have to find out where she's keeping herself during the day and hope to hell she isn't at full power. I think we have a good shot at it – her not being fully charged I mean. So far she isn't coming out during the day and if she was killing to feed or for some sort of ritual she hasn't had any supplies in a while."

"Good," David nodded. "Excellent work Kealey. So where is it hiding?"

"I have a theory on that too."

The four stood in a field just outside the town, ready for battle. They were dressed all in black, carrying weapons on their backs

25

and in holsters all across their bodies. Pockets held clips of ammunition full of bullets made of unusual materials – silver, lead, iron, wood. Different bullets for different weaknesses. The fireman helmets with caving torches attached looked out of place, sticking out garishly with their reflective bands.

They stood on grass a couple of inches long, flattened footprints trailing behind then to the van on the road. The grass hadn't been cut since everyone had starting hiding indoors and the road, although too narrow to have a van parked on it, had not been used in that time either. Road blocks had been put up around the area before the group had arrived for 'electrical and gas maintenance.'

They were standing around a large mound of stones that was in the centre of the field. It had always been there, so the townsfolk said. It had never bothered them (as you would expect from a pile of rocks) and they weren't bothered by the opening in the flat end of one side. They didn't feel its eerie pull as you looked at it and thought about what bogeyman could be lurking in there, waiting for you. Maybe this was because they had spent their teens egging each other on here. Maybe this was because the eerie presence had only recently moved in.

"A tumulus is a stone grave," Kealey told them as they stared at it. Calling it a grave didn't make it any less creepy. "They have various names and shapes depending on the culture… This one looks like an eyebrow dormer."

The laughter was nervous, the banter between the friends getting thinner. Eyes on the goal, they all knew this had the possibility to be the most dangerous mission they had ever experienced. They all silently prayed to themselves that Kealey had been right about everything.

Inside, the tumulus was dark, as expected, and damp. Gus took point, Kealey middle and David rear. Ferb stayed in the van, watching on a monitor and recording everything.

The light from Gus' helmet led the way. They were in a tunnel directly under the stone that could be seen above, but it went a lot further back, seemingly the length of the field.

"I wonder how many kids have ever had the guts to come down here." Gus whispered. Even without the present danger this was a place where you would never raise your voice.

"Who knows? If they did and survived it would mean she hasn't been here long."

They came to the end of the tunnel and were faced with a plain flat wall. The whole tunnel had been extremely dull, plain walled, unadorned. The opposite of what you would expect the creator of gods to dwell in.

"We're at the end of the tunnel Ferb. Do you still read?" David asked.

"Copy boss, everything's working fine up here and we have three hours until the sun begins to set," Ferb's voice was still clear in their earpieces. While they spoke Kealey was examining the walls. She looked along the tops, in the corners, searching for any -

"Bingo. I think I've found it."

There was a small stone sticking out of the mud wall. Touching it, a section of the wall pulled away, swinging out like a door. They had to double over to get through it. David did another check with Ferb and although his voice was slightly tinny they were all still in contact.

They were now in a stairwell. The steps were long enough for them to all walk down at once but, apart from that, were completely average. They still kept their formation as they walked down, noticing the walls were becoming more and more ornate as they went down. Every few minutes David would check in with Ferb but once they hit the bottom the monitors were no longer working. Ferb could hear them but not see what was going on. Gus turned the recorder in his helmet on. As point, he had the 'wide shot' that could be used to zoom in on specific things later and hopefully give the best view of everything that was going on.

The room they now stood in was illuminated by hundreds of

candles in alcoves. At the end of the room was an altar. There was a figure lying on it.

Dread filled Kealey, anticipation David, and Gus felt antsy as the adrenalin pumping through his body begged to be used.

They crept up to the altar slowly, Gus watching the altar, Kealey and David focused on the walls and their exit. The gold fixings, rough pictorials and candlelight made this more difficult.

They reached the altar finally and peered at Beira, divine hag, ancestral deity, deified ancestor, ugly as sin. She looked peaceful on the flat stone, dead.

They knew it was a lie.

Her arms were crossed over her chest, covering her heart. "I don't have a clear shot," Gus muttered, pointing his gun at her.

David kept his gun up as Kealey went around the back of the altar to pry the arms away.

BANG! David's gun was fired. Kealey whipped her head up to look at the back of the room, the stairs. Something was coming down them quickly, zipping left and right, almost too fast to see.

"Dammit!" David shouted as the gun clicked empty.

"Covered!" Kealey shouted and, dropping her current task, she started firing at the thing that had now jumped to the bottom of the stairs and was weaving towards them. While she fired David reloaded and in a second his arm was back up and he was aiming at the thing, missing it by millimetres as it dodged and dived. Gold streaked in front of their eyes as it ran back and forth.

The moment David had fired again Kealey had holstered the gun and pulled out one from her other side. She grabbed Beira's arm and yanked it. It was stiff with what you would call rigor mortis had she been either dead or human. Kealey yanked again and with a crack it came down, exposing her torso.

Once he had heard the arm break Gus had started shooting into her, making a giant gaping hole where the heart normally stays. Green and dark red oozed out, making a blackened colour that dripped down the side of the body and hid on their clothes.

At the same time this was happening, the creature attacking them had stopped and screamed an anguished: "Noooooooooooo!"

The group recognised the voice and gold streak they had seen before. Now that he was still they could see the ornate detail; the giant stones in each section of his Mayoral necklace.

Mayor Adams became even more aggressive. Fury curled his face, skewered his feature as he ran again, still fast but not the blur he had been before.

"He's just human!" Kealey shouted when she saw who it was. "Any bullets will kill him!"

While everyone else seemed to be screaming Gus was still working. Three rounds had made the crater in her chest, and as soon as they had left the barrel and another was chambered Gus turned it on her head, shooting until his clip went dry and there was just a pile if mush. He then ditched the gun and turned to fire at Beiras' accomplice.

It didn't matter what they used - lead, silver, wood. Now that Beira was dead anything would have an effect on the mayor and with her head blown to bits he was just a mortal again. Fire from three people stopped him in a matter of seconds.

With it over they walked over to check the Mayor's pulse. With the room cleared of any danger they holstered all their weapons, found the ones that had been dropped.

They were about to leave when another figure leapt from the stairs in front of them. Silver flashed off the candlelight as the machete he was wielding stopped in front of them. The knife handler was the only one with a weapon at hand.

"Anyone moves and I will behead you all," he told them. He smiled at them, taking them in, deciding what to do first when there was a small ping! And his face slackened. The three looked up and saw a starburst on his forehead. A couple more pings and his chest opened in a similar fashion. He slumped to the ground, machete glinting underneath him. Ferb was standing on the step behind him. He blew the barrel of his gun, silencer pointing up in the air and smiled.

"Your cavalry has arrived."

*

"I saw the Mayor from the van," Ferb told them all. The foursome was sitting in a circle in the main hall eating home-made shepherd pie and lemonade. Mrs Fogg had made it all from scratch as a thank you. The sun had recently begun to set, the sky that they could see from the open double doors blue with burnt orange clouds. Sitting with them were most of the townspeople, the children running about outside, playing fetch with the dogs and terrorising cows that were just happy be asleep on some grass. "He went in and then a few minutes later three guys went after him. I decided to follow them to see what the hell they were doing when they stop in front of the tumulus and pull out all the big knives. Two guard the entrance and the third follows the Mayor down. He must have assumed we were all down there because I got the two guards no problem and then I followed the third one down and when I got to him he was holding you guys up."

"Good work Ferb," David told him. Kealey smiled at him.

"What I don't understand," a woman in her mid-thirties asked them. She had been appointed temporary mayor until they could find an alternative. "Is why Mayor Adams did it and why he called you in if he was the one behind it?"

"I think I can explain," Kealey said. "Firstly, I believe he was a man obsessed with power. Once he was mayor he wanted more and he found a way to summon Beira and get her to either make him a god or give him that kind of power. And then when people started to go missing and you all wanted action, he had to be seen as doing something about it. It's like when a husband reports his wife missing, a large majority of the time he's the one that did it. I would even go so far as to say that if the boy who found us hadn't then he would have done something completely different."

"And how did you kill it? I thought gods were immortal?"

"They are. Immortal doesn't mean you're indestructible. It means you will live on forever unless someone kills you. We took a gamble with the Norse idea that mistletoe will kill a god because it was the only plant that didn't promise to never harm Baldur. We used bullets fused with mistletoe and it worked."

"Thank you, thank you all, you saved our village."

"You're very welcome," David said. "It was just our job."

With the mystery solved the group packed up in the morning and made for the van.

"Stop, *wait!*" A little voice shouted. They all turned to see a little girl with pink bits in her hair run towards them. She hugged Kealey, who hugged her back. "Are you leaving already?"

"I'm afraid so honey. Remember what I promised you?" Isla nodded. "Well, we've kept the promise, so now it's time to go."

"My mummy's the Mayor now. What happened to Mayor Adams?"

"He had to go away for a while. That's not anything you need to worry about."

"I'll miss you."

"I'll miss you too," Kealey wiped the tears from Isla's face as her mother came out the town hall that was also the church and picked her girl up.

"Mayor Adams had to take a leave of absence; a holiday because of the stress. He left a letter and we expect to hear from him soon," she told them.

That's the thing with a village this small, where everyone's families have grown up together since its founding. A village where everyone knows everyone else's business in the nicest way possible and they have a true respect and love for their fellow man.

A village like this doesn't take someone disrespecting it very well.

WINTER'S GIFT
by
Mark W Duncan

The woman writhed on the bed. Her surgically enhanced body, accentuated by the lack of clothing she wore, arched and fell. A raised finger beckoned. Peroxide blonde hair cascaded about her. He jerked awake. The half drunk bottle of beer jumped from his hand, some of the contents spilt on his trousers.

"Bugger it."

Jumping from the chair he crossed to the open fire and stood before it, holding the damp patch of his combat trousers out to dry. The woman on the television began removing the last visages of her clothing. He watched for a moment before shaking his head, taking the remote, he flicked over to a music channel. He had no problem watching porn on moral grounds, it was just at the moment the mood for that kind of entertainment eluded him. The day-to-day frustration of his inabilities to produce anything of significance caused him to spend his time worthlessly. Watching trash TV or daydreaming. Only using his exercise equipment gave him a sense of achievement. That and the merciless killing he could inflict in the virtual world of his games console.

Throwing himself back into the seat he retrieved his laptop from the table. *'Aspects and Perceptions'* by Michael S Morgan.

The rest of the page was painfully blank. The cursor's blinking state of ever readiness mocked him. Like some dog eager to be released for the chase, it strained, yet there was no prey. His attempt at writing the difficult second book was falling short of the mark, striking the seemingly impenetrable wall of writers block. It was an affliction, which he could not afford. His publisher had begun applying subtle pressure on him for a sample of his new writings. He could provide none.

The office where he sat was filled with objects that had inspired him at various times in his life. They failed him now in his hour of need. Scowling at them one at a time, he scanned the room.

The coal fire brought him back to happy times as a child. Several paintings on the wall, the almost exact replica of a wrestling championship belt; two swords crossed and the four-foot high statue of the Egyptian God Anubis stood sentinel. The obsidian eyes observed everything, yet remained impassive. All were expressions of his personality. Still they failed to aid him in his quest. Michael found his eyes beginning to close; maybe it was the heat of the fire, or the need to escape his failures. He felt the gentle wave of sleep begin to subdue him.

No more than a few moments passed before a sound tore through the house. It was the doorbell that howled. The terrible electric shriek, 'Got to get that fixed,' he thought as he began to rise from his chair. He made his way from his office through the house, turning on any lights that were not already on. The house became reborn into life. Reaching the front door as the second sonic attack struck him he shouted through the door.

"Just a minute!"

Quieter and to himself this time he said: "Keys, Keys, where are the damned keys?"

A quick and frantic search revealed their location. The fruit bowl by the mirror.

Before unlocking the door he checked his watch. 00.47. Damn it was late. Who could be calling at this time? He glanced through the peephole. The view was obscured by the frenzy of the storm outside. If it were a burglar, he reasoned, they would hardly be ringing the doorbell. By that logic he inserted the key, unlocked the door and opened it to the cruel night. Snow swept in forcing Michael to turn his face away. From the storm a figure emerged.

"Michael I am so sorry, I know it's late. I just didn't know where else to go." The female voice was very familiar but out of place at his house.

He sealed the door behind her. Taking a moment he observed her. "Amanda, what's wrong?" Obviously there was something amiss. She wore a thin denim jacket, ineffective against the storm. Her face was stained with tears and running mascara streaks.

33

She tried to speak, but emotion threatened to overwhelm her. Pausing and taking a deep breath she crossed the distance and attached herself to Michael. Her arms snaking round his waist, she began to weep, her face buried deep into his chest. He took her in his own arms and they stood there silent. Offering the comfort of his closeness, he held her.

Michael had not seen her for almost six months. Before his first book was published they had worked together. A bond of friendship had quickly developed. Finding themselves very much alike, a fierce closeness enveloped them. Rumours flew round the workplace. They were secretly seeing each other. They were having sex outside the building. It was fuel to their fires and more often than not they would do things to suggest more was happening than really was. When Michael became successful and it was time to leave it had been difficult, for secretly, her very presence in his life was a calming factor. Everything seemed to make sense when he was with her. He knew not to say anything as Amanda had a fiancée and a daughter to him. Yet deep down in some dark corner of his mind he hoped she felt the same.

Holding her at arm's length he spoke softly to Amanda.

"You must be frozen. Come and we'll get you warmed up."

Helping her out of the sodden jacket and hanging it by the door he led her silently through the house to his office.

"Sorry about the mess, I haven't had many visitors for a while. I kinda have been living in here the last few days," he kicked a crumpled newspaper for emphasis. "I'll get you a drink. Tea or coffee? Something stronger?"

"Coffee will be fine, just sugar please," Amanda had regained enough composure to cease her crying. She wiped away the remaining tears on her cheeks.

"Sure thing – will be a couple of minutes."

Michael hastily began to pick up some random things in an attempt to tidy up. Finding himself looking at her, he caught his breath. She was striking despite the tears and her distress. Her black hair, windswept as it was, fell to her shoulders. A perfect frame for her face. Pale skin resembling the flawless snow outside. Perhaps her most striking features were her eyes. If Michael were in a poetic mood he may have described them as moonlight reflected in the midnight water. They were a pale blue and drew Michael in. Large and captivating, he was enthralled. This coupled with a ready smile and open nature, her beauty glowed from the inside and radiated to the outside. There was little need for cosmetics.

He caught himself as she became aware of his gaze.

"Please Amanda, make yourself at home," he swept a hand towards a chair. "I'll be back in a moment."

Leaving the room he made his way to the kitchen. Making both tea and coffee he returned to the office, the steaming mugs in his hand. Amanda had removed her soaking shoes, sitting in his armchair her legs were outstretched, warming her feet at the fire. He handed the coffee to her and took a seat on the other side of the fire. Sipping, she sat back.

"You're such a caring guy Michael. Here I am at your house at stupid o'clock and you haven't pushed me and asked why I'm here. Always ready to help."

"Well I figured you would tell me sooner or later, besides for you I would do anything...to help." He had the good grace to blush.

"I tried calling your mobile," she sipped again. "In the end I just decided to come here. I didn't know who else to turn to."

Standing, Michael went to the fire and threw on a small log building up the flames. "I'm sorry about that; I haven't had my mobile on for a while. Anyway, it's always great to see you. I just wish it was under better circumstances," he hesitated a moment fearing to voice the question. "What's wrong Amanda? I hate to see you like this."

"It's Peter...I can't go back to him, not to that house, not anymore."

"What happened?"

She looked downwards unable to hold Michael's gaze. Letting out a deep sigh she began to speak. "When we worked together I never told you but...Peter and I. The only reason we are together is for Jenny. Our daughter means the world to me. I wanted her to grow up with a mum and dad but he changed."

She gazed down into the coffee. Black as her life had seemed to become. There was silence for a moment. "There is nothing between us. Not anymore. Not for a few years now. He started drinking heavily. Sometimes he would do pot. We argued about it. I didn't want her to see him like that. Tonight we argued and...and... he hit me."

"What?"

"It's not the first time. I just know I can never go back, not even for Jenny's sake."

Placing her mug down, she stood and lifted her top up revealing a dark purple bruise scarring her left side.

Clenching his fist Michael spat his words out: "The bastard! You have to call the police get him put away for this…"

"Michael."

"No he can't get away with this. Not you. If I were there I would have…"

"Michael!"

Her voice was stern and commanded his silence. He had never heard this side of her before. He was used to her laughter, not the sadness that pierced her words.

"I just want to be away from him. No police, not right now anyway. I just want to feel safe. Please."

From the fire Michael crossed and on bent knee took her hand. She sat back in the chair. "I am sorry it's just, well, you know. I care about you. I couldn't bear the thought of anything like that happening to you."

He released her hand, suddenly fearing that he had overstepped the bounds of familiarity with the gesture.

"I know and that's why you are such an amazing person," she took his hand back. "And that's why I have a big favour to ask of you."

He squeezed her hand gently. He knew the question before it had been voiced. "You are welcome to stay here for as long as you want. My house is yours. What about Jenny?"

"She's with my mum and dad for the weekend. If I could just use your phone I should really let her know what's happened and where I am."

"Yeah no problem, it's through in the living room, you can talk privately there. Not very warm though."

He let her stand and they walked in silence, reaching the phone Michael began to leave. "More coffee?"

She nodded and began dialling the handset. Michael walked out, closing the door behind him, he waited a moment. He could hear her talking. "No…It happened again mum. I just can't go back… I'm at my friends… Yes that one…No no…You will have to keep her until I sort things out…"

He moved from the door. Guilt stabbed him, the last thing the woman needed was to have someone eavesdrop on her. A thought occurred to him. Dashing up the stairs to the guest room he retrieved a bundle of clothes from a chest of drawers and laid them on the bed. He placed a warm housecoat over the pile before returning to the study. She returned a few minutes after.

"Thanks for that. My mum told me I have done the right thing. I guess I'm going to have to move back with her for a bit until I can sort things out."

"Well for now treat this place as your home. It's the least I can do. Oh that reminds me; I laid out some clothes for you. Thought you might be warmer out of your damp ones."

He tried not to smile at the obvious innuendo.

A beautiful smile lit up her face, one that commanded the pace of his heart. The order was quick march.

"Are you trying to get me naked?"

Her old spirit still remained. The verbal sparring between them had been frequent and intense at times. It was testament to her strength of character that she was able to joke after the events of the last twenty-four hours.

Letting out a laugh Michael replied: "Yeah but this time it's for your health's sake."

They both laughed. "Up the stairs and second on the left. It's not my habit to keep women's clothes, just so you know, they were my sisters - she left them when she stayed. Might be on the large side but they are warm and dry."

"You think of everything don't you? I will be back in a sec."

He tried not to stare at her retreating form. Failing, his gaze dropped. Her wet trousers clung to her form revealing the contours of her hips. Shaking his head he forced himself to concentrate on the objects that still littered the floor.

She left the room and climbed the stairs to the guest room. True to his word, a neat pile of clothes sat folded on the bed with a warm thick housecoat. She quickly stripped off. Shivering, she dressed in a garish combination of a white t-shirt and jogging bottoms. Fashion would have to suffer. Wrapping herself in the housecoat she left the room. Chancing a look into Michael's bedroom she found everything in surprisingly neat order. The only sign it had been occupied was the bed, unmade, and a games console controller left on the pillow. She smiled.

As she returned Michael was sitting by the fire, two fresh mugs of tea and coffee respectively sat on the table. More of the random clutter had disappeared. He poked at the fire. "Better?"

"Mmm, much better thank you."

Being dressed like this before him did not bother her whatsoever, the ease of their friendship saw to that. She returned to her seat and took the offered drink.

"You have such a wonderful house. When you left work and texted me saying you had bought a house I didn't imagine it would be like this. You've done very well for yourself. I'm really proud of you. Remember I always said you would make it."

"Yeah you did. You were one of the few people at work that I trusted enough to see my writing. I mentioned you in my author's foreword in the last book. Obviously I couldn't name you in case Peter...Ah, Sorry."

"Hey it was a lovely thought. No apologies, not from you. What are you working on now?"

"Supposed to be my second book; having trouble with it though. Anyway how about you? How's work?"

"Shit. It's always shit now."

He laughed: "I remember. We always got each other through the day. I hated it when you were on holiday and I had to be there. Wasn't the same."

"Yeah Mr Big Shot author, you dropped me like a stone when you got published."

"I didn't want to. To tell the truth I missed you like crazy. More than I probably should if I am honest."

The words should not have come out. He knew he had said too much.

"I missed you too."

The four words rocked him. Nothing could have sounded more splendid to him. They left him in amazement. Still, he should try to not overplay his hand.

"We were close, weren't we? Crap. Listen to me. What a twat. It's really great to see you again. I just wish things were different for you."

She nodded, her smile dimmed slightly. "Let's not talk about that no more tonight. You still like your wrestling I see?"

"Yup, still a geek if that's what you mean and I know it's fake before you say it."

They shared a laugh.

"What's that thing?"

She pointed at the dog headed and human body hybrid statue.

"That's the Egyptian God, Anubis; he was involved with the mummification process."

"He is kinda creepy."

"I guess I can see how you would think that. To me it's just cool." He crossed over and put his hand round the shoulders of him. "I suppose I have come to accept him for what he is. Plus I had a little accident last month, the fire spat out some coal which burnt the carpet so I needed something to cover it up."

Again they laughed. The sound of her laughter was sweet, he had missed it dearly.

"You know Michael, I have something to apologise for."

Before he could mount a protest she raised her hand. "I couldn't keep in contact after you left. Peter would go through my mobile, phoning me all the time when I went out. The drink and drugs made him paranoid. I wanted to, I really did," her voice was laced with regret.

Michael shook his head. "It's alright. I wasn't the best either; I was so busy with writing. I knew if I asked to meet you or phoned you it would cause problems back home. I backed off for your sake. Just promise me that when you leave here you won't be a stranger."

"No danger about that, darling," she used their pet name, one used for comic affect for each other. The English accent she retained sent a shiver down his spine. It was another thing he had missed.

When their mirth died she spoke again. "You know you really are so lucky living out here. You managed to get away from city life. Oh don't get me wrong, Aberdeen is fine – the shops are good and all. It's just out here you have no one to bother you. It's quiet."

Michael nodded. "When I was younger..."

Amanda laughed at this. Michael was just turning twenty-six. "I always wanted to escape the countryside, it was boring and I couldn't wait for city life. Now I can't imagine living anywhere other than out here. It does get very quiet here though."

The clock on the wall gave a brief chime announcing the time of 01.30. "Dear God. Check the time. Amanda you must be shattered and here am I talking your ear off."

"I am quite tired. You know you really are a caring guy."

"Flattery… I was going to have bacon, sausage, egg and toast for breakfast tomorrow, hope that's alright with you."

"Sounds lovely to me."

Oh, before I forget, you can have the guest room tonight. There is an electric blanket on the bed so make sure you put it on."

Smiling she nodded. Her hair fell about her face.

Michael walked to the window and looked out. The snow fell continuously and the wind swept it in every direction. "I saw the weather earlier. They said this is supposed to last for the rest of the week. If it keeps up you might be stuck here. Driving back to Aberdeen could be difficult. I bet it was dangerous in the first place. Don't worry though; I think I have plenty of food to last. Good job, otherwise we may have had to eat each other."

Winking she replied. "Whatever works best for you."

They laughed again.

"If you need anything through the night my room is next door to yours. Bathroom is at the end of the hall. There should be new toothbrushes in the cabinet. Help yourself."

Shaking her head in a friendly way she said, "Stop worrying I'll be fine. You know for a guy you're really well prepared."

"I put the toilet seat down after I am finished too."

"Living on your own too, I am impressed darling."

She crossed and embraced him. They both laughed. Her eyes looked up to his and she closed in and delivered a kiss lightly to his lips. His heart felt as though it might stop.

"Thanks again, for everything."

Then she was gone. From the hall, Michael heard. "Goodnight."

The sound was magical. Never in his life could he have imagined that he would hear those words coming from her. In the house he owned. Mute, he stood for a moment before he turned himself to the task of preparing the house for sleep. He moved to the fire and began damping it down, placing the mesh guard before it. He slammed the laptop closed, no more mocking for tonight. Moving through each room he turned the lights out. Locking the front door he risked one final glance at the storm. Still raging. If it kept up, Amanda would be stuck here. It had been a while since he had enjoyed the company of anyone for more than the briefest of visits. He knew that together they would have endless amounts to talk about and their similar natures would call to one another. Besides she deserved to be taken care of after what she had been through of late.

"Wait till morning. See how things stand."

He left the hallway and climbed the stairs to his room, where he undressed swiftly and made a dive for the shelter of his bed. The light went out as he lay shivering under the covers. He spoke quietly to himself, a by-product of his isolated lifestyle.

"Crazy day."

It was something that he loved. Ever since childhood he remembered lying in bed, listening to the uncontrolled anger of the storm in its futile attempts to reach him. He listened to the howling wind and the occasional scraping of a tree branch against the roof. Tired eyes began to fail him as they sought to close. He surrendered to their demands, lost in memories of old. Sleep almost overtook him when a slight noise alerted him from the dark. Fearful for a moment, he heard something fall to the floor.

A form slid under the covers with him. Was he dreaming?

Amanda's voice came from the dark. "I was cold in my bed."

"There was an electric blanket, all you had to do…"

Her lips pressed against his, interrupting. Not a friendly kiss as before, this time it was filled with passion and desire. He let himself respond, years of longing for this moment clouded his judgement, until reason regained control. Gently he moved her away. She raised herself up on one arm, watching him in the dark.

Her words came out in a flood. Her breath rushed.

"What's wrong? We both have wanted this for so long. Do you really think all the flirting at work was just fun and games? I wanted you for so long."

The words almost drowned out his beating heart. He took a moment before he could reply.

"If I had known I could have…" he struggled for the right words. "It's just…" Nothing he could say seemed appropriate.

She kissed him again. This time her tongue found his mouth and she pressed her body close to his. Michael's skin tingled at the touch of Amanda's naked body. Her breasts pushed tightly against him. His passion ascended. He returned the kiss. Turning his body to face her he wrapped his arms around her slim naked form. Skin as smooth as silk greeted him. Amanda let a hand trace shapes down from his smooth chest to a toned stomach. Promising to drop further it waited with trepidation, quivering. Waiting for the sign from Michael to continue. His body ached to guide her hand further, screamed even. Years of wishing, dreaming and he could have it all yet a tiny voice of reason nagged at him. For the second time he regretfully pulled away. He spoke, his voice filled with emotion.

"Amanda, wait and just listen a moment."

He cautiously touched her cheek.

"I don't just want to fuck and you leave in the morning, you're not just sex to me, never have been. If we do…I don't want to get this close and you leave. I couldn't handle that. I would rather never know what it's like than have you and lose you again. Does that make sense?"

She let her breath out slowly. "It does Michael. I don't know what the future holds. Me, with a kid and you, here. If you want me like that…" she fumbled for the right words. Letting her breath out she again spoke. "Just hold me tonight, hold me and make me feel safe. Please."

She turned in the bed and Michael moved his body next to her, wrapping his arms around her, they shared in the comfort of each other. Gently he moved his mouth next to her ear. Whispered something. Amanda turned her head, they kissed

43

briefly. Whispering a reply she turned back at ease and they both settled in for sleep. For the first time in months Michael felt content. Although the situation was strange he allowed himself to be enveloped in the tender embrace. The scent, touch and her presence filled him with desire, and a longing for a future he never thought possible. Whatever the future held, for the moment life could not have been more perfect.

FORE!
by
Jennifer Shand

Nothing ever happened on our street until the day aliens landed on the golf course at the back of Mrs. Clegg's house. She was far from happy, as Thursday was Ladies' Day and she had been waiting all week to be the first to tee off.

Mr. Leghorn, otherwise known as Foghorn, but not to his face, the President of the Paul Lawrie Appreciation Society Golf Club was spitting feathers. How dare they land on his greens? Couldn't they have landed on Little Chorttles? Their greens are not as well maintained!

The police arrived en-masse, all three of them, soon after it was reported. Officers Dibble and Jones were followed by P.C. Wimple on his bike. No P.C. Lee as it was her day off. They met with the Council, the Golf Club committee, the W.R.I. and the locals from our street in the Gym Hall at the primary school.

Something had to be done. Aliens had never visited Roswell before, and no-one knew what to do. How do you tackle the unknown? Mr. Leghorn spoke first, why would they come here? What do they want? How do we get rid of them?

Officer Dibble asked for calm, which I never understood as no-one was too bothered apart from Mrs. Clegg and Foghorn himself. But I suppose Officer Dibble had to be seen to look as though he were in charge. "We need to find out why they are here. Did anybody see it land, and has anyone seen anything come out of the spaceship?"

Old Jed, our resident loner and Oxbridge academic spoke quietly: "I saw them land at Midnight and three very small men walked down a lowered platform; they had a large dog-like creature on a lead too. They headed in the direction of the River Twerp and jumped in and had a splash around."

"Why didn't you tell us Jed?"

"Well Officer Dibble, they seemed to be doing no harm and were enjoying themselves."

"How long were they there for?"

"About 45 minutes till P.C. Lee turned up, and joined them in the water"

"Jed, did you just say that Lee was taken by these aliens?"

"No Dibble, I said that she joined in quite happily, and went with them back to their space ship at her own free will. Nothing much happens here, that's probably why she's gone."

"Are you making this up? Why weren't you spotted? Where is Lee?"

"Officer Dibble…"

"Yes Mr. Leghorn."

"Why don't we just go up to them and ask them to return P.C. Lee and for them to go home and we will forget they were ever here?"

"Officer Dibble, tell Mr. Leghorn that it's rather a dangerous and risky idea, and that he should stay well away. Anyway, shouldn't we wait until they make their demands?"

"Yes, we could wait Mrs. Clegg, but what if they don't make any demands, and just happen to be passing through. What if they take off to wherever and still have P.C. Lee with them, I would be beside myself for not trying to rescue my dearest Rosie."

"I'll go."

"Jed, as an officer of the law, I can't let you do that. But on this occasion I will. I don't mind saying that it's rather all too much for me."

"Yes Dibble, everything usually is. I always said that it was a bad mistake to twin up with a small town like Spockton. Anyone else want to come with me, Mrs. Clegg?"

"Yes Jed, count me in, and the ladies from the W.R.I. too. Safety in numbers eh? We can't have these sorts of people coming here and taking over. That's our job."

P.C. Wimple was all for a mass intervention at the space ship to get his colleague back, and was happy to agree with Mrs. Clegg for once. Nearly everyone went with him except me and Buster, Jed's old sheepdog.

"Actually lets all go they've got my fiancé in there."

That was the first time Officer Dibble had taken command of the situation, actually come to think of it, any situation, and about time too. I followed the crowd, I may be a kid but I'm not daft. Buster and I watched from the attic in his master's house. They all walked slowly towards the space ship, Officer Dibble, Jed, Mr. Leghorn and Mrs. Clegg leading. No-one was talking, but they all had a determined look on their faces. It was quite touching that they wanted to rescue one of their own.

They stopped about twelve feet from the space ship. They stood there for at least ten minutes and I began to wonder if they had changed their minds, I wouldn't have blamed them. Suddenly they started chanting, and from the mass huddle went into pairs and began skipping towards the space ship.

It was at that point I saw the platform lower again, P.C. Lee came to the door and shouted for Officer Dibble, he ran up to the platform and yelled out his undying love for Rosie. She smiled, stepped back inside and the crowd followed her in.

The platform slowly raised and closed, the ship silently hovered above the ground. The only noise was Buster whimpering for his master. I kept watching, transfixed. The ship kept climbing; their window was parallel to the attic window. P.C. Lee waved and smiled at me, and then they were gone.

Sure is quiet here nowadays.

47

THE GULLS
by
Amy McMillan

Baz and Mental walked down the lanes next to the harbour, on the lookout for prostitutes, daring each other to ask what she'd do for a fiver. Baz took another slug on his bottle of Buckie, his gold sovereign rings glinting in the weak Scottish sunlight, while Mental unwrapped a chocolate bar, took a large bite and chewed on it.

Suddenly his round, acne-scarred face screwed up in disgust and he spewed it out onto the pavement. "Urgh! Man that tastes boggin'," he spat and wiped his mouth.

He looked down at the wrapper. It was bright neon green and boasted energy boosting ingredients from darkest Africa. He sneered at it and, turning round, flung it with a grunt at a large scabby seagull that had been standing near them. The gull swooped over and hurriedly gulped down the half chewed chocolate, wrapper and all.

The boys, finding a new distraction, decided to chuck stones at it. Baz, with a fluke throw, landed a hard pebble right off the birds head, the gull dropped down with a strangled squawk and lay twitching on the road, green drool dribbling from its beak, until finally it lay still.

The boys looked at each other and ran over to the bird, prodding it with their trainers.

"Dude! You killed it!"

"Shut it knob head! It was that manky sweetie that killed it! No bloody wonder too, it was rank!"

Bored with playing with the fallen bird, the boys lost interest and started to wander off. They hadn't got far when a noise behind them made them stop. The street behind them was empty apart from the seagull's body.

"Did you hear something?"

"Nah! Come on mate, let's find some prossies!"

Just as they were about to go, something caught their eyes, the bird moved!

"Come on! It's not dead yet, quick, get a stick or something."

"Nah, go get that big brick over there," Mental pointed to a pile of discarded bricks. "We can drop it on its head!"

"Nice one," grinned Baz, running over and searching through the pile for the largest one.

Grinning to himself, Mental hunkered down next to the bird. Sniffing and snorting he hacked deep in his throat bringing up phlegm, and spat at the birds face. Laughing, he opened his mouth to shout to his friend, only to find a strangled scream come from it as he fell back onto his behind. The seagull had lifted its head and opened a red, spit-encrusted eye, and was now looking right at him. Slowly, to the horror of the two boys now silently watching it, the bird gave a strange high-pitched squeal, its pink sharp tongue lolling from its open, dripping beak.

"Quick, chuck the brick at it," Mental yelled at his silent friend, who was standing there with a mixture of disgust and fear on his face.

The gull pulled itself up in a series of disjointed moves, it stretched its wings out and half staggered and hopped towards the two now very frightened boys.

With sudden speed it flew at them, landing squarely on Baz's face, pecking at his eyes and clawing at his face as he wildly tried to pull it from himself, shrieking for help, blood pouring from the gashes on his face and hands. With a deadly lunge, the gull plunged its beak into the boy's eye socket, pulling and twisting till out came the glistening globe, snapping itself free from the dripping nerve. A quick gulp and swallow and it was gone. Baz was left a twisted, gibbering, screaming ball clutching at his face on the pavement, blood oozing from the mess that once was his face.

Mental could only stand there in shock, a warm wetness running down his leg as his bladder gave up on muscle control.

"Fuck that," he whispered to himself, turning and breaking into a panicky run for safety, tripping over his feet in an effort to leave behind a scene which he knew he could never forget.

An image of his mum and sister flashed through his head, a barbeque last year on a day much like today, his mum's laughter and the water balloon fight, granddad burning the burgers, all this was flashing through his head when the wind was knocked out of his lungs by a large heavy feathery body landing on his back, a high pitched squeal was the last thing he ever heard.

The seagull was confused, he felt like he was underwater, the waves crashing in his ears as he dived for fish, the pressure on his body that made his lungs itch for air.

But he wasn't in water, the hunger and the need for food was there, the pressure pushing in from behind his eyes, the feeling like a hundred sharp beaks tearing his body apart, and the rage, the rage that made him attack the human, the human that he had been happily feeding from until a man had come running and screaming and flailing its arms at him. He backed away from his food, hissing at the man and flapping his wings menacingly. The man was now screaming into a phone, only stopping to vomit on the pavement. Blearily wiping his mouth on the back of his hand, he looked up in time to scream as a ball of fury-filled zombie seagull hit him square in the face.

Three weeks later...

A hush lay over the town, cars sat abandoned in the middle of Union Street with broken windows covered in seagull droppings. The only sound to be heard was that of a thousand zombie seagulls' high-pitched shrieks as they circled the city looking for victims.

From a boarded up window on Union Street, Michelle peered through a crack, watching out for any sign of feathery movement. Jay had ventured out for supplies over four hours ago and still wasn't back yet. She sighed; worry setting in more so now, she wished she'd gone with him instead of staying here. She looked back at the others in the old office store room they'd converted into a makeshift base.

Mary was in the corner staring blankly ahead, still mourning the loss of her husband and son, winding her finger round a strand of lank hair muttering to herself under her breath, Mark and Amanda were stocking up bags of aerosol cans and baking soda bombs, their hushed banter a welcome sound. Sitting close to Mary, the punk kid Davie was messing around with the radio trying to get a signal, and lastly Alex, the oldest of the group and her father, who sat beside her eating cold baked beans out of the can.

Licking the juice off his fingers he sat up a bit and stretched, looking up at Michelle,

"Well love, any sign of him yet?"

"No nothing, you think I should go out and look for him?"

"You tried the walkie talkie?"

"No the batteries ran out and I've not been able to find any more yet."

Alex looked down at his watch. "I don't want you risking yourself going out there to look for him, he might have just holed up somewhere for the night."

"I hope so Dad I really do. I don't see any birds out today, maybe if I'm quick?"

"No! We go out together as a group, you know that, remember what happened to Mackie?"

His raised voice alerted the others who were now staring at them quietly, a nervous glance passed between Mark and Amanda before they carried on testing spray cans.

"Shush dad! Yes OK I remember, I'm not stupid, I just wish the phones were working or something, just to see if he's OK." She sank back on her haunches next to him, a tear of frustration threatening to spill, she blinked her eyes and rubbed at them, her dad pulled her in for a hug and kissed the top of her head.

"Try not to worry love. He's a clever lad who can look after himself."

Michelle could only nod in silence.

Jay wasn't feeling particularly clever right now. In fact to be honest he was a bit pissed off with himself and life in general! He should have been more careful and watched the time, but the sun had risen sooner than expected and now he was stuck, hiding under this van on the other side of town until it got dark again. Michelle and the others would be getting worried by now and he hoped they weren't going to risk searching for him.

Sighing to himself, he shifted around in an effort to get comfortable and wait out the long day, wondering briefly how the hell he was going to be able to go to the toilet under this thing, when a glinting flash caught his eye. It came again and again... a signal? He shuffled round to see where the flash was coming from - and found it! A paper shop across the road which miraculously still had all its windows intact, and from the half open door, a girl crouched with a mirror in her hands.

Seeing him notice her she gestured to him to quickly get inside the shop. "How?" he mouthed at her.

The girl pulled out from around her neck a chain with a short silver tube on it which she put to her lips and blew through. Jay heard nothing, but barely three feet in front of him behind a pile of rubble, unseen before now, a giant seagull took off in fright, cawing angrily.

"Hurry," the girl shouted from the doorway.

Dashing frantically from under the van, his eyes never leaving the door in front of him, feeling sure that any minute now death would land on him from above, he practically tripped over the girl in his haste to get inside. Once in, the girl slammed the door shut and pushed a chair up against it.

"How did you do that?" he panted, looking up at her.

"With this," she replied, showing him the dog whistle around her neck.

"It's the only thing that seems to scare them off, which is useful if you're being an idiot and wandering around outside in full sight," she said, giving him a withering look.

"I got caught out by the sun when I was getting supplies! Are you the only one here, or are there more of you?"

"There's just me and Mr Ged who runs the shop," she pulled him to his feet. "I'm Rachel," she said, smiling at him for the first time.

"Jamie, my mates call me Jay," he said grinning back. "Thank God you were there. I'd have been stuck under that bloody van all day if not! Speaking of which, you don't happen to have a working toilet here do you?"

Rachel's throaty laugh echoed round the dusty shop as she led the way.

Michelle was getting tired of waiting, angrily pacing the floor, the cigarette dangling from her lips trailing smoke behind her. She stopped abruptly.

"That's it! I'm not bloody waiting anymore! I'm going to go find him," grabbing a bag of spray cans out of Mark's hand she darted out the door and down the stairs. Shouts trailed her, quickly followed by her dad and the rest of the group.

"Michelle stop," her dad shouted, grabbing her shoulder. "This is not the way to do things you silly girl, running about outside's going to get you killed."

"Dad I know that! But you can't expect me just to sit around here twiddling my thumbs! Jay could need our help!"

"And how do you expect to find him then? Search the entire length and breadth of Aberdeen?"

"If I have to… yes."

Mary sighed to herself. "Alex control your child, all this shouting's going to bring those blasted birds right down on top of us! If she wants to go kill herself then let her!" And with that final remark she stomped back upstairs again with Davie fussing around her.

Watching her retreating back, Michelle tutted to herself and turned to the rest of the group. "Look, I'm not asking anyone to come with me, if I keep to the buildings and car hop I should be fine," she shook the bag with the cans at them. "Plus I've got these if I get in any trouble."

"Shut it Shell, you know you're a crap aim with them," Mark grinned at her. He took the bag off her and passed it to Amanda. "You leave the birdie toasting to the experts, me and Manda have got your back."

"Damn straight girl!" grinned Amanda, punching her playfully on the shoulder.

Alex looked at the three of them, and smiled.

"Well I guess I could do with the fresh air after being cooped up in this place," he made to move, until Michelle's arm on his hand made him stop.

"Don't think so pops," she said smiling up at him. "I've got enough to worry about with Jay being out there, I don't need to be worrying about you too. I need you to stay here and look after those two upstairs for me OK?"

Alex smiled, ruffled his daughter's hair and laughed. "You know you're getting old when your children turn into your parents," he pulled her into a bear hug and lifted her off her feet. "Take care Shelly bear, I love you."

He let her go and headed up the stairs, but not before Michelle could see the tears running down his face.

Struggling not to cry like a baby, she sniffed hard and turned to face the others with a weak smile. "Come on then guys. Let's go kick some seagull butt!"

Jay and Rachel stood together behind the grimy shop window staring out. Looking over at the girl next to him, he rested his hand on her arm. "You can change your mind if you want; I'm not asking you to come with me."

"Hey I'm not giving myself sleepless nights knowing that I let you go out there to get turned into bird food," she grinned up at him. "Besides, I could do with the exercise."

A wheezy cackle from behind made them both jump and turn to see a small Chinese man come smiling out towards them from the back room, in his arms he carried packets of crisp and juice.

"Can't let you two young things run off and have adventures without supplies now can I?" he said, handing the packets to them.

"Hardly an adventure Mr G," Rachel said, packing the food away into her rucksack then opening one of the bottles and drinking from it. Wiping her mouth she handed the bottle to Jay who drank from it gratefully.

"Thanks, and thank you Sir for the food and batteries, I just hope I can get back in time before they start searching for me." He looked over at the clock above the counter, it was already five o'clock, Michelle would be frantic by now and he knew he couldn't waste time.

"You're welcome sonny Jim, just you promise me that you'll look after this one," he nodded to Rachel, who pouted at him.

"Hey! Cheeky git!" she laughed pushing him playfully. "It's me that's gotta look out for him you mean."

Mr Ged held his hands up in mock surrender. Laughing to himself, he turned to Jay. "Be careful with this one Jimmy boy, she's a firecracker."

"Yes Sir I will be," Jay laughed along. Giving them both a hug he went back the way he'd come, still chuckling to himself.

A body pulled itself across the cobbles on Castlegate, blood pouring from the many lacerations over him. Gulls circled tauntingly, before he, struggling for breath and through blood encrusted hair, thought he saw two figures run past Archie Simpson's and duck behind a car. He struggled to raise his hand in a final gesture of help, until a mob of blood-hungry gulls descended on him from above and silenced him for good.

Watching from the relative cover of the car, Jay and Rachel could only look on in horror as the man was torn apart not twenty metres in front of them, the blood staining the greasy feathers of the birds that squabbled amongst the gore.

Jay pulled on Rachel's sleeve, gesturing down the rubble covered road with a jerk of his head. "Come on, while they're distracted."

With a final glance over her shoulder she followed him down the street.

Michelle and the others ducked into the library after narrowly missing a group of scout birds on the edge of the park. Scanning the book strewn floor, the group shouted on anyone that was still in the building. Finding no-one, they began to rake through drawers and cupboards for anything of use.

"See if you can find batteries anywhere guys," Michelle shouted up to the others.

"Got some!" A cheerful Amanda ran down the stairs two at a time waving a fist full of batteries around. "Found them in a couple of TV remotes upstairs," she said passing them over to Michelle.

"Nice one dude, let's just hope they fit in these now eh?" Pulling out the walkie talkies she flipped open the back and pushed them in, pressing the button so the speaker crackled into life.

"Oh you beauty" she grinned at Amanda, who slapped her on the back triumphantly and made her way back up to Mark to replace the batteries in their own walkie talkies.

"Right, let's just hope Jay's ones are still working," closing her eyes she pressed the button and hoped.

"Um Jay, your bag appears to be talking," Rachel threw the bag across the floor of the café they'd stopped off in.

Fumbling for the zipper, Jay pulled the bag open and emptied the contents out on to the floor, the walkie talkie skittered across the shiny surface, trailing Michelle's voice behind it. Pouncing on it he pressed the button.

"Michelle! Michelle I'm here! It's OK, I'm OK, where are you?"

"Jamie! Oh thank god! Are you OK? We're in the library, where are you?"

Sinking back down on the floor, hugging the device to his ear, relief flooded him, she was OK, and she was safe and not too far away. "It's OK babe, we're next to the Music Hall, let us come to you though, who's all there?"

"I've got Mark and Mandy with me. Are you alone? Who's with you?"

"A friend, Rachel, we'll try and get there as soon as possible, sit tight hun."

"OK, but please be careful babe, there are some nasty birds out there; we nearly walked right into them!"

Looking down at the whistle in his hands, he smiled over to Rachel. "Don't worry about that hun, see you soon. Hey! I love you."

"Love you too babe, take care," Michelle smiled, pushing the walkie talkie into her pocket as Amanda came downstairs.

"Everything cool dude?" she asked.

"Yep, just heard from Jay, he's not too far away so he's going to meet up with us here."

"Nice one! See, told you he'd be fine."

"Yeah I know, thanks hun."

Michelle grinned at her friend and looked around. "Where's Mark?"

"I left him looking through the DVDs upstairs, any idea where the loos are in this joint?"

Michelle gestured with her head towards a set of doors and Amanda had just disappeared through them when Mark showed up stuffing DVDs into his bag.

"Borrowing them are we?" she raised an eyebrow at her friend. Mark laughed, bringing one out to show her.

"Course I'm just borrowing them! What do you take me for? Hey check this one out." He pulled out one that had a snarling vampire on the cover and handed it to Michelle.

"Vampire Zombie Killers II," she gave him a quizzical look, a half smile on her face. "Interesting viewing hun, haven't you had enough of zombies, considering what we're dealing with just now?"

She handed the box back to him, he took it, shrugging his shoulders and grinning at her.

"Always room for some more, I always say! Did you manage to speak to Jay?"

"Yeah him and a girl called Rachel should be showing up soon, I just hope they get here OK."

"Rachel eh… she cute?" They both burst out laughing just as Amanda walked through the door with Jay and the girl, she assumed to be Rachel, in tow.

57

"Hey guys, look who I found loitering outside."

Both Michelle and Mark ran to them, shouting, hugging and laughing. Introductions were made, and soon the group settled down to talk and eat among the books.

Mark and Rachel were happily sharing crisps and looking over the DVDs from Mark's bag, when she pulled out the vampire one.

"Oh! I remember this one," she turned it over to read the blurb. "It's really gory, haven't seen it in years though," she looked out into space, thoughtful for a moment, and then looked around. "Don't suppose this place has got a TV?"

An hour later in one of the small cramped back research rooms the movie played silently, lighting the group's faces with a blue-green glow. Rachel had the remote and was fast forwarding it in places.

"Here it is; this is the bit I wanted to show you."

Watching, the group saw a bunch of teenagers confronting a large dangerous looking vampire surrounded by minions. Rachel spoke over the sound.

"See that big guy there? He's the head vampire, watch what happens when they kill him."

The group watched as, just as the head vampire was killed, all the smaller vampires started dying off along with him, in a series of twisted jerky movements, then finally the head vampire exploded, showering everyone with blood and glop.

Rachel switched off the movie and Jay was the first to turn to her.

"OK so what was the point of showing us that?" he asked confused.

"Well, I just thought if it can work with vampire zombies, why not seagull zombies too?" she replied with a shrug.
Amanda laughed. "You're kidding right?"

"Hey, I just figure that there must be a seagull out there that started this whole fucked up situation! It's worth a shot isn't it?" she looked at the others for support.

"How would we know which one was the leader?" Jay asked.

"And where would find him? There are a million birds out there!" piped up Michelle.

Mark got up and switched off the TV and turned to them, "Didn't the papers say it started with those two Neds down by the harbour? Maybe that's the best place to start?"

Jay looked round the group, who were all nodding. He turned to Michelle sitting beside him. "Shelly, what do you think?"

Michelle covered a yawn with her hand and stood up to stretch, she looked around. "I think we'd better all get a good night's kip, because we've got a big day tomorrow."

The morning was grey, wet and misty. Dampness clung to the group as they made their way quietly through the deserted streets. Rachel blew on the dog whistle every so often, Mark and Amanda scorched a bird that had taken them by surprise next to the graveyard as the group picked their way through the deserted shops and corpse-filled streets, the stench of death getting ever stronger the closer they got to the harbour.

On Guild Street they stopped to eat and rest awhile, Jay pointing out with grim humour how bird shit on the street sign had changed Guild Street to Gul Street.

"Must be getting close then, eh dude" Amanda laughed nervously.

They were all on edge now, picking off a few birds here and there was dangerous enough, but who knew what lay around the corner in wait for them. Mark put down his sandwich, brushed the crumbs from his mouth and looked through the binoculars at the skies and building tops.

"There are a lot of those buggers out there," he shouted down to the rest, who were grouping their meagre arsenal together.

"A couple of spray cans, some soda bombs and a dog whistle!" Rachel looked around at the group, worry etched on her face.

"I think its safe to say that we're fucked!" she swore under her breath, running her hands through her hair she stormed off to kick moodily at the concrete wall behind them.

Jay picked up the dog whistle, it glinted in his hand.

"Pity we didn't have a giant one of those," Michelle laughed pointing to it.

Jay looked up at her and then back down at the whistle and a smile broke over his face. "I think you just might have something there gorgeous," he shouted laughing and hugging her.

Thirty minutes later he had finished explaining the plan to the group, they looked at him like he'd just gone mad. Michelle had a slight smile on her face.

"You want us to get on one of those big ass boats that are surrounded by killer zombie shithawks and do what again?" Rachel asked chewing at her nail distractedly.

"Use the boats fog horn to amplify the dog whistle's sound, to stun the seagulls nearest us so that we've got a clear path to wherever the top bird is… simple." Jay sat back on his haunches and smiled at them.

"Dude you're crazy," Rachel laughed.

"Crazy like a fox," Jay gurned a funny face at her, which started the rest of the group off in fits of laughter. The sound of it bounced and echoed off the walls surrounding them, a shaft of sunlight broke through the mist, enveloping the laughing group and for a second everything felt like it was going to be OK.

The sound of a hissing gull broke the laughter off abruptly. A small beady eyed gull dropped down into the middle of the friends, hissing at them, trickles of green drool dribbling from its beak, its feathers around its head stained black with blood. Mark was already pulling out a spray can but Amanda's lighter had stopped working, she cursed it, red in the face.

Michelle scrabbled around in her own pockets for her one. "Amanda! Here, catch," she said, throwing the lighter over the hissing seagull's head, which was being kept back by Jay waving a piece of broken pipe at it.

"Mark! Now! Spray!" she screamed at him.

Covering his eyes with his arm, Mark aimed the spray can at the bird, the flames caught it and a jet of white hot fire torched the gull, turning it into a shrieking fireball. It finally slumped down and lay still, Rachel delivered the final death blow under her army boot with a satisfying crunch.

"The sooner we kill these bastards the better," panted Amanda.

"Then let's get going guys, its getting on, and I don't want to be caught down by the harbour in the dark," Michelle said, pulling on her backpack.

That thought drew a collective shiver from the group and getting their stuff together, they set off towards Market Street and the upper dock.

Getting on the boat had been tricky and now the group found themselves in what they hoped was the main control room. Amanda looked around at the millions of buttons, wheels and dials and ran her fingers through her hair, making it stick up. "OK…anyone who's a boat expert, raise their hands," she joked.

Michelle smiled at her, "Don't worry dude, there's always an idiot's guide to places like this, we've just got to find it."

"We really just need to get to the loudspeaker controls and hook the whistle up to it," said Jay, helping the rest of them search the cabin.

"Found something," shouted Mark, holding up a large important looking manual. Flicking through it while the others crowded around him, he ran his fingers though the pages until he came across what they were looking for.

"Here we go, Ships P.A. and speaker systems," he smiled triumphantly and handed the book to Michelle.

"Nice one dude," taking the book and reading quickly she looked over to Jay. "Says here that the P.A. and fire alarm system are linked, so we shouldn't have any problem blasting those bastards with enough noise to make their ears bleed!"

"Great, so we'd better get cracking before it gets too late then guys," Jay said, checking the manual for the ships P.A. layout.

It was three hours later and after much crossing of wires, swearing, one small electric shock and miles of duct tape, the dog whistle was finally rigged up to the ship's speakers. Mark and Amanda had been keeping a lookout over the harbour as the sky turned to twilight,

"Um, guys you might want to take a look at this," Amanda motioned for the rest of the group to look out the windows.

All along the quay, the walls and sheds were gradually being covered with a sea of gulls coming in to roost for the night. Worryingly, the front of the ship also had a heavy layer of bickering gore-slimed birds.

Michelle looked over to Jay and Rachel. "It's time, blow the horn."

Nodding, they headed off to the rigged speaker. She shouted after them. "Get ready to follow us down to the harbour guys. I don't know how much time the whistle will give us."

Grabbing their bags and what few weapons they had left, Mark, Michelle and Amanda ran out of the room and down to the dock side, just in time to see a wave of shrieking birds fly up into the sky, colliding into each other in a effort to get away from the sound that was pounding into their skulls. Two seconds later Jay and Rachel came running out to join them.

"Where we heading?" Rachel panted. Michelle pointed to a row of large industrial sheds that lined the dock side.

"If we can get to the shed and find shelter, the whistle should give us a bit of time to work out our next move."

Moving as one, the group pounded across the tarmac keeping their eyes peeled for attacks.

"Don't you think we should have thought about our next move before this?" panted Amanda to Michelle.

"Probably would have been a good idea, yeah," she gasped back.

Diving through the doors of the shed, a quick scout round confirmed that they were seagull free and could catch their breath for a second, behind a pile of crates.

"Ow, think I twisted my ankle a bit back there," Rachel said taking of her boot and gingerly prodding her foot. Mark knelt down next to her, pulling a small white toilet bag from his backpack.

"Hold still, I've got something that should fix that right up," holding her foot in his hands he began to wrap a bandage gently around the swollen ankle. Rachel smiled at him, a blush tinting her cheeks,

"Thank you," she whispered.

The rest of the group grinned at each other and rolled their eyes.

Ten minutes later the group had left the shed, after checking for birds, and were headed in the direction of a large building which held the lifeboat offices and also where the smell of decaying meat and bird shit was strongest. Keeping to the shadows the group peered through the dusty windows into the building.

"Fucking hell," gasped Amanda turning pale.

The sight that greeted the group was sickening. The seagull that had been the beginning of the end sat before them on a rotting pile of human bodies and bird waste. Transformed, as the mutated ingredients from the bar of chocolate pulsed though its body, changing it into a large, bloated monster the size of a dog. Featherless, its veins protruding though pale translucent skin, its sightless pink eyes roamed the room for any sounds, a high pitched wailing came from its gaping maw, its now useless wing stumps flapped in frustration as its demands for food went ignored. Heart hammering inside her chest Michelle dragged her eyes away from the window to join the others.

What the hell man!" groaned Jay sinking down next to Amanda.

"Was that him? Rachel stared at her in disbelief.

"That's defiantly the lead gull, damn ugly bugger ain't he?" Mark said looking back worriedly at the window.

"Jay, how long do you think the whistle will last? Michelle said turning to him.

He checked his watch. "I'm not sure, five minutes, maybe less, we need to do this now if it's going to get done at all."

"You think we brought enough lighter fluid?" asked Mark.

"Let's go find out," Michelle said, shoving cans into her pockets and handing the rest around.

The group was silent as they nervously made their way inside the building, grimacing as the fetid stink in the air choked them and made them gag into their hands. As they got closer to the room they stopped suddenly, a group of seagulls stood guard around the front of the door, in obvious discomfort with the sound the whistle was making, but the loyalty they had to their master was too strong for them to dare move any further.

"Shit! Now what?" sighed Rachel.

Michelle looked over to Mark and Amanda. "You guys got any spray left?" she asked.

Amanda shook the last can. "A little; might just be enough though."

"Think you two could blast them out the way?"

Shaking the can, Mark grinned. "Come on Mandy my girl, let's go toast us some bird flesh."

"I think you enjoy this way too much dude," Amanda laughed, following Mark as he ran towards birds that started up hissing venomously at them, only to be abruptly cut off with a blast of liquid fire. The rest of the group followed them through the burning bundles of birds and into the main room where they stopped dead in their tracks, their eyes needing time to take in the full horrendous sight before them.

Rearing up before them, drool and blood spraying from its beak, the king bird screamed his outrage.

"Blast him!" screamed Jay, spraying lighter fluid over the bird and its rotting nest pile. The rest followed his lead, and soon a petrol haze blurred their vision and covered the room in its scent.

Michelle was just about to flick her lighter when a deafening sound of gulls filled the air and several crashed through the windows to land at their feet.

"Shit!" Rachel screamed "the whistle must have stopped working, Michelle quick!" Pressing her thumb down, the lighter burst into life and she threw it towards the king seagull's face. It screamed in anguish before bursting into a mass of flames and painful squalling. All around them the smaller seagulls took up the cry, until it filled the room.

"Guys look!" Mark was pointing to the smaller gulls, now twisting and convulsing all around them.

"It worked! Rach was right!" he raced over to her grabbing her in a hug, and spun her round laughing.

As small bird bodies popped and turned black all around them, they stood together surveying the scene before them, the setting sun casting a shimmering haze through the broken windows.

"I don't know about you guys, but I could sure use a drink right about now," laughed Amanda.

"Good idea dude," grinned Michelle, "but I fancy a lie down first, before I fall down!"

Laughing amongst themselves the small group of friends made there way back towards the ship for a well earned sleep as the bodies of seagulls rained from the sky around them.

Epilogue

The girl walked along the path, hurrying home from school, looking forward to her dinner, *Fish and chips tonight, can't wait!* She thought to herself, though she had been very hungry so she didn't see the harm in popping into the local paper shop on her way and buying a chocolate bar to keep her going on the trip home.

Jingling the change in her pocket she looked along the rows of bright shiny bars of gobstoppers and fizzing candy, until she spotted a box on the bottom shelf, dusty and pushed to the back, the neon green had caught her eye, and *bonus*! They were selling them off for ten pence a bar! Grabbing a handful she went up and paid for her sweets and walked back on to the street unwrapping the bar and quickly taking a huge bite.

"Burgh!" Her face screwed up. "No wonder they're trying to sell them off cheap!"

Throwing the bars down on the pavement, she stormed off home lamenting having wasted the last of her pocket money on that crap.

As the girl disappeared round the corner, a small, grey scruffy pigeon fluttered down next to the chocolate bar and started to eat.

HARBOUR ANNIE
By
Sharon Hawthorne

"*Lalalalala la –merica... I like to live in America... Ok by me in America...,*" Harbour Annie sings, stamping her shoeless foot and clapping her hands in time to the rhythm.

A crowd has gathered. Some clap and sway along with Annie as she sings her favourites from the musicals. Others look on horrified at the grime that seeps into the lines on her sunken face and coats her hands until her translucent white skin is all but diminished. Harbour Annie finishes with a twirl that raises her hem-less skirt to show skinny thighs and bare buttocks.

"Bravo, Bravo," the crowd cheer. Even those, whose faces were a moment ago full of scorn, are overwhelmed by Annie's performance and are drawn happily into the applause.

As her cap fills with coins and notes Annie's smile lights up her face, showing the world a glimmer of the beauty that once was. *No tricks tonight.* She smiles, relieved, and spins away from her audience to stare across Union Terrace Gardens to the theatre in the distance. Pieces of a life flash before her and she wonders if the woman she sees in her mind is her or an actress from a film. When she's ready she turns back and fixes her gaze at the young man calling out for more. She recognises him, but doesn't know his name.

"Sing Maria," he yells.

"No, Annie always sings that. How about that one from 'My Fair Lady'," an older woman says. She recognises her too. These are her regulars and if Annie had an ego she would know them as her fans, she would know that people travel to Aberdeen from far and wide to hear her sing and she would know that she had become something of a legend in the city.

Annie steps into the middle of the semi circle that begins at one end of the bridge and ends at the other. She takes a deep breath, straightens out her spine, raises her arms out wide like a Broadway star and lifts her chin ready to start.

"Why not Moon River?"

The words stop her stony dead. Without moving her arms she shifts her head a fraction to see who has interrupted her. She looks him up and down, his expensive suit and soft hands, her quizzical eyes asking the question that her tongue cannot.

"Hello Annie," he says.

Her eyes widen and she shakes her head, moving her arms slowly back to her sides as graceful as a ballerina, defying the tremble inside.

"Annie, you ok?" The one who wanted a song from 'My Fair Lady' asks.

Harbour Annie shakes her head, more fervently this time, and kneels down to gather her things and to pour the coins into her bag.

"Do you want to go?"

Annie nods. She snaps her head, searching for the man in the nice suit, but he's gone. She looks right then left, she stands on tip toes, but he's definitely gone. She knows him, but can't remember why. All she remembers is the fear and the pain that now tumble through her heart like boulders from an avalanche. She pulls on her coat. It's inside out and filthy, but she likes people to see that it once came from Chanel. She thinks it makes her look elegant and stylish. She grabs her bag, nods a thank you and dashes through the crowd, ignorant of the disappointed cries that follow her across Union Street and down Bridge Street. She's forgotten about the man already. All she can think about is the money she has in her bag which means the cleaning lady in the station toilet can't tell her to piss off. Not today. Today she can wipe her backside with soft paper and wash her hands afterwards, just like a real person.

Later, as another lonely ship docks in the harbour, Annie counts her money.

"How much you got Annie?" Mac asks.

Mac is her friend. They curl up together under the bridge to keep warm. He is short and skinny and always has a knife in his

68

belt for protection. That's why he's called Mac, Mac the Knife, Mac for short.

Annie shields her eyes against the strong evening sun with one hand and holds out her bag with the other. Mac lets out a long whistle.

"Fuck me Annie, I cannae mind far they sell champagne, but we'll be drinking it the night."

Harbour Annie laughs and nods enthusiastically, rattling the bag for Mac to take.

"Alright me lady," he says, like a butler. "And what would Madame care for?"

Annie stands up, peers over the harbour wall and points to the chipper on the other side of the road. Then she pretends to drink so that Mac knows to go to the off licence too. As if he needed reminding.

"Very well Madame," he says. "Please take a seat and I will be back in a jiffy."

Harbour Annie can't stop laughing as Mac spreads out his jacket on the shingle for her to sit on. She knows she's been happy before, but she can't remember when. As she plays with the edge of her skirt, a smile refusing to leave her face, she hears footsteps along the stones. *That was quick.* But when she looks up it isn't Mac.

"Annie?" It's the man from earlier, the one who wanted to hear Moon River. She doesn't sing Moon River anymore. She doesn't know why. She just knows that it hurts. Her heart beats faster and her breath fixes in her throat as she stands suddenly and turns to run away. She crashes straight into Mac who drops their dinner so that he can catch her.

Annie runs behind him and points to the man in the nice suit. Mac pulls his knife and brandishes it at the man, but it does nothing to persuade the man to leave.

"I danea want to hurt ye," Mac says. He's afraid. He's never pulled his knife on anyone before.

69

"I'm not here to hurt anyone either," the man says. He glances briefly at Mac, a little bemused. "I just want to talk to Annie. It's been so long."

Annie cocks her head to the side, a faint glimmer of recognition passes across her eyes and she wants to cry. Instead she motions for Mac to gather up their supper and offers the man a chip. He accepts despite her filthy hands. Annie sits back down, Mac still has the knife in his hands, but it's pointing down toward the earth.

"I dinnae ken fit ya got to say to Annie, but ye can say it to me as weel," Mac says defensively. Annie nods her agreement before stuffing the battered fish into her mouth.

"I know why you ran away Annie," the man says. He's down on one knee so that his face is level with Annie's. He looks as though he might propose.

"Annie didnae run away," Mac says, sitting down so close to Annie that he might as well be in her lap.

Annie puts a finger to her lips to silence her friend.

"It broke my heart too, losing Lawrence like that, but he would never have wanted this."

Annie feels all the blood rush from her head as she struggles to her feet. She doesn't understand. Who was Lawrence? Why does the mention of the name cause an agony to rise inside her, urging her to scream like a banshee? She points to the man, then Mac, then back again, insisting that Mac speak for her. Tears stream down her face, creating rivers through the grime.

"Aye, quine, it's alright," Mac says, drawing her head to his chest as he wraps his skinny arms around her shoulders. Annie pushes him away.

"Annie, I'm sorry," the man says. He has tears in his eyes too. "It's taken fifteen years to find you. I've been on my own for fifteen years. First Lawrence, then you. Annie, please."

Annie looks up at Mac and nods her head in the man's direction. She knows that Mac understands, but he doesn't know what to say.

"Me and Annie hiv been a'gether for aboot ten year min," Mac says, defending his friendship. "Ye cannae just come here and tak her awa."

There is a long pause. The three of them look down at the pebbles beneath their feet. Annie wonders how the man makes his shoes so shiny.

"She's my Annie now," Mac finally says.

Harbour Annie remembers now. She falls to her knees, as though an invisible force has pulled away her legs. "Lawrence," she mumbles, hiding her face in her hands. She hears a gasp from Mac, he's only ever heard her voice in song.

The man holds out a small red book. "Here," he says.

Mac snatches the book from his hand and opens the first page. It's a photo album. "Is that you, Annie?"

Annie nods and runs a broken nail across the young face of the singer in the photo. She remembers that her dress is made from velvet and swishes against the floorboards as she walks. In the photo she crouches down by the piano, her arms open wide for the little boy to run into. A younger version of the man stands in the background, so much pride and love etched on his face that Mac has to look away. He isn't usually moved so easily, but he loves Annie and now he's sure she'll leave.

"Our son died," the man says, but his words seize his throat and he looks across at the big ships for a moment. "He was seven. He ran into the road and a car hit him. It wasn't your fault Annie. It wasn't anyone's fault."

Annie can't bear the pain. It runs slowly through her like hot lava spewing from a well hidden volcano. She wishes he hadn't come, she wishes she couldn't remember.

"You can come home now Annie," he says.

Annie shakes her head and reaches up a hand for Mac. Mac is her home now. She feels safe resting her head on his shoulder, drinking cider from a bottle and singing on Union Bridge. Sometimes her feet hurt, sometimes she throws stones at the women in the toilets and sometimes it's so cold that she feels as though her face has been bitten off. But here she's safe and she forgets the pain. She shakes her head again and hands the photo album back.

The man looks crushed, devastated. She remembers he's called George and in the life they shared together they were happy, but that happiness came at a cost that was too high for Annie.

"Please," he begs, his tears washing his cheeks.

Harbour Annie shakes her head again and gestures for both men to sit on the stones. She coughs to clear her throat, raises her arms out to the sides, lifts her chin high and starts to sing.

"Moon River, wider than a smile, I'm crossing you in style someday..."

It breaks her heart to sing those words again, but Lawrence loved it when she sung him to sleep and now she sings it to George as a parting gift. When she's finished there is silence, as if the whole world is in mourning for the end of her song. George lifts himself from the stones, steps over to Annie and kisses her cheek. Annie smiles as she watches George take the steps two at a time up to the main road.

The summer sky in Aberdeen never truly gets dark and even though it's nearing midnight the twilight blue lights their way to the bridge. They settle in their usual spot, Mac leans against the brick wall and Annie leans against him. She lays awake until the sun reclaims the sky and finally her thoughts are lost to her dreams.

In the morning Harbour Annie forgets the man with the nice suit and the shiny shoes and, as she wanders up to her spot on Union Bridge, she hums the songs she plans to sing and squints against the bright sunshine that bounces from one building to the next.

LIVING THE DREAM
by
Russ Alexander

He sliced the knife through the alabaster stem of her neck, watching in amusement as spurts of frothing blood sprayed him. She stared up at him like a startled deer, eyes shocked and incredulous and he smiled, a lop-sided grin smeared over his crooked teeth. She struggled beneath his body weight, hopelessly trying to escape the thick bonds that tied her hands and legs together.

"Goodbye, dear wife!" he purred as he began a frenzy of slashing...

"Walter! Walter!...are you sleeping again you lazy little good-for-nothing!"

The words thundered up the stairs and penetrated the bedroom door, pierced his subconscious and dragged him back to reality...away from the recurring happy dream he was having. Walter got up from his bed, where he was trying to have a nap, and looked at himself in the mirror. Looking back at him was a person he did not recognise...a slight, balding man in his mid-fifties, with what hair he had left rapidly going grey. Sad puppy dog brown eyes met his gaze and he could not recall what the young man he used to be looked like, or how he had once felt – had he ever felt anything? Love? Happiness? Lust? He knew he must have at sometime but now, and for so many, many years, he had been in limbo, his own personal level of purgatory. All he really felt now was...hate...but not a burning, passionate, fiery hatred, his hate was a living, physical, breathing thing, his hate had a name and a body, his hate had a life all of its own. His hate's name was...Patricia...he spat her name and a little spittle hit the mirror and run down the glass, he wiped it off with his fingers. All the man in the mirror really cared anything about was his job at the library and the books – all the glorious books, each one an escape tunnel to another world, an emergency exit from the tragedy that was his life. Walter had the ability to pick up a book, almost any book, and within less than a minute he was immersed in the story and the characters became real people around him as he "lived" the book. Walter remembered what his mother had taught him as a child: *"books are our friends and we must look after them,"* she used to say as she sat on his bed reading him a story before he went to sleep, it was just as well he had many books as a child, as Walter had no friends as such, either at school or in the streets around the small terraced house where he lived.

Walter's mother had brought him up alone and had told him that his father had been a soldier who had been killed in the war, although the truth was that his father had left them shortly after Walter was born and she had not heard from him since, but Walter gladly accepted the lie as fact. He had contracted polio as a toddler and it had left him with a pronounced limp and the need to wear a calliper and, when he played alone in the back garden he fantasized that he had somehow inherited his bad leg from his father and that his unknown father had been shot storming up a beach on D-Day.

The children at school, being children, latched on to anything or anybody 'different' and called him 'Frankenstein' and 'Captain Peg-leg.' The only island of friendliness in this sea of misery was Mr Chalmers, his English teacher, who saw the sadness in the small boy and decided to introduce him to the world of books; 'Treasure Island', 'Swallows and Amazons' and 'Great Expectations.' His teacher placed the stepping stones for Walter's journey into the world of books. Mr Chalmers wisely guided him towards a place and career which he thought would shelter Walter, to a certain extent, and where his passion for books would perhaps cushion him against what the world had to throw at him. Mr. Chalmers went that extra mile for his unfortunate pupil and, like some wise eastern Guru, he decided to take the fatherless child under his wing, talking to his young charge about the libraries of the world and about the Great Library of Alexandria and the loss to the world when it had burned down. They talked of ISBN numbers, the Dewey Decimal System and the major Publishing Houses of the literary world and he was introduced to the school library. This became Walter's second home, he got there early before the school day started, to avoid the bullies, and stayed late until he was sure all his tormentors had safely gone home – the cleaners often had to prise his face out of a book and remind him to go home. It was no surprise to anybody when Walter left school and started as a junior at the large library in town, he was a 'natural' with books and before long stunned the older librarians by being able to put his hand on any book they cared to name. Walter quickly climbed the ladder in the library and went from making the tea to the heady heights of Chief Librarian, he was very well respected and liked in his little world of the library and it was said that he had read every book in the place and many more besides and he would talk passionately about books and their authors, many of his colleagues said he should try to get on 'Mastermind.' Walter would laugh and say he was too shy, the truth being that despite his encyclopaedic knowledge of the literary world he knew very little about anything else, he could not tell one football player from another and, as for films, he didn't know De Caprio from De Niro! If he ever went to the cinema it would be to see a film adaptation of a book and it would inevitably be a huge disappointment to him and he would always say that no film could ever be as good as the pictures you see in your imagination, when you actually read the book.

Walter regarded the man in the mirror and noticed what he thought was some spit on the glass that he had missed the first time, he put his fingers up to wipe it and realised that there was no moisture there – what he saw was the reflection of the tears that ran freely down his face.

Another screech came rolling up the stairs and through the bedroom door. "Come down here this very minute...you little runt, your supper's getting cold!"

Walter sighed and limped his way downstairs, it was like descending into Hell, where his own personal live-in Satan waited to torture his soul, his wife, Patricia. It had been only thirty four years since that fateful day at the Registrar's Office, his twenty first birthday as a matter of fact, when he had signed his name in blood and made a pact with this she-devil, he winced at the painful memory of that day, it seemed like an eternity ago, several whole lifetimes – an ice age.

He reached the bottom of the stairs and took that long walk to the kitchen – a condemned man making his last walk to the noose could not have moved with such reluctance. He arrived at the kitchen door and sighed, he knew exactly what was about to happen, a premonition of doom, his stomach started that old familiar empty churning; he raised his hand and pushed open the gates of Hades.

"There you are you ungrateful little man! I hope you know I've been working my fingers to the bone cooking this dinner for you..." her lips kept on moving but Walter was imagining her bones, her bleached white bones lying in a box six feet under. His lips twitched at the thought, into the closest thing that Walter could get to a smile, but his face and lips did not move.

"Are you listening to me? You poor excuse for a man..."

"Yes dear, I'm listening to you..." Walter switched his mouth to auto pilot while in his mind he screamed: *"Yes, I'm bloody listening to you. I've done nothing but listen to you for thirty odd fucking years!"*

He listened to the real words trickling out of his mouth as if they were the words of another, or maybe he was just a ventriloquist's dummy...he felt that way sometimes...do these poor unfortunate manikins ever get pissed off having to say other people's words, words people expect them to say, instead of their own? But they're only dummies, he mused and suddenly had an awful thought – he was her dummy. It was her hand thrust up his arse making his lips move, what an awful picture, Patricia with her arm up his backside, to the elbow, and his mouth clacking open and shut: *"Yes dear…no dear…three bags full dear"* – came the wooden words and he saw his face painted on with large red cheeks and eyebrows moving independently, up and down.

"What's the matter with you now? You pipsqueak, seen a ghost?"

"No dear…" came from the dummy's mouth but Walter heard just two words in a strange deep voice: *"unfortunately not."*

The voice took Walter by complete surprise; it seemed as if there was another person in the kitchen. He looked around and there, standing at the kitchen sink was his mother, his poor dead beloved mother.

Walter collapsed rather than sat down on the seat at the dining table, he felt the blood drain from his face as he whispered… "Mother…?"

"What did you call me? Mother? I'm not your bloody mother. I would be ashamed if I had brought something like you into the world! Fat chance of that. You couldn't even manage that, you couldn't even give me a child – you sad sperm-less little sod!" Patricia's face distorted with disgust.

Walter's eyes looked past her to the sink where his mother stood. He couldn't understand it, his mind just couldn't take it in – his dead mother, she had died a year before that dark, fateful day he had married Patricia. Walter had nursed her through a short illness, she had lasted only eight brief weeks from the doctor's diagnosis but he had treasured that last, two oh-so-short months with her. It was the only time he had ever been off work and away from his beloved library haven. His thoughts tumbled over those last days he had spent with his mother…his only parent…his best friend…

She had gone suddenly at the end, Walter had been downstairs preparing her dinner and was taking it upstairs on a tray when he heard her cry out, dropping the tray he had pushed open the door and made it to her bedside.

"Walter…" she said as she felt his hand grasp hers "Walter, I'm afraid I'm leaving you and I don't want you to be alone, you're a lovely thoughtful boy and I would hate to think of you on your own," she patted his hand, her veins and bones clearly showing beneath her thin translucent skin. "I think you should marry that young girl you've been seeing. She'll look after you and I don't want you to be alone."

Walter kissed the back of his mother's hand, the hand he had known so well all his life, it had bathed him as a baby, tenderly washed skinned knees when he had found it hard to walk, at first unaided, after the polio and the hand he had nervously held so tightly and had to let go of, on that first terrifying day at school.

"Be brave my little soldier," his mother had said as the teacher's hand had replaced hers and led him into the classroom, he clearly remembered glancing back over his shoulder at his mother.

"I'll always be here for you, my boy," he heard her words resounding in his head, and she blew him a kiss as he was led away.

He felt her hand slowly relax as her strength ebbed, and he had looked up through the tears to see her head bow slightly to one side and heard her last breath escape her lips as her soul, at last, left her body.

He suddenly felt so alone, an orphan of the storm; his grief cut him to the bone. Suddenly exhausted he had curled up and slept next to his mother that night and only phoned the doctor in the first light of the morning. The next few days passed in a sort of a haze and he only really came to as the last few mourners were leaving the house after the funeral, he shook their hands limply, as empty words of sorrow were uttered, and he lay there on the carpet. Then he had felt his hand taken by a hand very reminiscent of his mother's, he looked up and there stood Patricia, the young lady he had been seeing these past few months.

"I'll stay and help you clear up and wash the cups," she seemed to smile gently…almost his mother's smile.

What had been just a casual relationship seemed to take on a new serious depth and over the next few days she had come round and helped him out with the house and had bagged up his mother's clothes and taken them round to her favourite charity shop. She seemed to do this with undue haste as she packed and stuffed the clothes with his mother's own unique smell still clinging to them, into a black bin bag – she never had that many clothes but what she had was of good quality and well looked after. He had tried to take a silk blouse he was particularly fond of, out one of the bags, just to keep, he thought, but she had seen him and said that a clean break was best and it would be better if he had nothing of his mother's around him to remind him of her, and had snatched it from his grasp and returned it to the bin liner.

Over the next few weeks she had changed the old house a lot, the old curtains in the living room, the blankets on his bed for a duvet and an old black and white picture of him and mother on holiday at the seaside was changed to a coloured one of Patricia and himself at a library function. He never said much, especially as the changes did brighten the old house up a bit, she was also coming round and cooking his meals – as he was not very well versed in the ways of the casserole dish – his mother had always been there to cook for him. Then came the fateful night that she had announced after supper that she was *'staying over'* he said that, of course, she could have mother's room. Moving a little closer to him on the sofa she had whispered that she would decide where she slept.

Walter's all too obvious virginity was well and truly plucked that very night and lying warm and close on the single bed of his childhood, Walter decided that he liked this new found intimacy but at the same time was a little uncomfortable about something and it was not only the relative overcrowding of his old bed. He thought about his mother's dying wish that she didn't want him to be alone. He glanced at the sleeping woman at his side and her hand on his bare chest in the moonlight and thought again as he drifted off to sleep that her hands were really rather remarkably reminiscent of his mother's.

Before Walter realised it, Patricia had installed herself in the house like the new cooker and fridge she had insisted he bought to modernise the place a little. He grew used to coming home from the library and smelling supper as he opened the newly repainted front door – it reminded him of happier times when mother was alive and Patricia was really quite a decent cook.

Walter couldn't quite remember much about that fateful Saturday night, Patricia had announced that she was preparing a special meal, her Steak and Ale pie, she said that she had also got a bargain at the supermarket…a 'BOGOF' apparently – buy one bottle of Shiraz and get one free. He was not a great drinker, only sharing the odd sherry with mother at Christmas, but that night, between the two of them, they had managed to polish of both 'BOGOF' bottles! And that is how Walter had felt in the morning 'bogging awful.' He awoke with the unfamiliar feeling of having a small man inside his head trying to escape with a hammer, slowly making his way through a very delicate skull and a thirst that could be seen from space! He felt a cold sweat cover his brow and his mouth seemed to fill with saliva, he threw off the new duvet and ran to the bathroom, which soon echoed to the sound of retching, and in the cold light of day, which filtered through the window as he knelt as if in prayer, at the toilet bowl, he began to remember the previous night. His befuddled brain seemed to release small pieces of memory of the previous night, which played like an old flickering film on his firmly closed eyelids. He really wasn't sure who had brought it up, but he remembered agreeing that it would be such a good idea if they got…married! And they had both raised a replenished glass of ruby red wine in a toast. Then his brain finally released the final piece of the jigsaw of the previous night, it was a clip of the two of them laughing together and Patricia saying that wouldn't it be great if they could get married and every night could be like this? He had only managed to say "yes," in agreement when she had let out a squeal and had said well in that case I accept, and I will marry you. Glasses had clinked together and Walter, full of steak and ale pie and Shiraz, had felt that it was such a good idea, in fact, the best idea that anybody had ever had, but in the back of his mind he wondered if it was he who had come up with it.

"Well then, aren't you going to eat your meal? You always said my Steak and Ale pie was your favourite – so are you going to bloody well eat it, you little tosser!"

Walter looked up at his wife across the table, two opposing armies, deadly enemies sizing each other up over a battle ground of china, cutlery and linen. He couldn't remember quite when she had changed, her slow metamorphosis into the snake-haired Whore of Babylon. He remembered the happier times...oh so long ago...she had said that she was broody and wanted a baby more than anything else in the world and he had come round to her way of thinking, it was the natural way of things, a small boy perhaps to inhabit his old room with all his memories of childhood. They tried and tried for months which turned into years, his failure punctuated by her period every month. Although they never consulted a doctor, she considered it was his fault that she could not conceive a child and Walter wore the blame like an overcoat, heavily hanging around his shoulders.

Slowly, little by little, she had changed towards him, there was no more intimacy and all he would see of her was her cold back turned to him in bed. Whenever he was at home she would look at him with contempt and she would only open her mouth to snipe at him or belittle him, calling him some terrible names and making his time at home a misery. Since he was Chief Librarian he started to stay late at the library, deliberately spending less time at home with the enemy whose hate and detest seemed to grow inside her, like the baby he could never give her. Walter moved out of his mother's old room, where they had shared a bed, and moved into his small bedroom. What had been his childhood refuge had now become his adult refuge, and he slept in same comforting single bed where he had experienced two types of love – the love of a mother tucking him in and reading him a story and the first physical love of his wife. At least there he could read his precious books, his door at the back of the wardrobe leading him into a different world, without her complaining of his bedside light keeping her awake. It struck him that he had only ever seen her read one book, 'Anna Karenina,' and it had taken her months! She had never wanted to talk to him about if she had enjoyed the work of Tolstoy, he wondered if, like the heroine of the book, she felt she had an empty life or was she thinking of emulating Anna and was looking for her own Count Vronsky to have an affair with? He concluded that he didn't really care, and that she had the depth of a puddle. He wished he had someone who he could talk to about his life and books, which were the same thing really. Instead his hate and contempt for her grew, a bubbling mantle of loathing ready to break through the surface and, one day, become a volcano spewing molten hate that would burn them both to ash.

He snapped back to the reality of the kitchen as he heard the voice again, the odd, low tones which seemed to come from this apparition of his mother, which stood, large as life, at the sink.

"Come to me, my brave boy," his mother's lips moved in slow motion. Walter pushed back his chair and stood up from the steaming mass of steak and ale pie, potatoes and gravy in front of him and moved to the sink.

"Where the hell do you think you're going? Sit down and eat the food I prepared, you ungrateful little bastard," Patricia loaded her fork up with a large lump of steak and pie crust and shoved it in her mouth. Patricia had always loved her food and had grown with every year of their unhappy marriage, so that now she was the size of a large mountain gorilla, dwarfing Walter and making him feel even smaller and even more insignificant than he already felt.

"I'm just going to wash my hands dear," Walter limped his way behind his wife to the sink. He stood there looking at his mother, she looked just as she had in her prime, and Walter felt his eyes welling up with tears. He saw his mother's lips move…

"Why don't you kill her?" the voice said matter-of-factly. *"Why don't you just fucking kill her?"*

82

He had never heard his mother swear before but then, he had never seen a ghost before either and the voice wasn't his mother's loving tongue, it was a low, deep monotone.

"Pick up the knife, my brave soldier," his mother's kind eyes looked down at the chopping board where Patricia's favourite carving knife lay. It had a good ten inch long stainless steel blade with a wooden handle and she kept it razor sharp so it would cut through any meat she had decided to prepare. It gleamed in the sun and still had traces of the steak she had cut up for the pie.

"Remember your dream my lovely boy. No one will blame you and afterwards we can be together again, just like we were in the old days. The neighbours hear her screaming at you every day. Everybody knows that she deserves it. She has made your life a misery. Live the dream my lovely boy."

Walter felt as if he were in a trance as he watched his right hand reach out and grab the handle of the knife. He felt the weight of the weapon in his hand; he held the knife in his fist the blade pointing downwards at the floor. He raised it to eye level and slowly turned to face his wife's back; reminding him of how her back always turned towards him when they shared a bed...always turned towards him...she would not turn her back on him ever again.

"Do it my brave soldier...do it for your old Mum."

Walter's fingers gripped the knife, draining them of blood in a deadly grip. He raised the knife above his head, he would savour the downward strike, it was just like his dream. His eyes focused on her neck and he wondered if he should say the words he said in the dream. His lips started to form the words: "Goodbye, dear wife."

Patricia's body seemed to jolt and tense as if she somehow sensed the knife about to plunge into her. She seemed to growl and her head shot backwards. Walter looked at the knife in his hand, a cobra about to strike, a deadly motion but frozen in time – his fingers opened and the knife fell to the floor, embedding itself in the laminate flooring with a thunk!

Walter walked around the table and looked at his wife, she too seemed frozen in time, her mouth wide open in a silent scream but only a strangled gasp escaped her lips and her face was blood red. She dropped her knife and fork and both her hands went to her throat, as if she was trying to strangle herself. Walter sat down slowly in his seat and watched. Patricia's eyes were bulging now and bloodshot he noticed her colour had changed to a deep purple and her tongue stuck out of her mouth as far as it possibly could as she desperately tried to take in some life giving oxygen. Walter smiled, she did love big pieces of steak in her famous Steak and Ale pie and one of them had done Walter a big favour and, it occurred to him, also saved him the all the unpleasantness of spending years in prison!

He leaned forward in his seat and said: "It's all for the best, my dear. I retire in a few years and you would have made that a misery for me too, like you have the past thirty odd years. It'll all be over soon, for both of us."

Patricia's eyes still just stared at him, pleading him to do something.

Walter looked at his pocket watch as her eyes finally glazed over and her head fell forward heavily onto her plate, her face, now blue, buried in the food.
Walter winced.

"Will we go upstairs and you can read me a story?" he raised his eyes up to look at his Mother but she was gone.

Walter picked up his untouched plate of food and walked across to the cooker and gently, with a spatula, he replaced the portion of pie in the pie dish, as if it had never been served. He would heat it up and eat it later after all the fuss was over – but he made a mental note to chew it well. He placed the boiled potatoes back in the pan too, carefully wiping off the gravy, and then washed the plate and placed it on the drying rack. It would avoid any awkward questions being asked if he just said he had felt unwell and had gone upstairs to lie down for a while, which is when he had fallen asleep and heard nothing. Bending down he pulled the carving knife out of the floor and placed it back on the chopping board – that was indeed a close shave.

Walter decided he would read for a while as he climbed the stairs and perhaps think a bit about his future for an hour or so before coming downstairs to 'find' poor, dear Patricia and phone the authorities. If he just stayed very quiet perhaps that would be interpreted as grief. As he lay down on the bed and opened his book he thought about one of his colleagues at the library, Mrs. Harper – Susan. She had been widowed about a year ago, was very pleasing to the eye with a lovely soft quiet voice and she could talk at length about books and authors, in fact she ticked every box really.

Walter smiled…for the first time in a long, long time.

FLYING
by
Ann Miller

"Courage angels, please come."

Jeanette said angels always came when you called on them, and not just at parties. Jeanette said you didn't usually see them with your eyes, but Alice badly wanted to see them.

"Courage angels, **please** come," she repeated a bit louder, peering into the darkness, hoping they might pop up – all in white, with wings and haloes like the ones in pictures – next to her wardrobe, or in the corner where her case sat packed and ready for tomorrow. She didn't need the courage angels here in her room, of course. She didn't need courage. Mum said Alice wasn't scared of anything. But if only she could see them, know that they were here, she'd send them into Mum. Angels worked when you were asleep too, Jeanette said. That was good, because Mum would be sound asleep, for sure. She'd taken an extra half tablet.

The doctor says I can take an extra half if I need. And I need tonight. That's because she was going to hospital tomorrow.

How long for, Mum?

Maybe for a wee while. You'll be all right, darling, won't you? Your bus'll drop you off at Bridge House after your Day Centre. You like Bridge House, don't you? Maybe some of your mates'll be there.

Mum had started to cry then.

Alice went to Bridge House for a weekend or even for a week or two, when Mum needed a break, but it was a break for Alice too. Sometimes Alice wished she lived at Bridge House. It wasn't that she minded living here, though Mum hated it, said it was what made her sick—being stuck in this damp smelly box way up on the tenth floor, with other boxes through the walls and ceiling and floor—all so thin you could hear right through them, hear the banging doors, shouting, swearing, TVs, music, even people going to the toilet.

All of that didn't bother Alice so much. It was how Mum was these days that she didn't like. She'd got used to a lot of things, like

86

Mum still being in her dressing gown when Alice got home from the centre, and having Rice Crispies and Coke or even just crackers for tea almost every night, Though Mum hated it here she could hardly manage to go out any more, not even to Somerfield. Mum couldn't help it. What Alice hated was seeing Mum slumped on the sofa all evening, not watching the TV, not looking at anything, not really listening when Alice chatted about her day at the centre. Usually Mum had her fingers plugged into her ears to shut out the blare of the neighbours' TV or the blast from their Hi-fi. Sometimes she closed her eyes, but Alice knew she wasn't sleeping.

Angel party evenings were different, of course. Every second Tuesday, Mum used to get dressed, ready for Jeanette to pick her up. She even let Alice stay on her own. Alice wanted to go to the angel parties, but Mum said not yet —wait 'til you're a bit older. She was eighteen, she reminded Mum, and Jeanette wouldn't mind her going—why couldn't she? Mum never said why.

Never mind honey, she's just a little scared. Jeanette said Mum was scared of lots of things. But why angels? They were good. Mum wanted them. *People are often scared of good things, things they want.* Alice had given up arguing and begging to go. Anyway, it was almost as good, having the place to herself for the evening. She could turn up the TV or Hi-fi to drown out the neighbours, look at her magazines and try practising the new movements she'd learned in creative dance. Apart from turning the volumes up, she could do these things other evenings, but it wasn't much fun with Mum always lying there in her gown, like she was sick. But on angel party evenings, Mum would be all dressed, even smiling, though she had to keep on at Alice about not going out the door, not opening the door, not answering the door…

OK, Mum, OK… Who'd come to the door anyway? Nobody except Jeanette ever did.

I know, darling, you're eighteen. And don't open the balcony door. I know I've said it before. Not just before; every time. Jeanette, waiting there, would smile at Alice over Mum's shoulder, and mum would wag her finger.

No flying, remember!

That was a joke, the only joke Mum ever made anymore. Maybe the angels did help just a bit sometimes. Joy angels, Jeanette called them. Alice had thought it was joy angels that Mum needed, or maybe health angels.

Yes, those too, honey. But sometimes folk are too scared for joy. We'll call on the courage angels for your mum.

Before Jeanette, Alice hadn't known there were different kinds of angels. Calm angels, love angels, joy, health, courage. Alice couldn't remember all the kinds Jeanette talked about. She hadn't known, either, that angels came to parties. She'd hardly known anything about angels, except what she remembered them looking like in pictures. When Jeanette first started coming to see Mum, Alice had been full of questions. Mum had said to give Jeanette a break, but Jeanette didn't mind.

The parties aren't exactly like the ones you have on your birthday or Christmas, honey, with balloons and cake and all that, but they're just as lovely, just as happy. And yes, angels do bring presents—not things like bubble bath or chocolates all wrapped up. They bring things people need even more. Love. Peace. Joy. Courage. Whatever you need the most, they bring. But you have to really want the gifts they bring... All dressed in white...haloes? If you like, honey. Wings? Maybe. Oh yes, they can fly. Definitely. 'Cause they're free spirits. They can go anywhere they want, anytime. But you know what honey, we can all do that, not just angels. If we truly want to. If we let ourselves. We don't even need wings. We can all fly.

When Mum went out and told Alice "no flying", it wasn't really a joke. She said it because of two things that had happened a long time ago, just after they'd moved in here. Alice remembered as if they'd happened yesterday. The first was the time Alice had wandered out of the flat onto the landing and into the lift. Alice knew from the time she and Mum had been taking up their cases and bags that one button moved you up, one moved you down, but she'd forgotten which was which. She tried pressing first one, then another. She kept on. Up a bit, down a lot, up, up, way down, down, down, way up... She was screaming with laughter, could have gone on all day, but the door suddenly opened and she was yanked out by Mum, who was screaming too.

But Mum, it was fun. I was flying.

The other time was when Mum had said she was going to get rid of the damp, fusty smell in the flat once and for all. She opened, as wide as they'd go, all the windows in every room, even the two big windows in the lounge that had never been opened yet since they'd moved in. They were funny windows, one next to the other, that reached right up to the ceiling and down to the floor—more like doors. You could see out of them onto a little bit of floor with a sort of fence around it. Mum had got a key from the linen cupboard, turned it in a hole in the middle of one, and slid the two windows apart. She had to shake and pull. They were stiff, she said, but she managed to slide them until they each disappeared into the wall on either side and a huge space opened up where they'd been.

Don't go out there, darling. Mum had gone to open the bedroom windows.

Alice stared. They **were** doors, not windows. A cool breeze wafted in, and she thought she felt a spot of water on her face. What was behind the little fence? She had to see, she'd jump straight back in when Mum came back.

There was nothing behind the fence—only space and more space. She ran her hands up and down the cold, hard rails. Her chin just about reached the top when she stood on tiptoe, she was smaller back then. She looked—down, down, down—onto rooftops, treetops, cars, buses, people and dogs—all like toys. Voices floated up, but she couldn't tell what they said. A long, slow buzz grew louder and louder until it drowned out everything else. She craned back her neck, peered upwards. A plane was streaking across the sky that was changing from drizzly grey to blue. She could see stripes of colour—red and blue—across the wings. Maybe it could see her. She leapt up and down, waving.

A seagull swooped down in front of her. She didn't know why people said they were horrible, it was something to do with rubbish bags and mess, but she liked the way they wheeled around in the air and cried. *Keeee-aaaaye*…She keee-aaayed back at him, laughing. He soared back up into the clouds, higher than the plane. If she climbed on top of the fence, maybe she could reach the sky too, maybe she could fly…

No flying! It wasn't funny then. Nothing much ever frightened Alice, but the look on Mum's face almost had, after she'd hauled Alice back inside. Mum had locked the balcony doors and never opened them again.

Mum was scared of more things now than she was back then. Jeanette said she was even scared of getting better. Jeanette didn't only take Mum to angel parties. Sometimes she came and sat beside Mum on the sofa and put her hands on Mum's head. They'd stay like that for ages, both with their eyes closed but not asleep. Afterwards Mum always said it felt nice and warm, but the nice feeling wore off and she never really got better. *You want the healing, honey, but you're scared of it.* Alice couldn't understand. How could you be scared of something you wanted? Alice hated being off sick from her day centre with cold or flu. But Mum's kind of sick wasn't cold or flu.

The courage angels almost helped. The morning after one of the first parties Mum had gone to, Mum was up and dressed even before Alice. She said she was going to ring the housing office and pester them about the transfer. Mum was always talking about the transfer she said she'd put in for a long time ago. Transfer meant moving somewhere else – *not a box, not damp and smelly and noisy, not high up.* She was going to ring the surgery too and ask about getting to see the special doctor. She'd said no to that for a long time because she didn't want to be a mental case. But last night at the party, she'd got the feeling that's what the courage angels were telling her to do.

When Alice came home that day Mum was back in her dressing gown. The housing officer had said the transfer was a long way off; she didn't have enough points, was nowhere near the top of the list. And when she'd rung the surgery, they said they'd get her an appointment with the special doctor, but it might take a while. It took about a month. The first time Mum went, she said it was hard. The doctor had asked her a lot of questions and stared at her and expected her to talk, and she'd tried but didn't get very far. She carried on, and took the new tablets he put her on, but they didn't make her feel any better. After a few more times, she stopped going to the special doctor.

It just made me worse. Maybe it was my fault, Jeanette. He said I didn't open up.

Well honey, I've never had much faith in these head guys. Or pills, either, for that matter. He had a point, though, honey. You don't open up. No, don't take it wrong, honey. We'll carry on with the parties. And what about going with me to the church?

Alice didn't think it was the sort of church some of her mates at the centre talked about going to. At Jeanette's church, dead people spoke to you.

Nothing spooky, honey. Just your friends and relatives who've passed on and want to help you.

Like Nana?

Mum laughed at that, but not as if it was funny. *She didn't like me when she was alive. Why would she want to help me now?* She caught Alice's eye. *Don't look gob-smacked, darling. You don't remember Nana much. Not everyone's close with their Mum, like you and me.*

Alice wondered how dead people could help you. Did they turn into angels?

Yes, in a way, honey. When we die, we're free spirits, like angels—free to go anywhere, do anything. Like we said about flying. So we're free to help people we love who're still on earth.

*That's if they loved you when **they** were on earth.* Mum sounded angry. Jeanette said it was OK to be angry, and maybe she'd like to talk about it, but Mum said no thanks, and no more about dead people either. So Mum didn't go to Jeanette's church, and Jeanette never mentioned dead people any more when Mum was there. But Alice had a lot of questions about them, and sometimes she and Jeanette managed a whispered conversation when Mum went to her room to get changed for the parties.

Mum kept going to the parties, but didn't want any more talk about them when she got home. She just took her tablet and went straight to bed, usually without even undressing. The next morning she didn't always get up, not even to go down in the lift with Alice to meet her bus. When the escort buzzed to pick up Alice for the centre and Alice went in to say bye, Mum would be lying on top of her bed in her going-out clothes that were all rumpled now. Sometimes she didn't change them until the next party, or not even then. One day Jeanette came to take her and said why didn't they help her take a nice shower and get into some fresh clothes before they went, but Mum said it didn't matter, she didn't feel like going anyway. Jeanette tried to talk her into going, kept coming every party night to try, but Mum never went again. Jeanette said that was OK, they'd leave it for now; Mum would come back to the parties when she was ready. She still came to talk to Mum, though Mum hardly said anything now, just lay silently while Jeanette held her hands on Mum's head. But finally, a few days ago, when Jeanette arrived at her usual time, Alice had to tell her that Mum had taken an extra half tablet and gone to bed, and not only that. The doctor said Mum should go to hospital.

Well, that might be the best thing for her just now, honey.

Mum had said it might be the best thing too. *The Rice Crispies have run out. What have you eaten, darling?* Alice didn't know what that had to do with hospital, but Mum often got confused and jumped from one subject to another, when she talked at all. Alice mumbled that she'd found some crackers at the back of the cupboard. She didn't tell Mum that she'd been nicking fruit and nut bars and packets of crisps to take home from the canteen at her centre, ever since the Rice Crispies at home had run out weeks ago. Mum hadn't noticed, because she was never hungry and didn't look. Alice sometimes put one of the bars or a packet of crisps on the coffee table, or more often on Mum's bedside cabinet, planning to say her mates gave her them if Mum asked – she never did—and was glad when she checked and saw that Mum had at least eaten a bite or a half packet. Mum was getting very skinny. Alice knew you could die from not eating.

Why couldn't the angels help Mum, Jeanette?

Maybe they still can, honey. We'll have to keep calling on them, even if your Mum can't just now. You can help her. You're a big help to your Mum, you know. You're the only one she's close to. And probably you're the only thing in life she's not scared of.

Mum often said Alice was a big help, too. Alice wasn't sure. She washed up the few dishes, and Mum had shown her how to run the Hoover through the flat. Alice had talked Mum into letting her try to cook dinner once, in the days when they'd had proper food in the flat. She'd learned how to cook a few things at the centre. But the one time she'd tried at home, the mince had burned and the water in the tattie pan boiled over onto her hand; she and Mum had had to rush to A&E in a taxi. Mum had said never again, although she let Alice make toast, until the time she'd caught Alice using a fork to pry out a piece that was stuck, while the toaster was still on. Making cups of tea she could just manage. She wished Mum would at least let her go shopping for some nice food, she'd gone with Mum often enough to Somerfield, though not since Mum had stopped going out. She'd pestered Mum into letting her walk the few blocks to Mace for milk and bread once. Mum said OK, she'd wait for Alice to buzz and go down to take her up in the lift, though Alice would like to have come up in it herself. Mum waited and waited. Alice found Mace and bought the stuff no problem, but took a wrong turning and wandered about the roads and circles and half-circles of houses that all looked the same, until she finally got home. She didn't think she'd been that long, and couldn't understand why the bobbies were there and Mum was crying. Anyway, like with cooking, it was never again.

Still, at least once, she'd been a big help to Mum.

I'm so sorry, darling. I'll never do it again. It was a mistake, you know, I only wanted to sleep, I didn't want…but you know, I might've taken the whole lot if I didn't have you. I maybe wouldn't have woken up. You're my angel.

Angel. That was before Jeanette. Alice knew now that she couldn't be an angel. You had to be dead to become one.

Alice's eyes were getting used to the dark. Her case loomed in the corner, packed with enough stuff for a long stay at Bridge House.

A few hours ago Alice had been looking forward to going. Kim and Julie might be there. They'd have nice dinners, watch DVDs and go out in the minibus on weekends. Last time they'd gone ice-skating. When Mum had told her she'd be going to Bridge - that was the first thing Alice had thought of – ice-skating. Alice brushed the tear away roughly. Crying was stupid. But she didn't want to go to Bridge House, not any more.

Mum wouldn't get better in hospital. She hadn't the last time, after she'd swallowed all those tablets, although she'd said then that she didn't need to get better—It was just a mistake, she wasn't a mental case even if the doctor thought so, and no way was she going where he wanted her to go. In the end she had gone there—*just for a few tests, darling, so the doctor can prove I'm OK.* She'd stayed almost a month, but she'd just gotten worse and worse after that. The doctors and nurses couldn't help her. Jeanette couldn't. Alice couldn't. Live people couldn't help like angels could. Nana couldn't, even though she was dead and a sort of angel, because Nana and Mum hadn't been close or liked each other. Even the courage angels hadn't managed to help.

You're the only one she's close to. Probably the only thing she's not scared of.

When we die, we're free spirits, like angels…like we said about flying …free to help people we love…

If we only let ourselves. It doesn't take wings. We can all fly.

Alice didn't remember falling asleep, but it was light when she opened her eyes. She threw back her duvet and got up. Jeanette said angels sometimes came to you when you were asleep. You didn't always remember them coming but you could be sure they'd been with you, because they made you know exactly what to do when you woke up. You had the answer you were looking for before you went to sleep.

They'd come to Alice. She knew.

She even knew, without thinking, where Mum kept the key, though she hadn't paid much attention when Mum had screwed a

94

hook high up in the airing cupboard. Alice only had to stretch a little now to reach it. She tiptoed past Mum's room, but Mum was snoring quietly, sound asleep from her extra half tablet.

She had to fiddle and turn the key different ways before it worked. The doors hadn't been opened since that one time long ago, and they were stiff, but she managed to prise them wide enough to get out on to the balcony.

After the carpet, the cold hardness under her bare feet made her shiver. Keeeee-aaaye… She peered up and waved her arms at him, just remembering not to kee-aaye back in case she woke Mum. He was alone in the sky this time. There was no plane, no clouds or drizzle. Everything was pink and orange, not only the whole sky but the balcony floor, the paving stones way down below, the houses, streets, bits of grass—only there were no people—it was too early. She jumped from one foot to the other, laughing quietly. Keeeee-aaaaye, she mouthed, craning her neck, waving and watching until he soared out of sight

She grabbed the top of the railing. She didn't have to stand on tiptoe now, she was bigger. It would be easy. In a few seconds she could help Mum get better. She'd be a free spirit, an angel.

"Courage angels," Alice whispered. In a few seconds, she'd be flying.

UNSEELIE

By
Vic Gordon-Jones

The faint creaking of that chair was the only sound. He just sat there, as always, deathly silent and only staring ahead, rocking slowly back and forth at the window, in the corner of the dimly lit room. Ian didn't dare reach for the light switches. He would always sort of snarl, whenever they did that, clenching his fingers tightly, as though secretly wishing that there was a neck within reach to grasp them around.

"How are you today?"

Not expecting an answer, and receiving none, he inched towards the clinical metal table at the window, and hastily placed down on it a glass of water and a small plastic cup, holding two pills.

"Here's your painkillers, right there, you can take them when you need."

He tended not to answer, most days – he would usually only ever groan, in a way that always made Ian's insides squirm with deep discomfort. And that night, he let out one long, rattling sigh in response, eyes narrowing slightly in that familiar, lizard-like way. His gnarled, skeletal fingers crept their way along the blanket draped across his knees and towards the table. The fingernails, Ian now noticed as they reached out into the bars of light cast through the half-closed window blinds, were yellowing and split, with something brownish still decaying beneath them. Shaking, he slid the pills into his mouth and wrapped his shrivelled lips around the rim of the glass and gave another laboured, hoarse breath.

Mr Andrew was now the only one left – the last out of twelve patients, the rest of whom had eventually passed away in the short space of only two months. There hadn't been much time to prepare for new arrangements, new patients. So, until more were admitted to the hospice, Ian and one other nurse would be the only ones working nights. And the nights, they were the worst;

because with the nights, when the traffic stopped and the chattering and laughter from the streets outside faded away, came nothingness. Now, there were no more volunteers, no more relatives at bedsides or children or grandchildren scampering through the halls. No more noise. If it had been any other patient left, anyone with somebody to hang around them, anyone that talked, even to themselves, or liked to have their television turned up to almost full volume all hours or who constantly and loudly shuffled cards, then perhaps the almost empty building may not have felt so horribly desolate. But instead, there was only solitary, silent, Mr Andrew.

But clearly, this man was soon to follow the rest. Ian knew, from the sunken eyes and pale, papery skin, the way his shoulders poked so fiercely out from the dressing gown that seemed to swamp him that he was wasting to nearly nothing. His lips were now an unhealthy shade of blue, branches of tiny, almost black veins beginning to blossom along his cheeks. He had seemed to hang on with some strength, over the last few months, enough so that he could leave his bed and sit almost vigilantly in that chair all day long. But now, more than ever, he seemed to be teetering on the edge of mere consciousness.

A thin trail of water ran down from Mr Andrew's mouth and sat glistening on his chin, he made no attempt to reach up and wipe it away. Taking a piece of tissue paper from his pocket, Ian leant down over him, reached one hand out towards his face. And as he did, he noticed, the old man's lips moved slightly. A faint, inaudible whisper was all that escaped them.

"I... I'm sorry?"

"Need... more..."

"What is it, *what* do you need?"

A sharp and sudden pain shot through his arm. Jagged nails sank deep into his flesh, a grip surprisingly, terrifyingly tight. Lips still barely moving, he drew closer, rasping breath slightly louder as he whispered again, eyes unblinking and gleaming viciously.

"I need... yours..."

The sudden, loud thud of the table against his arm as he wrenched it free from Mr Andrew's grasp made his insides jolt. The plastic glass went clattering to the floor and rolled underneath the chair, the water spewing across the carpet.

"*What's going on?*"

At the sudden sound of her voice he spun around to see Jillian, standing in the doorway. Her eyes flicked down to the water spattered across the floor, then back up to meet his.

"What happened?"

"He… he's asking for more, for, something… I think he's…"

"He must be wanting more medication – maybe we can find something to help him sleep…" reaching out one latex-gloved hand and nodding towards the glass. "Pass me that?"

He hesitated, feeling suddenly frozen as those fiendish reptilian eyes bore into his own, those bony fingers clenching tightly.

"Come on."

He could feel every inch of his body quiver as he slowly edged towards the chair, trying almost desperately not to look up at that wretched face, and bent down. A feeling almost like relief crept through his chest as his hand closed around the cold plastic, and he shot straight up onto his feet.

It was only as he stood back, releasing one shaking, relieved sigh, that he felt the sudden surge of pain tearing into the side of his neck. As he turned, he caught only a quick glimpse of her – wielding the empty syringe in one hand and grinning viciously back at him, before he collapsed, face down, on the floor. Somewhere close above, he could hear her voice.

"Not again…"

Her gloves stuck to his skin as she yanked at his arms, with a tight and painful grip, turning him over onto his back.

"What did you go and scratch him for… Want to get yourself caught…"

He attempted to struggle against her grasp, to move his arms, his head… but finding his body drained, could only stare helplessly up whatever that old man was, up into its' glinting eyes, as it crawled on all four contorted limbs above.

Cold fingers pressed against his face, pinning him to the floor, while he stared upwards in frozen terror. Those repulsive blue lips parted, mouth widening abnormally, further and further into some enormous scarlet abyss as the throat inside shuddered and an inhuman, rattling cry escaped, its nostrils twitching madly... He tried to somehow scream out as it drew closer, stale breath flooding his nose and catching in his throat, tried frantically to breathe, but every breath seemed to be caught in his throat, his lips growing colder and his heart twisting tightly, agonisingly in his chest. With every moment he could feel himself becoming weaker, increasingly numb, as though he were being torn from his own body as those eyes bore down into his own. A horrifying shriek sliced suddenly through the room, causing his insides to recoil.

The sound had come from him.

And at that moment, as that last breath escaped and the last ounce of warmth rushed from his body, eyes slipping back into the darkness of his own skull; that was when he saw them. The mass of withered faces; hollowed, haunting eyes staring down at him, the stench of decay overwhelming as they drew in close around him. The twelve pairs of shrivelled lips, gaping hungrily, their piercing screeches ripping through the calm of the night, and right into his soul... Twelve pairs of greying, gnarled hands- all clawing madly, all reaching out for him; all waiting to take him away.

CORPORATE KILL
excerpts from a novel
by
Ian Beattie

Corporate Kill is a crime thriller focusing on a series of grisly murders of the directors from an energy company. These are the first two chapters as they currently stand and an expansion of one of the main murders from later in the novel.

Chapter 1

Mt. Fuji could clearly be seen from where he sat. He always returned to this spot overlooking Fujisasano Heights, one of the more exclusive and prestigious golf courses just outside of Tokyo. It reminded him of time with his father, now long since dead. His father had been a respected but not particularly successful businessman who had an electrical store in the Blade Runner-esque Akihabara district. Due to the ever warming climate the usually snow covered top of Mt Fuji had receded somewhat in recent years. Not that he believed any of that pseudo science nonsense about global doom coming to destroy humanity for its sins against mother earth. Personally he thought it was a load of eco-hippy crap. The air was warm, dry and had that particular kind of freshness only experienced in the spring as the season changed.

New life was appearing all over the predominately volcanic landscape with energetic enthusiasm. His car had ticked itself cold long ago as he pondered his unwanted new found predicament. He pulled a half used packet of Ligier cigarettes from his inside jacket pocket. Gently tapping one on its end he lit it up and inhaled. This was the worst part, the waiting, the seemingly endless waiting. He pulled his shades back down from his forehead and glanced at his watch. 3.30pm, still only 3.30pm. Another ten minutes before he would begin.

He offered a unique and discreet service for his clients who needed his particular talents and training. His Ninja skills were always useful in his cleaning job. He knew he could perform a wet op from start to finish and never be detected. His sensei had been a powerful samurai from the traditional school. A hard taskmaster but he had taught him well. His cigarette was almost down to its butt and he threw it to the ground and extinguished it with his left foot. Time to go. Opening the car door he got in and drove off. He likened his GTR as being a 'spaceship between the stars' even though it was positively earth bound. If he got into trouble, it could get him out. No one could even think of catching him if he floored the loud pedal. Though it looked stock and had a few scrapes from its previous owner it had a very special specification. The usual 3.5 litre lump stretched to 4.5 litres. Polished ports. Lightened flywheel. Carbon propshaft. Carbon vented discs and Brembo calipers. Fully adjustable suspension. Quad turbos. Remapped engine management. A Tubi exhaust system and best of all Nitrous. 900 horsepower on tap if he needed. He had his instructions and now it was time to carry them out

Martin Connon had to die. He was a liability that the president of The Darrow Corporation could do better without. Too many embarrassments to the company of late and they had had a tough enough time adjusting to the global downturn and the increasing competition from Korea. The episode with the prostitutes was not disappearing from the papers soon enough. He had become completely power-mad and seemingly immune to the hurt and pain he created on a daily basis. Stories had already begun to circulate in the gutter press about his more salacious desires, of how he had a substantial collection of torture devices, S & M gear and enjoyed looking at inappropriate photos of children. This was not going to be tolerated. Martin seemed to be the epitome of respectability and had started out as an idealistic college graduate then went onto to study at Aberdeen University before completion of his Oxford Masters degree. He decided that travel in Europe was for him before returning to his beloved Scotland to pursue his business ambitions.

The black GTR rumbled through the tunnels of inner Tokyo's road network towards Sibuya. Police sirens wailed in the distance as a KLM flight made its way onto the tarmac of Narita airport about a mile to his left. Despite the twenty five million people who lived here there was always a courteous order to proceedings in Japan. Only the madness was hidden for its shame. Cumulus clouds beckoned a change in the weather. The forecast had said thunderstorms later with a definite chance of lightning too. Just as he approached Sibuya the first spots of rain started appearing on the windscreen, within a minute they had turned torrential. No matter, this amount of rain would wash the blood away. Sibuya was a glazed urban jungle teaming with young bloods out admiring themselves before the coming weekend. All styles and influences went here from 50's Rock-a-Billy to ultra modern Plastics brainwashed by the US invasion that happened after Japans defeat at the end of the last world war. Rugan always thought that the Metal-heads had to be the weirdest, but that was what made living in Tokyo so interesting, there was always some teen trend to follow that created its own unique look in this part of town. Rugan glanced at the time, 4pm. Only half an hour till Martin Connon was due back at his hotel. Then it would be done.

Making his way through Kasumigaseki district he drove along Kojimachi and skirted past the Imperial Palace and its many walls, moats and cherry blossom filled gardens. At the end he turned right down Sakuradamon in the direction of Tokyo's central station. Then his sat nav flagged up an accident on his pre-planned route. Thinking quickly he turned left again and proceeded via Yurakucho and Maranouchi and northwards to Otemachi before stopping nearby Martin Connons hotel in Kanda Nishikicho. That was the problem with technology; it was never as fast as the human mind.

By now the rain had begun to stop being quite so fierce. It was almost a pleasure to be out in this weather. He had become gentle and quiet, as he had to enter the hotel without arousing the suspicions of the staff. That was the problem with wealth - it made you nervous about your possessions and you spent all your money to protect it once you had it. The hotel was a serene oasis in amongst the chaos of the city. Once inside its protective walls you'd never know you were in one of the busiest, most congested cities in the world. Checking the perimeter cameras for the right moment, he swiftly reached the cover of the many trees which surrounded the imposing hotel. Another twenty seconds and he was in. He would have the place to himself and had plenty time to lie in wait. He walked at a leisurely pace through the kitchen where a delivery of fish was waiting to be prepared into sushi for tonight's meals. Vegetables awaited the same fate. Duck and chicken hung from the hooks in the kitchen as if Connon had tortured them himself earlier. The smell of fresh coriander wafted up his nostrils as Rugan walked through the hive of activity that was the hotel kitchen. He was not challenged or checked. Everyone assumed he was simply a lost guest. Without arousing suspicion he assuredly made his way up to Martin Connon's room. There he would wait. He checked his watch again 4.45pm Connon was late. No matter. Plenty of time to contemplate and reflect. Achieve stillness. This was the art of a ninja after all. Stealth and surprise used in conjunction with expert, swift swordsmanship. Green goddess would not let him down. Forged by a master sword maker from Hokkaido in the 16th century Green Goddess was the ultimate weapon. No loud and crude guns here, far too Hollywood, thought Rugan.

Moments later the front gates to the hotel opened and a dark green Lexus hybrid parked up in front of the imposing hotel. An athletic figure emerged from the car's back door and was obviously worse for the wear. His face characteristically pock marked and soft tanned. Dressed in an expensive black Armani suit with close-cropped hair he was the epitome of the modern businessman. His driver closed the car door and then drove to the hotel's private underground car park. He hazily swaggered towards the glass doors of the entrance and past the bustling reception swiftly walking to the lift. Once in he quietly enjoyed the view of the cities skyline as he ascended. A gentle ping notified him that his floor had been reached and he walked onwards to his room.

Martin ignored this on his way towards the door of his hotel room. Travelling on business always seemed lonelier now that his wife had left him, but home it was and it brought him much needed peace from the stress of business life. He entered the suite and poured himself a large Drambuie and settled in one the leather chairs. Rugan waited motionless in the bedroom ready for his prey. He reached around for his sword grasping with it with both hands and toyed with it as if he was a child pretending to be a Jedi Knight. Martin decided that it was time to remove the day's stresses and made his way to the bedroom and the tranquillity of his daily bathing ritual. He walked into the bathroom unaware that he had seconds to live. The silent figure of Rugan slid silently up behind him, raised his blade and in one swift move it was done. He didn't even scream such was Rugan's stealth and skill. Connon's body lay motionless on the floor; his stomach was cut from back to front in one smooth movement disembowelling his intestines. Blood spattered the back wall of the bathroom and pooled on the elegant stone tiled floor. Rugan cleaned his blade, returned it to its elegant sheath and pondered his next move. Martin Connon lay on the floor, his own blood drained onto the darks stone surface beside him, but Rugan had not finished with him. After removing Martins trousers he expertly placed him on a chair, and began to tie him to it securing the bindings tight whilst silencing him with a handkerchief from Martins own pocket. Men like him deserved much worse than the incisive swordsmanship he'd just received. Below Connon Rugan began cutting out the chair so that his genitals were accessible. He brought out a smaller knife and began to castrate Connon. No more would this man torture innocents. Martin's screams were muffled by the handkerchief and the rooms sound insulation. He would later bleed to death in a slow agonizing way fitting for someone who took pleasure in raping children. Once done, Rugan cleaned himself and his blades and calmly walked outside into the dark that would hasten his escape.

On his way out he noticed that there was hardly anyone around to blend in with but it made no difference now as no alarms were triggered by his entrance to Connon's room despite the hotels high level security. He calmly walked into the garage towards his Skyline glancing around for signs of trouble but there were none. He plipped the alarm on the GTR and drove off. The neon glow of the coming Tokyo night awaited him. Time for rewards thought Rugan.

Chapter 2

Shu Lian the chambermaid started her duties as usual at ten o clock the next morning. She had arrived by underground half an hour earlier and was eager to get her job done as she had planned to see her boyfriend in the afternoon. She had spoken to her manager and been told of the day's most urgent tasks and set about doing those first. During the course of her day she worked her way through the hotel on an ever-upward course, finishing up at the upper floors and the hotels most expensive suites.

It was on opening the door to the third one that her day changed and she got the fright of her life. She asked in her sweet and courteous manner was there anyone in, having seen a collection of suits and a Macbook Pro laptop on the desk near the window. In the bathroom she soon discovered the body of the man who she'd seen over the previous three days, now lying in a congealed pool of blood. Shu Lian screamed when she saw the dead man and ran out of the room leaving the door open, far too distraught to do anything sensible like phone the police.

Her boss discovered her in the stairwell some twenty minutes later when Shu Lian did not come for her break. She was shaking, something was clearly upsetting her and it seemed she was in no condition to talk due to the shock that still registered on her face. So her boss took her to her office to find out what was wrong. It took another forty-five minutes for Shu Lian to say what she had seen. It was not until another hour had passed that the grim discovery was to be known to all the hotel staff. The hotel manager, a Mr Leung ordered all staff to stay as he had called the police.

The Japanese police were swiftly on the scene after being informed by Mr Leung that one of his chambermaids had made a gruesome discovery in the morning as she went about her duties. Soon forensic officers and detectives were interviewing all the guests and staff but no one could report anything unusual. This added to the mystery surrounding the death of the European businessman. Press and Television attention rapidly followed as the search for the phantom-like killer began to intensify. The officer in charge, an experienced man by the name of Detective Hakayama decided fairly quickly to inform Interpol to see if anyone who fitted the murder style had been released in any other country. After a brief search of the hotel room it became obvious that the gentleman in question was a director of a Scottish energy company called The Darrow Corporation and that he was here on business to meet with various Japanese ministers and companies with a view of expanding their business interests in the orient. Upon further enquiry with the company it was also apparent that he had a wife and family that needed to be informed. Detective Hakayama contacted Grampian Police as he was of the opinion that the news should come from officers in the dead mans home country. His relatives would also need to confirm his identity prior to it being released to them for burial purposes.

One of the major concerns that Detective Hakayama had was that in this day of global news saturation it was going to be very difficult to keep the grim news from surfacing before his relatives could be informed. As it was the local Tokyo press were swarming like vultures and the local and national TV stations had rapidly shown up and were desperate for a scoop on the murder.

Rugan sat in his home patiently waiting for his next job to come through. The small farm on the north-western coast in the Toyama district had served him well as a base and no one enquired much about his business. He had bought it many years ago as it was suitably quiet and unassuming. It met his needs for privacy well. This was how he liked his life to be, plenty peace and time to practice his skills. Plenty time to tend his Zen like garden, his Coi and his *Somei Yoshino* cherry blossoms. Most of all he relished spending time with beloved Bonsai trees. He had rested well the previous night and awoke at the same time as before. Nearby the small fishing village of Nakajo was shrouded in a mist that had rolled in late last night when he had arrived home. Boats could be seen on the waves far out to sea on better days but today this was not to be. Only the sounds of eager gulls alerted you to the fact you were in a coastal village. This early in the day very few people were up and about and Rugan always enjoyed the solitude the farm offered him. It had many years since he moved here after having some trouble as a result of a local teenager seven years ago who discovered his secret life as a hired assassin. The unwanted attention meant Rugan had to leave his flat in Okinawa suddenly one night. Police attention was particularly undesired in his line of work. The fiercely thorough Japanese police had always taken a dim view of assassins and the government liked them even less. In feudal times this had often resulted in the torture and death of assassins who were caught and found guilty.

Three hours later BBC News 24 had somehow got a hold of the story from the website of one of the main Japanese dailies. This led to a number of European correspondents posting reports based on the many rumours that were allegedly connected to Martin Connon. This was going to get messy. Rugan walked

107

casually over to his computer, switched it on and accessed his email. The bank had confirmed that his payment was in his account. This would help with many things. But first it was time to check out the rest of his communications for his next set of skin jobs. A large proportion of his targets comprised hits for those people in the world who could afford to remove their enemies in an efficient and ruthless manner. The next target was another businessman who had caused his superiors rather too much bother of late and this was going to be just as much fun and possibly easier for Rugan to achieve than the last one in the hotel.

Chapter 3
(later in the novel)

Detective Dillinger opened up the door of his black Jaguar saloon blipped the throttle and drove out into the traffic. The vee eight engine burbled as he discreetly made his way through the busy city streets. The supercharger whined contentedly as the revs rose. He loved this part before a shift began. Driving through the city when day morphed to night. Tarmac and pavement glistened with the rainwater from the earlier downpour that seemed to refresh and cleanse the cities dirty streets. He made his way through the Tullos industrial estates and past some of the more salubrious establishments that the lower east side near the harbour had to offer. Neon signs from bars and takeaways gave the area an almost American feel even though he was in Aberdeen.

The darkness had descended about two hours ago and this was when the cities character seemed to change. Office workers were returning home, bar workers suddenly got busier. Patrons huddled outside pubs indulging in their smoking leprosy. The breeze had picked up, whipping litter into a balletic dance. The night had overtaken the day. Noises changed too. Frantic dance tunes boomed from max powered up Corsas, their colours clashing with the neon. Club promoters staked out their territory at the top of Belmont Street to entice people inside the warm welcoming premises. The promise of cheap booze and easy sex abounded everywhere he looked. As he made his way towards headquarters a message appeared on his pager. Meet Detective Marr at an address in the west end. Urgently. So much for a quiet night finishing the mountain of paperwork that needed doing he thought. Dillinger immediately performed a u-turn and in doing so almost stopped the oncoming traffic. He used the cars siren to full effect. The previously clogged traffic parted with ease ensuring his progress was as rapid as was safe to do at this hour.

As he sped towards the upmarket address he wondered what he was going to encounter. In his line of work it could be anything from a domestic gone out of control to a full-blown murder scene. Tonight it was to be the latter. The street had already been cordoned when Dillinger arrived and Marrs red Alfa Romeo 159 was parked on the road. Once there he met Detective Marr who was the first of the non-uniformed police on the scene. The house was one of the more traditional granite ones that the city's west end could offer. Well established trees lined both sides of the garden. A silver Volvo XC90 sat parked in the immaculate drive. By the look of things this was a fresh kill. It couldn't have happened more than three hours previously.

A neighbour had reported hearing a number of distinctly unsettling noises coming from the house a couple of hours ago. She thought it was just the couple having a party as they sometimes did. However it wasn't until about an hour later that she noticed a stranger, who did not seem as if he belonged, coming from the house and she phoned the police. At this point it also went deathly quiet and something in her told her there was something wrong. She had taken her mobile next door only to discover the front door unlocked and open. Marr said they were still awaiting Crime Scene to appear and that he noticed a few unusual things but wanted Dillinger to have a look and give it his expert eye. Of the two Dillinger was the more experienced having been on the force for a full ten years more than Marr. Together they seemed to compliment each other bringing insights that sometimes the other did not think of but mostly seemed to be on the same wavelength, making it quicker to deal with the unsavoury work they did on a daily basis.

Dillinger went inside and worked his way from room to room in the impressive granite property. It was obvious the owners had money to burn. In the living room a Bang and Olufsen Hi-Fi and television with surround sound dominated the large open space. Black leather sofas and designer pieces were arranged tastefully around. Expensive bouquets gave the room that feminine touch. Along one wall subtle wallpaper provided a luxurious background for some original contemporary art. A massive ten-seat glass dining table sat in the middle of the dining room, which was separated from the lounge by heavy oak doors. A huge self-contained barbeque sat on the decking to the back of the dining room that adjoined the lounge. He proceeded upstairs to the bedroom and it was there he saw the body of an attractive woman in her forties. There seemed to be no signs of a struggle but there was an open safe that was very much empty.

Arterial spray spattered the wall behind her slumped body. Karen Matthews's throat had been cut, apparently in one rapid cut from right to left. Dillinger was as disturbed by the method used to kill Karen Matthew as all the officers who had seen the body. She was showing all the classic signs of having been expertly and quickly killed, not unlike an animal in a slaughterhouse. The arterial spray suggested that she had twisted round in the remaining seconds of her life.

Her hands were covered in congealing blood, as if she'd tried to save herself. She had probably tried to scream as she gasped for breath. She had almost certainly seen her killer up close and it was possible the killer waited till her pulse disappeared.

It was apparent that the victim was the owner of the house. Karen could be seen with a man and two children in a number of photographs throughout the imposing property. They looked happy in the way that most 'contented' couples of their age did. Trying not to show the cracks in their relationship, which they hoped could be plastered over if they had babies.

Marr found out from the neighbour that Karen was a career woman by nature and had previously tried to do the impossible dream of having it all. The husband who adored her, the two kids, and foreign holidays and be successful in her work life, but this had ended up destroying the things that really mattered. Her family life had immediately suffered and she lost so many moments of her kids growing up due to being stuck in the office from early in the morning to late at night. This had effects on her in other ways and she had been in contact with her doctor about stress at work. She had links with C. Re-nu too. Up until yesterday she had been one of the senior directors responsible for the rapid growth of the company. It was becoming clear that specific company directors were being targeted, either by a particularly twisted individual, or individuals.

Her husband was not at home and Dillinger thought that it was time that he be found and informed. The kids were not at home and it was a worry that they might return home to the horrific scene that greeted him upon his arrival. Dillinger called Marr to make sure that her husband was found and that the family should be housed in a hotel till the relevant investigations could be completed. He would also interview the husband as he could give vital insight into Karen's home life and general state of health prior to current events in a way that most doctors notes never could. As the crime scene officers took measurements and photographs of the body where it laid, Dillinger excused himself from the room and wandered into the other rooms on the first floor. A study with two desks and expensive Apple computers on each could hold clues into recent events. Dillinger immediately ordered these to be removed by the tech guys for analysis.

Head office was not going to like this, a third unexplained murder of a director from The Darrow Corporation in as many weeks. The Incident room was already stretched beyond belief with the vast amount of information that had been gathered from the first two murders. Dillinger knew that a meeting with the Chief Inspector was absolutely vital. He needed more resources to sift through the various witness statements and simply to help look for clues. He phoned H.Q and demanded a meeting with the chief Inspector at the first available opportunity today. There wasn't the time for all the internal protocols, for he and his colleagues had to think fast and even more intelligently than with the murders of Martin Connon and Alexander McRae.

The first two murders had turned into high profile incidents due to the standing in the business community that the two victims had. On the face of it these were respectable men, with families and well paid jobs and they enjoyed their success. What puzzled Dillinger were the ever-changing methods of disposal. He knew that most serial killers tended to enjoy torturing their victims and killing them in mostly the same manner before disposing of the bodies at a later date. However this was not happening here. Dillinger wondered if he was even dealing with a serial killer. A number of thoughts entered his head, and not all of them were making sense just now. Either he was, with the killer being particularly clever by changing the method the victims were killed, or the victims were being targeted by separate perpetrators. Here he had someone who had managed to evade all possible potential witnesses and disappeared like a phantom. He also had someone who was highly skilled, very strong and able to inflict maximum damage to their victims.

Dillinger also knew the investigation would become ever more difficult, as more often than not if a case got mass media attention this meant that the crazies came out and professed to having done it. There were those members of the public that simply were deluded enough to believe that it could bring them their fifteen minutes if they confessed. Dillinger knew that those idiots were wasting police time, but as with all police work their claims would have to be investigated.

One of the uniformed officers came into the study and told him they had located Karen's husband at work. John worked in advertising for one of the more prominent design companies based in the prestigious West End of the city. He received a call informing him of the devastating news during a meeting to a new set of clients. He was on his way home now and could be expected in about ten minutes.

When John parked his sage coloured Audi A6 he saw the full horror of the chaotic mess of police cars, ambulances. The local press and TV had arrived not after someone who lived nearby sent them a video of their street. He had to struggle past the reporters and was clearly not in any state to drive himself home. His mind raced with thoughts of what he'd find of his beloved wife. Then he thought of the kids. What in God's name was he going to tell them? How would be tell his mum and dad?

Marr was the first to speak to him and led him into the lounge so that he could be interviewed. John slumped in one of the black sofas and was in shock. His normally white features had gone ashen. Dillinger sat opposite John on one of the single seats. Dillinger and Marr both expressed sadness for his and his families' loss and then started to ask the questions they knew they had to.

"When was the last time you saw your wife?" enquired Dillinger.

"About eight this morning; I'd just finished breakfast and had come upstairs with hers before I took the kids to school and they went off on their events day".

"Did anything seem different about her at all?

"No. She seemed to be the same as she'd always been. She was looking forward to having the rest of the week off. There was nothing unusual that I can immediately think of."

"What about her home life? Have you had any trouble in your relationship with your wife lately?"

"I hardly think that's any of your business," retorted John.

"We'll be the judge of that Sir," replied Alex.

"We simply need to know as much as possible about her life as this could give us a better understanding of the events that have led up to this horrific event," continued Dillinger seeking to reassure him that it was a routine question. "We don't mean to cause you offence but we must ask you these things."

"She's been a bit distant of late as if something was bothering her. I asked her about this around three months ago but she said it was nothing and that she'd probably made a mistake, then she talked no more about it."

"You got any idea what that could be?"

"No, not at all. It was all hush, hush and on the QT."

"How was her work?"

"Well as you know she worked for The Darrow Corporation as one of the only female directors the company had. She enjoyed the work and the challenges it sometimes meant for her, but in the last couple of year's things seemed to have changed," said John.

"Can you elaborate on that Sir?"

"The company changed its direction from one that specialised in the promotion and manufacture of cutting edge Power generation techniques, to one which seemed to be more focused on its financial interests."

"What do you mean?"

"It seemed that becoming a company that was financially secure and independent was rapidly the main business focus. The impression that I got, at some of the office parties I was invited to, was that hedge funds and the accruement of wealth was much more important to The Darrow Corporation. Some of the more arrogant directors like Alex McRae and Theo Akeson openly bragged as the nights progressed into a drunken abandon. Don't get me wrong, they hadn't all of a sudden decided to let the manufacturing side go it just became less of a priority. I have heard from other sources that these hedge funds that The Darrow Corporation have are part of an ongoing OFT and FSA investigation but as yet nothing has been confirmed or denied by either The Darrow Corporation or those looking into the allegations."

"Was your wife in any way involved in this process?"

"Not that I'm aware of, but she kept much of her career separate from her home life. She was very disciplined and professional about distancing the two, said it was bad for business."

"Right, right. We understand she was Marketing Director for The Darrow Corporation, is that correct?"

"Yes, she'd been hired by The Darrow Corporation about two years ago, having worked for Acergy in a similar role but with a bit less responsibility. It was definitely a step up the ladder that she had wanted to achieve. The Energy industry is still so male dominated that even in the more enlightened times we live in its unusual for a woman to get so far."

"Do you know if she'd made any enemies on the way up?"

"She must have done. There are still so many men who resent a woman being successful. And that's before you count all the women who want to be doing what she did."

"We have heard from some of the staff in The Darrow Corporation that there was a rumour linking her to one of the other Directors. Do you know anything about this?"

"I can say that she worked late rather a lot and was involved with all the large projects that the company was producing. Once they had secured that deal, to provide power for the Highland region using their latest renewable technologies, things changed with her like I said.

"Okay John thanks for speaking to us. I'll give you my card. If you think of anything get in touch with either Marr or me. Once again can I say how sorry I am for your loss. An officer will accompany you to a hotel."

With that Dillinger and Marr left the grieving man in the company of a Liaison Officer and walked to their colleagues in the portable Incident Room outside. Inside it was a mess of machines and phone lines. Police men and women from forensics and crime scene were using the cabin to start on their initial reports prior to the body going to the morgue and being given a post mortem. In cases such as these it could take weeks before all the evidence was carefully gathered using the latest techniques to prevent damage to D.N.A etc.

"So what do you think is going on?" said a perplexed Marr.

"Damned if I know. But I've got a few ideas. I'm not going to share them though till I've got further detail. All I know is that there have been three murders of three Directors from the same company in as many weeks. The method used to kill has changed with each victim and there is no apparent link apart from he or she all worked for the same business. What I need is the following."

Dillinger took a quick breath and then reeled off a list of tasks as Marr frantically scribbled his notes.

"I need information on all three victims, detailing what they did, what their hobbies were, what time they ate, what they ate, who they were friends with, who they were enemies with, what sort of coffee they drank and anything else I might have missed. I want to know what time they had a shit and what time they went to bed. I also need all the information you can get me on the deals The Darrow Corporation has made in this country and in Europe and Japan. Get me someone who can tell me all about the hedge funds too. I need all the company' financial records too. Plus I need someone to look at it and tell me if there was anything suspicious in any of those business transactions or deals. There has to be a link that we've missed, something not obvious, something hidden."

"Anything else?"

"Yeah, get me a decent cup of coffee I'm parched"

"Oh, and get me a meeting with the entire team. We are going to have to raise our game if we are to get to the bottom of this"

"Okay will do. When for?"

"Tomorrow afternoon. We have no time to lose. And warn everyone that none of us will be getting any time off till this is solved"

ABER DA-AEVIN
by
Tori Hill

Before the granite was unearthed the land was green. It was Aber Da-aevin, at the mouth of two rivers.

The settlers owed much to the provisions of nature and, with ritual and song, honoured the spirits who occupied the forests and waters. At one such dawn ceremony Kerr knelt where the Uisge Dè flowed into the sea and scattered his childish curls on the water. The group behind him sang their praises to the spirits as he bowed his head in the pretence of prayer. His mother's voice rang clearly from the crowd, filled with pride for her son, and he stifled a sigh.

As the voices reached their crescendo Kerr opened his eyes to meet the gaze of a face in the water below. The song faded from his ears until all he could hear was the rushing of the river. The woman beneath was beautiful. Her green eyes held him and her lips parted in a smile as she reached up for his hand. With no thought, he reached back to her and their fingers met in the air as the sun emerged above the horizon, flooding the sky with light. At that moment she slipped away.

119

Kerr was suddenly surrounded by neighbours and kin coming to congratulate him on passing into manhood. He accepted everyone's good wishes in a daze until Màthair Mòrag grasped his wrist.

"Marked," The old woman's voice was tremulous and her eyes were wide.

A murmur began in the crowd as the news spread. He looked at his hand and froze. The skin of the index finger, stretching up over the back of his hand, was a silvery grey. A chill spread through him but most of the onlookers were now chattering and beaming. Kerr's mother pulled him into a hug, away from Mòrag's grip.

"I knew you were special. The spirits themselves blessed you."

A celebratory meal was lain out for the people to break their fast, as was the custom. Children giggled and whispered the rumours that quickly spread to small ears while the adults marvelled at the good fortune Kerr had brought upon their settlement. The mark on his hand made Kerr queasy with apprehension. As soon as he was able, the young man sought out Màthair Mòrag. She had retired early from the merry-making and sat outside her home sewing. She nodded to him as he approached, then cast her eyes down on her work again.

"Màthair, you know something. Please tell me what this means. Who was the woman in the water? Why has this happened?" The words spilled out as Kerr knelt before the old woman. She picked at her stitching before whispering,

"The Ceasg. It's said they are half human and half salmon, but that's only a story to make them seem fanciful and harmless." Kerr's eyebrow twitched upwards but the old woman continued,

"My son was marked. She took him. My Aengus' shirt was all they found at the water's edge." Her hands shook, and her work fell to the ground. Kerr retrieved it and, as he passed it back to her, he saw tears in Mòrag's eyes. She met his gaze.

"Stay away from the river."

Màthair Mòrag's words stayed with Kerr, but three years went by with no strange events, the old woman passed on, and with no-one to remind him of it the young man forgot his disquiet. The incident became nothing more than a lonely old woman's imagination. As Aber Da-aevin's people lived their lives, gathered their harvests, fished and culled, and gave thanks for their bounty, Kerr grew fond of Elspeth, a fisherman's daughter who sang as she worked and smiled at his clumsy advances. Before long it was accepted between the two families that a union would occur.

Kerr dreamed. A familiar face smiled and a silvery hand beckoned him in the darkness. Fingers outstretched, he stumbled forwards into a fresh scent and a warm embrace. He sank into her arms and buried his face in her hair as she whispered strange, beguiling words that sounded like promises. Her grip tightened and he fought for breath, his lungs straining and his limbs afire as he sank.

As the weeks moved on Kerr grew thin and pale. The mark on his hand appeared more livid as he grew more sickly. Every look given was a judgement on him, every word spoken an incrimination. Though he had done nothing wrong his guilt pressed in on him, he flinched at shadows and spoke little. The change in him did not go unnoticed. Friends and family questioned him to no avail, he would not allow himself to be drawn out. His betrothed thought him to be sick and brought endless remedies that lay untouched.

Each night Kerr longed for sleep, to see her face again, but his body would tense and hold his mind hostage long into the dark hours, until exhaustion claimed him and the dreams finally, tantalisingly, began. Each morning he woke sweating and shivering, but by evening he was desperate to return, praying that this time the embrace would linger before the pain began. The day of his wedding approached, with talk of flowers and food, but when he looked at Elspeth he saw only the face from his dreams.

At last, two nights before his nuptials, he awoke with frost on his breath and the knowledge that she had asked him to come to her. The words she spoke finally had meaning and Kerr's mind was filled with only the sense of her. He swam through the day, surfacing into clarity at nightfall. When there was no-one to see him he entered the trees and made for the mouth of the Uisge Dè, to the place he first saw her. The water was black but something shone there. Words he heard nightly were on the breeze, and the scent that flooded his dreams surrounded him now. In the ripples and the moonlight her face took shape and at the thought of her touch he let himself go.

THE PRECIOUS
by
Sandra Smith

Libby had been married to Tom for over nine years before she unexpectedly fell pregnant. As her pregnancy progressed, Libby began to suffer from dark moods, feeling trapped and restrained by her pregnancy. She had morbid thoughts she would lose the freedom they had enjoyed once the baby was born. She had always been a wild character, but as her growing bulge increasingly reminded her of future restraints, she became almost claustrophobic in her own skin.

Tom was an easy-going character and he displayed no great expectations of the forth-coming birth for he was a soul that lived for the moment, not for the future, however, it upset him to see Libby so depressed. He wondered whether a holiday might be the answer as it might just lift her mood.

The baby was not due for another month yet and, as Libby was in fine health, Tom decided they would take a trip north and fulfil a wish both of them had dreamed about for years, but had never satisfied.

Tom arranged to visit several of the Outer Hebridean Islands off the west coast of Scotland, including Skrensay, one of the most remote of the outer islands. Many of the Hebridean islands were linked by causeways, but Skrensay remained aloof, and although inhabited, the sheep outnumbered the islanders.

It was nearing the end of September and the weather had been unpredictable of late, yet Tom and Libby were determined to visit their quota of islands as planned.

Skrensay was their last port of call, which was only accessible by ferry. They were the only tourists onboard for it was nearing the end of the holiday season. As they disembarked, the captain reminded them that the boat would return at five that afternoon, leaving sharp at six o'clock. If they were to miss their passage, they would be stranded on the island for four days until the ferry returned from Harris.

"Be aware," the Captain stressed, wagging his finger at them in the air. "There's no hotel on the island and nobody takes in lodgers, though I dare say they'd have to find a bed for you if it came down to it. But I'd be safe rather than sorry and return in good haste, especially lass, in your condition."

Tom did not like the sound of this and asked the Captain if the islanders were friendly.

"You're speaking to one and I think you can safely say I'm cheery enough. I was born on Skrensay and it's a beautiful island. We are just set in our ways. We don't like the trappings of modern day life – we will not have any internet, television or phones on the island, bar the telephone at the community hall, and even then it's a bit temperamental. However, don't let this put you off the island – appreciate the tranquillity, and if you can, have a look at the wee church and the beautiful graveyard. The islanders keep it awfully bonny."

The island had a population of forty-seven inhabitants, the majority living in the only settlement, Skara. Much of the coastline was rugged and indented, sprinkled with many caves that had been carved out by the harsh wind and rain. Tom and Libby chose to spend the afternoon exploring the island's sweeping, sandy beaches, which interspersed the rock formations, until the skies opened, cackling with thunder, and they were forced to return to the village to seek shelter.

Fortunately, the rain abated, and as they entered the village, they were welcomed eagerly by the island folk. The islanders were friendly enough, perhaps too friendly, as they all seemed much taken with Libby's pregnancy. Although Libby was happy to discuss her condition, she began to feel the attention was a bit invasive, especially when all the local women gathered around, taking it in turns to stroke her bulging stomach. Some of the women got down on their knees and began kissing the ground, mumbling soft Gaelic words in an almost feverish manner.

"Tom," Libby whispered, "can you tell them to stop doing this, as it's making me feel uncomfortable."

A hand clapped on Libby's shoulder and she turned to face a hunch-backed old woman, whose grey, marbled eyes shone from a weather-beaten face. Paper-thin skin stretched over her gaunt cheekbones as the old hag opened her mouth to speak, revealing rotten stumps of teeth.

"Ah, bonny lass, you should feel blessed, for children are very precious. Here, take this." The old woman thrust a twig into Libby's hand. Libby looked at it curiously.

"Please, humour us, 'tis a local custom. It's from the rowan tree and it will ward off the evil spirits. Being such an exposed island, we don't have many trees, thus the rowan is a special tree."

Libby looked at Tom for guidance.

"Perhaps," Tom insisted, steering Libby through the throng of women. "Now's the time to visit the church and graveyard, as I think we can safely say you have had enough attention for one day."

The church lay on the edge of the village, a short distance from the harbour and community hall. They had to pass the island school and Libby was amazed that there were only six children in the playground. As they strolled past, the children all stopped playing and stared at Libby. They whispered to each other, pointing at Libby's stomach, giggling.

"Weesh, children, where are your manners?" A grey-haired woman appeared at the doorway of the school.

"I'm Miss Angus, the local schoolmistress. You must be the couple that arrived on the ferry this morning. There has been much talk about you. Please excuse the children, as it is a rare sight to see a pregnant woman on the island. As you realise, we don't have much of a population, so the children get very excited when they see a woman with child. We have not had a live birth on the island for a long time, though we had hoped Jeannie would have been lucky this time, but sadly no."

A child broke away from the group and rushed up to Libby. Tentatively, the child reached out a hand and began gently caressing Libby's stomach. Soon, the other children emerged from the playground, and each child took it in turn to run their fingers over Libby's bulge, some even laying their heads on her.

"Come on, children," Miss Angus called. "Playtime is over. You have your studies to attend to."

As Libby and Tom thankfully continued on their journey to the church, they heard Miss Angus calling them from the playground.

"You are very lucky, so please remember this. Children are very precious."

The church was a ramshackle, white washed building, simplistic inside as well as out. It was furnished with plain, wooden pews all facing a raised platform which contained a font and a stone statue of a woman. Ribbons and pieces of cloth adorned the figure's open arms and Tom bent down to read the inscription at her feet.

"Who is she?" Libby asked, as she sat down on a pew, feeling drained with all the day's activities. She was exhausted. She stroked her belly, feeling a slight maternal instinct, followed by an overwhelming feeling of regret. Frowning at her betrayal of her unborn child, she studied Tom, who seemed oblivious to her emotions.

Grinning, Tom was absorbed with other things. "I can now see why you have had so much attention today, Libby. This is St Bride, who is well known in both Irish and Celtic folklore. She's an old pagan goddess, a symbol of fertility and a patron of pregnant women, amongst other things. The islanders obviously have a great respect for the lady, for they have left scraps of fabric and ribbon to pay homage to her. It is believed her powers will be transferred to the cloth and bring luck and good fortune to those who have brought their offerings. I think this explains today's adulation, Libby, as the islanders obviously look favourably on pregnant women."

Libby shrugged. "Tom, do you think the women of the island worship this stone statue in the hope they will produce children, to prevent their dwindling population heading the same way as St Kilda? The few remaining St Kildans chose to leave their island in

1930, as there was so few of them left due to emigration and child mortality. Perhaps the islanders here are worried about the same thing."

"Possibly, possibly, remember, children are very precious!" Tom replied. "But surely, it wouldn't matter how many children they bring into the world, who would want to stay on such an isolated island? The children are just going to grow up and leave!"

Libby smirked, aware of the solitude and remoteness. "It is all a bit strange, though, Tom. The old school mistress mentioned it was rare to see a pregnant woman on the island, yet there were a few women with toddlers and babies back in the village. Perhaps they leave the island to have their babies on the mainland? I think that's what I would choose to do, if I lived here in the back of beyond. It's frightening enough, the prospect of giving birth…oh, perhaps we have been foolish, coming here! What would happen if I suddenly went into early labour, here, on this awful island?"

Tom sat down beside Libby, stroking her hair reassuringly, trying to quell her rising panic. "Hush, everything is going to be fine. We're just a bit spooked that's all, and it won't be long until the ferry arrives. I admit, the islanders seem a bit weird, but put it down to inter-breeding! Joke! Cheer up! Let's go and have a look at their 'bonny' graveyard, then we shall better head back to the community hall and see if we can grab a bite to eat before the ferry comes. I don't know about you, but I think I'm looking forward to getting back to Harris and civilization."

Libby rose to her feet, and a sudden rush of dizziness caused her to stagger sideways and she dropped the rowan twig at the feet of the statue.

"Libby, are you okay?"

She nodded. "Tom, stop worrying. I'm fine. I think I have overdone it today, that's all. I just feel so frustrated waddling about like this. I need my body back! Let's head outside – I need a bit of fresh air."

The graveyard split into several areas. Older, crumbling headstones rested on the right side of the church and fresh, granite headstones stood together on the left. In the far corner of the

127

graveyard, a section was deliberately separated from the others and this area was sprinkled with identical simple crosses, each bearing a brief epitaph. Someone had obviously tended to this area with great pride, as the grass was neatly cut and fresh flower tributes lay at the foot of each cross.

Libby felt drawn to this plot of the graveyard and as she passed each cross, she read out the engraved words.

"These must be the most recent. Kirsten McGregor, 1996 - 1999, Mhaire Murphy, 1999 - 2000, Alisdair Campbell, August, 2001 - December, 2001, Ellon McGregor (stillborn) 2003, Katie Anderson (stillborn) 2005, Stuart Murray (stillborn) 2006...Oh, Tom, this is dreadful! This must be the children's graveyard, and so many of them have died at such a young age. So many stillbirths. Oh, and look, a freshly dug grave. How sad. Let's get out of here as it is making me feel morbid."

The sky suddenly darkened above them, and bruised clouds smashed together, as rain slashed down onto the island. As Libby yanked open the cast iron gate, she thought she could hear childish, lilting laughter coming from behind her. She swung her head round and for a second caught a shadowed child-like figure darting amongst the headstones. Her eyes followed the ghostly figure as it darted between the grey slabs and for a moment, Libby stood, entranced.

"Come on," Tom cried, "this weather is turning wild. Let's head to the village."
Libby nodded, passively.

The storm that had threatened earlier was now in full force, snarling around them as they struggled down the little path to the community hall. Rain thrashed down on the two; a violent blast of weather.

"Libby, you're getting soaked. Let's get you out of the rain."

Exhilarated with the force of nature, they looked at each other and laughed, hysterically.

"Look at you!" Tom cried. "Are you okay? Sure?"

Libby whipped the strands of wet hair from her face, and shrugged. She mouthed something, but the noise was quenched by the wind.

They eventually reached the Community Hall, and Tom wrestled with the door handle but the door would not budge. He tried knocking, but there was no response. He began hammering on the door and a face appeared at the window.

"Will you please let us in?" Tom shouted. "Can you not see it's pelting out here?"

The face stared back at him, unresponsive.

"Oh hell!" Tom roared, and with a fury of energy, he slammed his right shoulder into the wooden door. The door flew open and Tom fell forwards, collapsing onto the floor.

Immediately, a group of islanders surrounded them.

"Oh pray, you must be soaked."

The old crone they had met earlier leaned over Tom, her face twisted and curdled.

"That's a wretched door. It's always causing us trouble. Come in, and get yourself warmed round the fire and you lass, must take more care of yourself. Remember, children are very precious, and in your condition…"

"I know, I know!" snapped Libby.

The old woman's face knotted into a scowl.

"There's no need to be sharp. I see you have lost your rowan twig. You will have to be careful for evil spirits abound. Now, you are most welcome. You must be chilled to the bone."

The old crone pulled up a pair of spindle backed, wooden chairs and beckoned for Tom and Libby to sit down. Tom raised his eyebrows at Libby.

"Hardly the most comfortable…will you be okay?"

Aware that the old woman was standing staring at them, Libby hushed Tom.

"Be respectful," she whispered, grinning at her husband.

As they sat round the fire, the islanders scuttled about them. One stoked up the flames and another brought them steaming, hot tea and strange looking bread. Tom looked at the bread, warily.

"This is a bannock, made especially for Michaelmas Day, which falls tomorrow. Michael is the angel who meets the souls of those who have crossed over and into the 'light of another time'. It is a day when we mourn for all our lost children. Enjoy the bread, but be careful, for Maggie still insists on hiding a silver coin in the mixture. It's supposed to be lucky, but not so lucky, if you accidently choke on it."

Laughter vibrated through the room, as Tom nervously chewed on the offering.

Libby drank the hot tea, gratefully, and gazed about her. Adorning the walls on each side of the fireplace were photographs of children and babies, many of whom had tightly closed eyes.

The old woman smiled.

"These are all the babies and children we have lost to the other side. It's very sad. We believe they are still with us, in spirit if not in body. Sometimes, if you are lucky, you can hear their childish laughter coming from the graveyard."

Libby shivered, remembering the shadowed figure she had seen earlier.

"Ah," continued the old woman. "We've been told these losses are probably due to interbreeding. It weakens the stock. We value our children for we need them to grow up and look after the old. It would be a real shame if our population fades away and we are forced to move to the mainland. Our island is such a perfect place in a world full of corruption."

Suddenly Libby felt faint as strange pains rippled through her stomach, causing her to wince.

"I think I need to visit the rest room. Is there somewhere…"

The old woman nodded, pointing to a door on the other side of the room.

"Be careful, lass, for your time has nearly come. Do you not think it was a bit foolish to be travelling in your condition? Children are very precious, as you know."

Libby sighed, too tired to retaliate, for she was more concerned about the pains that shot like tremors through her stomach.

Left alone by the fire, Tom's eyes skirted the room, trying to avoid the fixed stares of the islanders. The clock above the fireplace ticked solemnly.

"Perhaps I should check on Libby?"

"Hush man, she'll be fine."

Tom fidgeted, wondering what to do. He caught sight of a curled up newspaper wedged in a paper rack, and unfolding it, he noticed it was dated from last month. He remembered the glaring, front headlines about yet another toddler going missing in the Glasgow area. The child had still not been found, and he could not imagine what the poor parents were going through.

"It's very sad, when something like that happens," the old woman leaned over Tom and pointed a twisted finger at the photograph of the missing child. "We have to look after our children. I blame the parents myself."

"That's a bit harsh," Tom replied, staring into the old hag's cold eyes.

The old woman returned the stare and eventually she spoke.

"We don't believe those on the mainland appreciate their children. They are always too busy getting on with their own lives and their own interests to concentrate on their offspring. That's why so many go missing. There are too many distractions, such as alcohol, pornography, television and the evil internet, which is spreading the devil's words throughout the world and destroying our existence."

Tom shrugged, unsure how to answer the woman. He wished Libby would hurry up, as he felt uncomfortably alone in this room with these strange people and their odd beliefs.

The old hag began to circle Tom, flicking a piece of seaweed back and forth.

Tom adjusted his spectacles, nervously.

"What are you doing?"

She stopped abruptly in front of Tom and held her hand under his chin so that he had no choice but to face her.

"We like it here, on our island, but it's been difficult of late. Take Jeannie Murphy, sitting over there in the corner. She tries hard to bring children into this world, but only three days ago, she gave birth to yet another dead child. Her breasts are aching and her heart is heavy. We have no other choice but to bring in fresh stock. Oh, we could always try to persuade others to come and live on the island, but no, we don't want adults, thank you. Adults from the mainland are tainted, but bairns are innocent." The old woman tapped her finger on the newspaper.

"Usually we visit the mainland every now and then and 'borrow' a child. We believe we can give the child a much better life than the one he would have suffered. Given the choice, would you not rather grow up here on this beautiful island, or be trapped in some Glasgow slum?"

Tom stared at the old woman, with a dreaded realization. Surely not? True, there had been a spate of toddlers and babies going missing in Scotland during the past few years, but this was too crazy a notion! Tom shivered, recalling the village women with their young children, yet, as Libby had reminded him, the schoolmistress claimed there had not been any births on the island for several years.

"You might think," the old hag sneered. "It would be easier to adopt or foster children, but we don't want any interference from the outside world. We don't want meddlesome social workers trailing all over *our* island, and that's why we have had to make our own plans. We normally have to take our wee trips to the mainland, only this time we won't have to make that journey. Today, indeed, has been most fortunate, thanks to your wife and yourself."

Tom shifted in his seat, aware that all the islanders had crowded round him, and he tried to turn his head to see where Libby was. Suddenly a pair of strong hands clamped round his throat. For an instance, Tom was stunned by shock, but as the hands exerted more pressure, he began to wrestle, panic shooting through him. The hands gripped tighter and tighter and Tom attempted to break free by prising apart the strong fingers that were compressing his windpipe. Frantically, he struggled to rise to his feet, but the islanders crammed closer, restraining him, holding him firm in the chair. Tom's body convulsed, as the hands round his throat crushed the life from him, and the chair Tom was sitting on clattered backwards and forwards on the floor, scraping against the floorboards in a frenzied death dance. Finally, the thuds ceased and Tom's body crumpled over – dead.

Jeannie Murphy cowered in the corner, embracing her heavy breasts.

"It will be all right now, Jeannie, that's the first part over," cried the old hag. "Your baby shall be born tonight even if we have to rip it from her womb. However, I don't think it will come to that, for we put some of the special herbs in the mainland woman's tea and, even now, she is probably starting her labours in the room next door. I have others attending to her. I know this baby can't replace your dead babbie, Jeannie, but you'll soon grow to love it, and we have to think of the island."

Jeannie frowned. "I'm just a bit frightened, for we've never done anything like this before. This is murder! I know we take other people's children, but that doesn't feel wrong. But this…"

The old woman crossed the room and laid a hand on Jeannie's shoulder.

"Weesh, woman, it was just too good an opportunity to miss. We had no choice. Jock didnae mind doing the deed – he's killed plenty of chickens in that manner, before, and Jock disnae mind disposing of the mainland woman as well, once the bairn is born. We can bury them in the grave set aside for your dead babbie, and if anyone comes looking for them, as far as we are concerned, they left on the six o'clock ferry. Just think, Jeannie, it's a very special baby, fresh from the womb! Come now, have a good cup of tea. We have a busy day, tomorrow as we have the baptism, on Michaelmas day, of all things. How fortunate. Have you thought of a name for the wean, Jeannie?"

Jeannie smiled, as her black thoughts drifted away as she began to imagine this new baby suckling her breasts.

"I'd like to call the baby Hope, if it's a girl, or Michael, if I'm fortunate to have a boy."

The old woman cackled, slapping Jeannie on the back.

"You can be clever when you want to Jeannie, naming the baby after St Michael, the archangel. You are not as stupid as we thought. Now, we have things to do and a baby to anticipate. Children are very precious, after all."

THE PERFECT SHOT
By
Russ Alexander

I first spotted the animal's tracks high up on the ridge, a few scrape marks here and there where it had tried to get a bite to eat, small plants bitten down to soil level, a sure sign. It would be a deer, perhaps a roe deer and well worth the hunt.

Although only just past five the day already warm with the promise of real heat later on, the air was alive with insects. It wasn't hard to guess where the deer was heading, I saw the trace of an animal track heading downhill into the fir trees. The animal paths are well worn tracks where a variety of animals through the years had worn a line, along the side of a forest or across a field, where they felt safest to travel, not always true as they were also the best place to set snares as many a trapper will tell you.

I stood up and re-adjusted the sling across my shoulder and decided this deer was fair game and headed for the trees, as I walked I looked up at a Buzzard high in the azure sky, its wingtip feathers spread out like the fingers of a hand touching and sensing the warm, uplifting thermal winds on which it see-sawed lazily, like a rice paper kite. One thing for certain, it saw me, its eyesight better than any telescopic sight made by man... we were both hunters but after different prey today.

Both light and temperature dropped as I entered the trees, sunlight mostly banished by the thick canopy of branches only here and there a shaft of persistent rays cut a diagonal path and found it's way to the padded pine needle floor of the forest. The thick carpet of fallen leaves denied my footsteps sound as I walked through this eerie gloom, no bird song here to lift my spirit because this was no natural forest of haphazard tree species but a specially planted cash crop of soft woods, tomorrow's newspaper pages or cheap flat pack furniture... no doubt a tax dodge for the local absentee landlord but what did I care, he could have all the expense of the upkeep of the land, I would still make a living from what didn't reach the rich man's table and make sport of avoiding his gamekeepers, who like bargain basement hitmen illegally slaughtered anything that endangered the Laird's other cash crop, the game pheasant, the only bird call to hear in this artificial place, one cash crop inside another cash crop, surely the stuff of an accountants' dreams.

I had come to the edge of the woods and was about to re-enter the world of light, I stopped to let my eyes readjust to the morning sun, gather my wondering thoughts and concentrate on stalking the animal. What I was about to do had no forgone conclusion, the deer was well armed with defensive weapons, hearing, sight and smell that had evolved over the ages in this natural prey animal to detect anything approaching from a great distance, but something else, a sixth sense when it came to predators... a feeling when something was just 'wrong.' All these coupled with an impressive turn of speed that, at times, could outrun a bullet made the deer a challenging prize.

I stepped out of the forests' welcome shade into the morning's stifling heat and at once felt the army surplus forest camouflage jacket I wore, was perhaps made for a colder climate than this July morning but it did its job and rendered me almost invisible to the most observant of eyes, but still the sweat prickled on my shoulders and back.

I would have to be as silent as possible from here. I guessed that the creature wouldn't be too far away and feeding, a little further on was an expanse of flat ground with lush green grass watered by a burn that flooded now and again after rainfall in the hills. If it was there it would be exposed and vulnerable and present a clear, clean shot for me. I walked quickly but quietly along the edge of the trees to my right and a bank of ferns and gorse bushes to my left, at the ready to duck into the trees if I saw any movement ahead.

After about fifty yards there it was, feeding about twenty five yards out from any cover. It was a Roe deer, a large one, perhaps three feet at the shoulders with it's reddish brown summer coat, a beautiful example of the species but one thing was wrong, damn it, the lack of short, three-tined antlers, it was a doe and not a buck, and this was the breeding season, but I felt I had to take the chance, I needed that deer and after all it meant money in my pocket and food in the larder for my family. I crouched down and edged forward silently, now an animal myself on all fours, my senses and hunting instinct going back to the caveman who had hunted with spear and stones and not the high tech equipment I had slung round my back. I reached a small break in the ferns, I would have to take the shot from here.

I lay still and watched my prey chewing the grass, its ears flicking now and again at the halo of black fly buzzing round its head. It kept nervously glancing in my direction, this was strange as I knew it could not have seen me or heard me behind the thick ferns. Then I saw it! Hidden in some long grass about four feet from me was her fawn, perhaps a week old. The only thing a fawn can do in a dangerous situation is to stay completely still, they do not move a muscle or even blink in the presence of a predator.

It was so beautiful lying there an ornament of a fawn sculpted in fine bone china, a piece of porcelain perfection in the grass, its ridged and spotted coat, fine features of the face, ears folded flat back against the head, and its long stilt-like legs tucked underneath it, I would have to take it right after the doe, it was too good a chance to pass up now.

Moving slowly and silently I lay down in the grass to take the shot, the doe was about twenty five yards from me and presenting its right side. My hands, clammy with sweat now, felt the weight and the cool metal against my cheek, I closed one eye and looked at the creature now through

137

optical glass which somehow made the creature an inanimate object. I slowed my breathing down now, slowly in, slowly out to stop the slight tremor in my hands... the third time I inhaled I held the breath in my lungs and felt the pressure build in my finger... The metallic click seemed to ring out like a gunshot through the morning still...I swung round to the fawn and squeezed again... another satisfying click from my camera. Glancing back to the doe, I saw she hadn't even flinched. I started crawling back from that idyllic scene, I just knew I had two great shots on film, they would surely sell to a nature magazine, maybe even a calendar if I was lucky.

THE LEGEND OF MAGGIE DUFFTON
by
Sue Baker

The painted exterior walls of the old building were now discoloured from years of grime and dust from the nearby quarry. Granite walls still held strong, keeping the roof firmly in place.

The evening sun blushed in the sky, promising another clammy night. As the evening descended, birds sat in the trees singing. The smell of barbecues filled the air.

A motorbike drove into the small uneven car park of the Burnett Arms, one of only two hotels in the village of Kemnay. A small collection of the village inhabitants stood outside, smoking. Inquisitive eyes watched the stranger slowly removing their gloves and helmet. A gentle breeze ruffled their long hair.

The young men in the gathering stared at the large bike, then they stared at the woman and then to back to the bike. Conversation between them stopped in mid sentence.

"Evening," she smiled, as she glanced around the group. "Do they have any rooms here?"

"Aye, we do," a middle aged woman wearing a black polo shirt and trousers pushed herself away from the wall. Throwing her cigarette end on the ground she stubbed it out with the ball of her foot. The name of the hotel was stitched on her shirt just below her shoulder and underneath that, her name, *Ada*.

Ada opened a single door to a small foyer, then through another door into the bar. The stranger unzipped her leathers to her chest as she followed Ada to the bar.

"How long you staying for?"

"About one or two nights, I'm not sure yet." She watched Ada as she flicked through the pages of a reservations book.

"And you are?" She asked with pen poised.

"Coleen, Coleen Jordan."

139

Glancing around the semi deserted bar Coleen noticed many of the customers were men still in their work clothes, chatting away in the pleasantly cool room. Just along the bar one woman stood out, her sad eyes scrutinized every inch of the activity. Coleen had no idea why, but she seemed to be out of place. There was something in her features that stood out as the light overhead reflected on her frame.

Ten minutes later Coleen was in her room, she placed her bag on the bed and set about putting her things in the wardrobe and in the drawers of the matching dressing table. Opening the window a little Coleen let some fresh air in to circulate around the room. She couldn't believe she was here, she was home. Her life's dream was to visit Scotland, now she was here. Her family originally came from Kemnay and the area had always intrigued her.

The black and white photograph on the wall above the bed showed an old Burnett Arms. It hadn't changed much over the years – only difference being the flat caps.

Locking the door to her room she walked towards the bathroom to get a leisurely hot shower. No more campsites with ice cold running water. She had a few days to rest.

Closing the door she turned on the shower. Perfect. Checking for the towel she quickly got undressed and stepped under the running water as it fell over her head. Holding her head back she felt the water trickle down her face and her back.

All the tension, which had been building up to a crescendo over the past few days, began seeping away. Coleen started to rub the shampoo gently into her hair.

She froze as she heard a rustling in the room. Her eyes flew open as she listened. Wiping the soap out of her stinging eyes she cautiously pulled back the white shower curtain to take a quick look around. There was no one in the room, but she could see the vapour from her breath swirl around her. The mist from the hot shower had steamed over the small mirror on the wall, it looked like someone had wiped over the glass with their hand.

A frosty shiver rippled down Coleen's spine, causing every cell on her body to prickle. Someone had been here.

Finishing her shower she wrapped a towel into a turban around her hair. Collecting her belongings she reached out her hand and grabbed the door handle, but she quickly snapped it back as if she had been electrocuted. The round brass knob was ice cold, and twisting. Someone was trying to enter the bathroom. Looking down, as the door handle turned from one way then to the other, her blood pounded in her ears. Using a towel to turn the handle, her hands shaking as she pulled sharply on the door. Stepping back she expected someone to fall in, but there was no-one there. Edging her way carefully into the icy room, not knowing what she might find, she leant against the wall she closed her eyes and tried to calm her erratic breathing. Her whole body shook. Coleen needed air. She rushed to the window but the room started to spin. The window had been open when she left. Now it was closed and locked.

"The window was loose and it dropped by itself," she whispered calmly. She opened the window again, she was able to explain how the window closed, but how did it lock?

Throwing her head forward she unwound the towel and started gently rubbing the towel over her hair. The towel fell to the floor – retrieving it she stood and pushed back her hair from her face.

She screamed!

Standing there at the bottom of her bed was a woman in a long pink dress. Staggering backwards as the icy air engulfed her. Her hands flew out to the side and behind to grab hold of anything for support.

The lady smiled watching the commotion. Coleen's mouth was agape as she watched the figure slowly vanish. When the last of the shape disappeared she sat down on the edge of the bed. Her body trembled; she couldn't believe what she had just seen. It was the woman in the bar.

"It wasn't real!" She told herself. "It couldn't have been!" Her heart beat faster.

An hour later Coleen sat at the bar. It had taken a while for her body to stop shaking. Her stomach churned as she thought of the woman. She drank a vodka and diet coke to calm her nerves. The air around her felt thick to breathe.

"Hello, earth to space!" A voice came from nowhere.

"Sorry!"

"I asked if you wanted a drink."

"I'm sorry. I'm away with the fairies, yes please vodka and diet coke." The large man standing beside her ordered her a drink.

"K.P." the burly man held out his hand.

"Coleen Jordon. K.P.?"

"Long story! You look a bit...I don't know... preoccupied."

"No, I'm okay just tired I guess." The pair talked for over an hour, K.P. introduced her to a number of the customers. Coleen was bought a number of drinks and as the night wore on she found herself wanting to tell someone of her experience in the bedroom.

Turning to her new best friend she smiled, one of the sweetest smiles drink would let her muster, hoping that she didn't sound too crazy.

"You don't know me so you might think I've lost it, but... I've seen a ghost." Picking up her drink she took a large swig. "I know... I've lost it!" She went on to explain what had happened in the bathroom and bedroom. What the ghost was wearing and the sad look in her eyes.

"No you haven't. That's Maggie, Maggie Duffton, one of our resident ghosts."

"One of!" She held her drink to her lips.

He nodded. "She's harmless. Been here 80 years or so. She used to own this place, till her death in 1931."

"And!" Coleen wanted to know more.

Margaret or Maggie and her husband, James, owned and ran the Burnett Arms Hotel. He died in 1925 and Maggie continued to run the pub till her own demise in 1931. The pair had two children, one girl and one boy.

"It's said she requested three coffins to be made for her. One for her body, one her fortune and the third was to be filled with stones. She asked for one of the coffins to be buried in the grave yard with her husband and the remaining two were to be bricked up in the cellar.

"To this day no one knows if the request was true. If so, where is she resting? Last July, the present manager, Malcolm, had part of a wall knocked down to see if there was any truth in the yarn. Unfortunately nothing was found, but he hasn't given up yet.

There are two more walls to try.

"Maggie's not the only ghost to be found, but she's the best known. There are a further four spirits that occupy this bar. One stands in the corner playing darts, another stands at the door and two sit in the snug. Maggie keeps them in order and they don't trouble the living."

Coleen listened intensely. "You're having me on?"

"No, it's true," Ada said, placing a drink on the bar. "Edna's heard her and seen her standing in the open door over there." She pointed to an archway that led to the snooker room at the far end of the bar.

"She's heard the sound of rattling bottles in the bar and in the cellar and an old hand towel dispenser makes a noise in the kitchen, yet the kitchen no longer has that machine. One morning a woman came into the bar while the cleaner was alone asking if she had seen Norman. The cleaner said she hadn't and when she looked up the woman had gone. When the cleaner left at the end of her shift the bar doors were locked. No one had entered that way."

Coleen felt a chill shudder run down her spine, thinking that some unknown person or spirit could be watching somewhere in the building without being noticed. Opening the door to her room Colleen popped her head around the doorway and looked around to see if anyone was there. She was alone. She felt silly looking for something she couldn't see. A glance at the window told her that Maggie had been into the room and closed the window again.

Now she knew she wasn't losing it, she just reopened it and felt the soft breeze on her face. She wasn't afraid if Maggie wanted to show herself again. After all it's the living you should be more afraid of, not the departed.

Getting ready for bed Colleen noticed the room had become cold again. Breathing out she could see her breath disappear into the room. Turning around she saw Maggie standing there at the bottom of the bed.

Watching.

Her heart beat faster with excitement as the pair looked at each other, both smiling.

Colleen felt honoured that she had come back. She felt comfortable to be with her. Slowly the vision disappeared and the room became warmer.

Waking early Coleen took a walk to the local grave yard where she had been informed Maggie was buried. Walking slowly up and down the rows of head stones she read the inscriptions. The she found what she was looking for and read:

Erected by Margret Duffton
In memory of her husband
James Duffton
Who died at
Burnett Arms Hotel, Kemnay
1ˢᵗ March 1925
The above Margret Duffton
17ᵗʰ February 1931

Bending down Colleen placed a small bunch of flowers on the well kept grass. Taking a step back she looked at the head stone once more and smiled. Her heart went out to the unknown woman.

THEY TASTE LIKE CHICKEN
By
Vic Gordon-Jones

On her knees on the floor and pulling the carpet back from the edge of the wall, the old woman was clearly just as anxious. She paused for a moment, apparently also trying to listen through the muffled sounds of the traffic and voices from outside for anything unusual. Obviously hearing nothing, she yanked the carpet once more with all the strength in her large and sagging arms, finally uncovering it.

"In here."

"You don't think they're going to know?"

"Probably," wrenching the trapdoor open, "might as well take the risk though."

She took the small plastic crate in her arms and swung her legs over the edge of the opening, peering down into the dimly lit room below. She looked back up at Janet who stood trembling at her side. "Want to see?"

It was much larger than she'd expected. The image Janet had built up in her mind from days of indecisiveness and wondering, had resembled some sort of dingy battery farm, damp and cramped and stuffed with tiny cages... With roughly twenty square feet of carpeted floor scattered with an array of baskets and plastic carriers, yellow painted walls and flickering light bulbs swinging from the low ceiling, it was hardly pleasant; but she knew it could have been much worse.

"There's so many…"

"Thirty eight now, I think."

"And nobody should hear them down here?"

She waved one spade-like hand in dismissal. "Very well built, this place and of course they must have been discouraged from making much noise…"

"Of course…" She watched old Mrs Kinnock as she shuffled ahead, thighs jiggling violently beneath her blue patterned nightdress.

"You needn't worry too much…. We always have someone down here to watch them, feed them and everything."

"I'm surprised you can find enough to feed them…"

"Plenty," glancing back at her, she cast a very solemn look. "But we certainly don't want to let them get too… *healthy*. Just in case."

The silence that followed was excruciating. For those few moments, Janet could hear the soft brush of their feet against the carpet, a haunting mixture of faint groaning and snuffling and the buzzing of the light bulbs. She could hear them breathing.

"If you'd prefer you can take your box home and I'll use one of mine… Will you be bringing in any more?"

"Everyone I know turned theirs in weeks ago and I don't have any more of my own."

"You're lucky, then," he said with a soft, but grim, smile. "And you're definitely doing the right thing."

"But a little too late. If I'd known what was going on, what they were doing …"

Kinnock snorted, an enraged, half-laugh. "Doesn't matter to most people. They'll all sit there over platefuls, talking and laughing like the whole thing's just perfectly normal. And it's everywhere now—you know that one, just two streets from here?"

Nodding slowly: "I talked to him, just last week. About serving the stuff, asked him how he could *possibly* want to sell that to people…" For a moment she almost choked, unable to repress the sickening feeling rising in her throat. "And he just stood there before he laughed and said they taste like chicken."

"And to think, you don't even need a licence to keep chickens… It's insane. They know fine that people just can't afford it. They'll be charging per kilogram to keep them before you know it."

Letting her head drop as she tried to hide her eyes and shield herself from Kinnock's penetrating gaze, her voice was only a whisper. "We couldn't come up with the money. But even if we could have, this time, what then? Higher costs every time?"

"Makes it easier for people to just hand them over," she shook her head in disgust, "I couldn't."

"Sometime we'll all have to."

Though it was something that she knew and had known for a long time, finally voicing the thought made it so much more haunting. "You know it'll never stop. One minute it's pets, dogs; and now... They couldn't even stop it from spreading here; soon it'll be the world over..."

The sudden thud from somewhere above wrenched her quickly out of her thoughts. She felt her stomach tighten, felt the sick feeling begin to tug at her throat once again, as Kinnock turned and hobbled slowly towards the wooden ladder.

"*What're you doing?*"

"Stay right here."

Only able to stand, frozen with horror, she watched as the very last thread of blue nightdress vanished, and the trapdoor closed between them. She listened to Kinnock's thundering footsteps, until they had softened to a vague shuffle, stopping somewhere at the far end of the floor above her and for a few seconds...nothing. Then, as what must have been the door creaked slowly, a man's voice, muted, but terrifying all the same. Trying to figure out what was going on. All she could hear were the two muffled voices, then the faint sounds of the two pairs of feet creaking above, growing louder and closer...

The trapdoor opened.

And with a loud, horrendous thud, he hit the floor, sending a light spray of scarlet across the room as he landed. A large, blood-soaked baton of wood followed, falling on top of him with a clatter as Kinnock's slippers reappeared through the opening. Instantly, the wave of cries began to spread across the room, from one basket to the next- they were all screaming, the unbearable noise echoing all around.

It seemed almost as though Kinnock couldn't even hear them. Calmly, she lifted the wooden bludgeon from the ground, and nudged the newly deceased's head with her foot. Seeing the expression on Janet's face, she gave a cold, flippant laugh. "Oh don't worry too much. It had to be done."

She hobbled towards the nearest open basket, humming softly to herself as she bent down over the child inside. It lay silent, speckles of blood dripping slowly along its cheek and a small droplet perched on its bottom lip.

"Just a little taste of the future," Kinnock brushed one fingertip across its lip, leaving a slight red smudge behind. "If he lives long enough to see it."

Janet could only stare wordlessly as Kinnock, so casually shuffled past her, chilling smile spreading across her lips, could only stare down at the carnage at her feet. Her eyes scanned the young man's body, taking in his blood-drenched hair, his wide, gaping eyes, frozen in lifeless shock, the way his arms and legs were sprawled gruesomely across the carpet- and stopped at the large grey badge, pinned to the left sleeve of his jacket. The badge that read, in small green lettering: *Anti Child-Slaughter Alliance of Scotland.*

THE TRUE CONFESSION OF MORAG MAGOON
by
Sharon Hawthorne

On February sixteenth Morag Magoon confessed to murder. She hadn't meant to confess, but pride and the sheer delight of what she had done overwhelmed her and she blurted out her crime before she had even realised what she was saying.

"Mrs Magoon," the policeman said. "Are you sure? Do you really know what you're saying?"

If it hadn't been for his patronising manner, DI James McDonald would have been right up Morag's street. Of course she was a fair bit older than him, but that didn't matter so much as she gazed at his lips, plump and ready for kissing, mouthing words she had chosen not to hear. He had a nice face too, round and well fed with a stomach to match and she allowed her eyes to follow the line of his navy blue tie that settled on his paunch like a ski slope. He was still talking, and Morag was still not listening, when she cocked her head to one side to see beneath the tie where a shirt button had given up the struggle against his belly and popped off, leaving a gap that exposed bare, hairy flesh to the world. Morag sighed, if only times were different, if only she had been eighteen when he had been twenty, if only they had gone to the same Christmas Ceilidh at the village hall in 1953, she would have been married and widowed by now.

"Mrs Magoon, can – you – hear – me?" DI McDonald said loudly and slowly.

Morag snapped her attention back to his face and nodded equally as slowly: "Yes – I – can," she said with a giggle, settling back in her chair and trying to remember the last time she had had the attention of two young men, although the other one wasn't as bonnie as she would have liked.

"Now then Mrs-"

"Oooh, before we start," Morag said, raising her hand to halt the DI mid-sentence. "I wonder if your sergeant would be a love and put the kettle on. I'd do it myself, but I've had quite a day you know."

The sergeant raised bushy eyebrows in protest but dragged his feet to the kitchen, DI McDonald smiled and Morag pulled a face at the state of his teeth. Thank goodness he wasn't there in 1953 after all. Bad teeth were the one thing she couldn't bear, hairy backs were OK, nails bitten down to the quick she could live with but teeth like the DI's, all crooked and stained brownish from smoking and drinking too much red wine, were a real turn off.

"Mrs Magoon," DI McDonald said with forced patience. "Can you tell me what happened this morning?"

Cups and saucers were clanging together in the kitchen as the sergeant prepared the tea things and the kettle began its long slow whistle.

"Well, I left home at seven forty-five and, och Inspector, I almost forgot there are butteries in the bread bin, would you mind fetching them on a plate please? No point having a dry a cup of tea is there?"

DI McDonald was about to complain, but thought better of it as he tripped over a low footstall on his way to the kitchen. A few minutes later they were, all three, settled around the coffee table, cups of tea in delicate china resting in one palm, butteries crumbling into their laps in the other.

"Isn't this nice?" Morag said with a smile and a nibble.

"Lovely Mrs M," the sergeant said, spitting morsels of pastry way past his knees and onto the carpet as he spoke.

DI McDonald did not look happy. "Mrs Magoon, please."

"Yes of course Inspector," Morag said. She blew on the hot tea and took a cautious sip, delighting in the sweet warmth that trickled down her insides. "I will tell you what happened this morning, but first of all you must stop calling me Mrs, I've never been married you know."

*

Morag strolled along the gravel drive at eight o'clock that morning, feeling small stones leap up to find purchase inside her sensible black shoes and excitement at the adventure she was about to have. She smiled, in fact she laughed out loud, enjoying the little skip in her step, the little flutter in her heart and the thin veil of sweat on her palms. The house was set back from the road and revealed itself as she took the corner by the fat fir trees, its majestic turrets fit for Rapunzel to let down her hair and its secrets as secret as the gardener, Mr Springer, and the cook come cleaner, Mrs Hyde allowed. As Morag drew closer, the house loomed taller and ominously captured the sun behind its chimneys, turning a bright summer's day into a chilly twilight. When she reached the front door she heaved the round brass knocker away from its resting place and let it fall with a heavy thud. Behind her tall bushes had been crafted into birds and animals and lined a wide stretch of lawn that Morag imagined the Laird used for afternoon tea. Now what was it they called the shaping of trees thingy, she wondered, completely forgetting that no one inside the house had yet responded to her knock. Propary? No. Flopery? No. What the devil was it?

"Who is it?" A voice from inside the house eventually called out, but Morag was lost to her thinking.

"What do you want?" the voice asked again.

"Come on Morag Magoon, you know what they're called."

"Are you still there?"

"Oh, I give up!" Morag tutted in frustration and turned back to the black wooden door, her hands fisted on her hips. All was quiet on the other side now, so she knocked again. No answer. She lifted the letter box and peered through, jumping in fright as a pair of large brown eyes stared back at her.

"What do you want," the owner of the eyes said, squinting suspiciously.

Morag fell backwards, her arms and legs scrambling in the air, as she landed awkwardly on her ankle. "Ouch," she cried, reaching down to rub the sore spot and silently cursing the damn eyes for frightening her. Then suddenly she got it: "Topiary!" she shouted, raising her hands in the air like a conquering football hero on championship night and, for a brief moment, she forgot all about her ankle.

"Are you mad?" the voice said, this time it was a little louder because the front door had been opened as far as the safety chain would permit.

Morag struggled to her feet and limped up the steps. "Hello, you must be Lady Ferguson, I'm Morag Magoon. Mrs Blair couldn't make it today, so she asked me to pop along instead. She said it would be alright, just a matter of getting you ship-shape for your party."

"Party?"

"Aye, that's it petal, your birthday party."

The door slammed shut and from inside Morag could hear loud sobbing and then a steady thump against the door, she hoped the poor girl was using her fist and not her head.

The step felt cold when Morag sat down, but she ignored it as the smell from the flower garden drifted across the lawn. She had never been one for gardening, much too much like hard work, but she loved flowers and always had a vase on her window seal at home. Minutes ticked past and Morag wondered what to do next, should she go, wait, force her way in? Mrs Blair did say that it wouldn't be an easy job, although she didn't explain much further than that.

"I don't know you," Lady Ferguson called through the open letter box.

"I know petal, but I've lived in the village all my life. You've probably seen me about, perhaps in the paper shop, or the pub. If I get there early enough I get the wee comfy chair by the corner so I can drink my Guinness in peace."

"I don't go to the shops or the pub for that matter-"

"Jeez Louise," Morag mumbled, easing herself up from the step. "Listen Madam, I've got a key, so it doesn't really matter if you want me to come in or not. I have permission and I have a job to do. A job that will be better for you if I complete it than if I don't."

"Why?"

"Why what?"

"Why will it be better for me?"

"Because petal your husband has invited half of Scotland's finest to your do and you want to look your best don't you? And you want to turn up on time and..." and she couldn't think of a third reason. Those were her instructions: make sure the lady looks her best and turns up on time. That's all.

"I don't want a party or a birthday," Lady Ferguson sobbed like a sulky teenager. "Do you think you could help me run away?"

"No," Morag snapped, her patience wearing thin. She dug around inside her bag and pulled out a set of keys, jangling them loudly. "That's it, you leave me no other option, I'm coming in."

But just as Morag was poised to place the key in the lock the door opened, creaking like an invitation to a haunted house, and Morag could not hide her shock at the state of the Laird's wife.

"Good heavens," she said, her face a confusion of disgust and disbelief. "You look like-"

"I think we might have a wee problem," Lady Ferguson said, interrupting what may well have become a very long diatribe of how, with all that money, a young woman could let herself go.

Lady Ferguson shed a tear and wiped her runny nose with the back of her free hand as she leant heavily against the edge of the open door. Her hair was wild and matted, black makeup had smudged from her eyes and crayoned thick lines down her cheeks. A man's shirt, which reached her knees, fell unbuttoned to her waist and was torn at the shoulder, as though someone had tried to rip the sleeve off. She sniffed and took a large swig from the bottle of red wine she held in her other hand: "Please come in Morag Magoon," she said with affectation, as she pulled the door inwards, swaying so violently from side to side that Morag felt sea sick.

Morag gazed warily at Lady Ferguson and the almost empty bottle of red wine. The pain in her ankle had increased and she considered calling that nice young doctor to pay a home visit once she had finished what she had come to do. The thought cheered her and distracted her, so much so that when Lady Ferguson tripped suddenly and fell on her back with her legs flying into the air, it came as quite a shock. But Morag was good with catastrophes, which is why Mrs Blair had recommended her.

"You're so calm Miss Magoon," Mrs Blair had said yesterday afternoon when she had popped round with a bunch of dog daisies and some Millionaire's Shortbread. "You're the only friend in the village that I could trust."

Morag had blushed to her hairline at such a compliment and decided there was no way she could ever refuse, and now her skills were to be tested to the limit. She rushed, as fast as her poor ankle could carry her and knelt beside Lady Ferguson, who had knocked herself out on the marble floor.

"Madam," Morag said, gently slapping the side of her face, although she was tempted to hit her really hard. "Madam, wake up."

She knelt back on her heels and looked up to the highest ceiling she had ever seen and a staircase that swept the whole side of the far wall, a wall that had been decorated with portraits from the first Laird to the present. Laird George Ferguson smiled back at her, he looked handsome and kindly, quite unlike the reality. In contrast to his wife, the Laird had spent many a happy hour in the pub, he had even shared a Guinness or two with Morag and so Morag could claim an authority on his bad teeth, rheumy eyes and balding pate. How on earth he managed to marry a woman half his age she couldn't fathom, unless it was the money? Even so, money or no, the poor girl still had to sleep with him.

Morag sighed and lifted the empty wine bottle from Lady Ferguson's hand, that was when she felt the damp seep though her stockings and onto her skirt. "Och no," she cried as she shuffled to her feet, fearing a red wine stain that would never come out of her favourite woollen day skirt. But it wasn't red wine that was pooling from beneath Lady Ferguson, it was darker and thicker than wine. It was blood.

Lady Ferguson groaned and lifted herself up.

"Are you alright madam?"

"Nothing that another glass or two of rioja won't fix," she said and tried to giggle, but the effort was too much and she fell flat on her back again.

"Madam, please sit up. You were right, we do have a problem, now let me see where you're hurt?"

Lady Ferguson pointed to her knee and made a sound that was caught between a cat trapped in a smokestack and a new born calf. There was a scratch on her leg, a small scab had started to form, but there was no cut that could warrant so much blood.

"Do you think you could stand up madam?"

Lady Ferguson sat with her legs splayed out like a rag doll that had lost half its stuffing, wiped her face with the corner of her shirt and nodded. She manoeuvred her limbs so that she was kneeling on all fours, then she straightened her back legs and miraculously stood up. But then she lost her balance again and slipped in the gooey blood that surrounded her feet, as though she were a monument on a dark red pond, and fell, this time face down. When she looked up, blood had mixed with old makeup and she started to cry.

"Oh what am I to do?" she wailed, slamming her fist into the puddle of blood so that it splashed across Morag's face and cardigan. "I know that something bad has happened. Oh why does it always have to be me?"

"Och now petal," Morag said, wondering if coffee would be best first or after she had hosed Lady Ferguson down. "You must get a hold of yourself. Now is there anyone else in the house?"

"No," she cried. "I'm all alone. I'm always alone, nobody loves me."

"Well now, you know that's not true. What about your husband?"

"He doesn't love me. He's having an affair you know, with the tart in his office, Sheila. Bloody Sheila. It wouldn't have mattered so much if she'd been an Isabella or a Georgina, but Sheila, from Torry of all places. Oh the shame."

Morag could only guess at the madness of the upper classes as Lady Ferguson slammed her tiny fists on her knees and raged

155

against her misfortune. "Well this just won't do," she said as she looked around the floor for the source of the blood and finally spotted drag marks that headed off under the door by the foot of the stairs.

"Now madam, you have to stand," Morag said, holding out her hand to help Lady Ferguson to her feet.

"I can't."

"You must, something has happened here and we have to find out what it is before we call the police."

"Can't we just call the police first?"

"Heavens no madam, just think of the scandal."

Lady Ferguson's eyes glazed over and just when Morag thought she had lost her again, she said: "You're right," and hoisted herself onto her shaky legs.

"Alright petal?" Morag asked when they reached the door.

Lady Ferguson shook her head. "I don't think I can go in there."

"You'll be fine, I promise. Now, on three."

She counted slowly and when she reached three Morag turned the door handle, pushed it inwards and stepped inside. Lady Ferguson was close behind her, holding onto her elbow as though a little old lady would be able to defend her against a monster. But the room was empty of life. A grand piano languished in sunshine that streamed through the back window and the usual grandeur lined the walls. The only thing that looked out of place was the blood that covered the furnishings and drew a crooked line all the way to another door in the far corner. The two women followed it, stepping lightly like sparrows, the smell of fear palpable as their hearts beat faster in their chests. At the second door they looked at each other again and nodded. It was the same routine, Morag counted to three and pushed the heavy door inwards. Only this time the room wasn't empty.

"So, Lady Ferguson was well when you first saw her?" The sergeant asked.

"As well as any drunk covered in red stuff could be."

156

The DI placed his tea cup back on the coffee table with a little more force than he had intended to show. "And by red stuff you mean..."

"Och, you know."

"Please tell me, just for clarification."

"Blood, inspector. The poor quine was covered in blood!"

"And the house, that was covered in blood too?"

"Yes, every room we went into had red stuff all over the floor and the walls and, well once we had discovered the source, then it all became clear."

"The source?"

"Yes sergeant, the bodies."

"Bodies? They were already there? But I thought-"

"Well if you didn't interrupt perhaps I could finish," Morag said huffily, she was getting to the good bit and like any good story teller she was just building suspense.

Three people sat around the kitchen table as though they were about to play cards. One leant back in the chair in a strange parody of laughter, another's head lolled to one side, as though peering at his opponents hand and a third had given up altogether and fallen asleep, his head on the table twisted awkwardly to one side. Of course none of that was true, they were all dead, each with a slit across their throat that had all but decapitated them.

"Oh dear," Morag said.

Lady Ferguson screamed.

Morag checked Lady Ferguson's profile and smiled, pulling her lips over her teeth to stop herself from laughing like the villain she was. "What have you done?"

Lady Ferguson fell over again.

When she came too, Morag was standing over her with a knife, she screamed – again.

"Is this what you used?"

"I... what....I didn't," Lady Ferguson crawled backwards, away from Morag, in a desperate attempt to escape.

"How would you know? You were drinking Scotland dry."

157

"But I'd know," Lady Ferguson was now suddenly and clearly sober, she got to her feet, leant against the wall and lifted her chin away from the knife that Morag had almost pinned to her face.

"How? Show me what you did," Morag said thrusting the knife into Lady Ferguson's hand.

Lady Ferguson let the knife rest on her upturned palm, as though holding it properly would be tantamount to admitting guilt. Morag was chuffed. It was all falling so easily into place.

"Who did you do first?"

"I... I didn't," Lady Ferguson was crying again and her gaze fled from one side of the room to another, resting anywhere except for the bloody mess that met her on the table.

"Did you take Mr Simpson first or Mrs Hyde? Did they come in and catch you in the act of slitting the Laird's throat, is that what happened? Is it? Tell me."

"I don't know, maybe... perhaps.... Oh God, what have I done? Morag you have to help me."

Morag reached a gentle hand out and stroked the Lady's face. "I will petal, I will."

And that's where it all went wrong. Suddenly there was a groan from the table and the sleeping form of old Mr Simpson raised its head, how that was possible Morag would never know, and Lady Ferguson snapped. In a blink of an eye she ran behind Mr Simpson, raised the carving knife high above her head and slammed it into the neck of the poor gardener. Then she pulled it out again, looked at the blood, looked up at Morag, screamed and stabbed herself in the heart.

"Oh bugger," Morag sighed as she watched Lady Ferguson flail from one side of the kitchen to the other, blood spewing out of her chest in a grand arc that swept across the cooker, pots and pans, plates, cups, glasses and the three corpses at the table. Morag waited until Lady Ferguson was spent and had fallen over for the last time before collecting her bag from the front door and limping home, it was almost eleven and time for a nice cup of tea and a buttery.

*

"So you're saying that Lady Ferguson killed the cook, the gardener and her husband?"

"No. Would you like another cuppa Inspector?"

"No. No thank you. Mrs, sorry, Miss Magoon, could you please focus. When you called us you said that you had murdered them, but now you're saying that Lady Ferguson did it."

"No I'm not, you weren't listening Inspector. I killed them and made Lady Ferguson believe that she did it. Of course, I had no idea she was going to top herself, that was not part of my plan."

"Your plan?" the policemen said together.

Morag was disappointed. In all her years she had never confessed and never been caught, and now that she was confessing no one believed her. She gazed down at her new slippers and wondered if telling them how she had killed them would help. She wondered if it would make any difference if the policemen knew that she was a keen genealogist and that she had now taken her family history all the way back to the sixteenth century. October 1579 to be precise and the weeks that led up to her ancestor, Laird Henry Ferguson, the third Laird, the one who's painting was missing from the gallery at the house, being disinherited. And why? Morag shook her head in sorrow. Henry had fallen in love with a girl from the village and in a whirlwind of passion and romance had married her. Henry believed at first that his father had given his new bride his blessing, but then he uncovered a plot to have her killed. Henry confronted the Laird and gave him an ultimatum, either his father accept his marriage or he would leave. Unfortunately that was his downfall and poor Henry died a penniless farm hand in Alford ten years later.

Hours upon hours of research confirmed that Morag was a direct descendent of Henry's only surviving child and she felt it was her duty to make amends for the travesty that had befallen her family.

Laird George Ferguson, the ugly one with the new young wife, the one with the bad teeth who liked to share a pint with the locals in the pub, was the last of his line. And no amount of wooing was ever going to make his drunken wife pregnant. It was easy, all Morag had to do was arrive at the house early, go home and change and come back as though nothing had ever happened. Of course daft Mr Simpson came in and caught her, so he had to go and then Mrs Hyde came in whistling Take the blooming High Road and that was the end for her. The problem with Mrs Hyde was location. She had died by the front door and it took Morag a good half an hour to drag her body into the kitchen and position it with the others. But when it was done it was done and Morag wondered how long it would take to prove that she was the rightful heir, get her books and clothes packed and move in.

The inspector looked closely at Morag and she smiled, he really was quite handsome when he kept his mouth closed. "Miss Magoon, we're going to go now, if you can think of anything else, just give us a call."

The two men stood, both towering above her, and smiled sympathetically.

"Would you like to see a doctor about your ankle?" The sergeant asked.

"That young one you mean, Dr Patterson?"

"I believe so, shall I call him and ask him to come round?"

"Oh yes please," Morag said. "That would be wonderful."

Morag waved to the policemen as they drove away and thought about what she would do for the rest of the week. As she closed the front door she noticed gossipy old Mrs McLain twitching behind her lace curtains. Morag smiled and made a note on her to do list.

SLEEPING
by
Vic Gordon-Jones

"You did something with her, didn't you?"

Glancing up at her from the sink with a line of mint foam still dripping from my chin, I spat a sharp laugh. "Bugger off."

"Glad you take me seriously…"

"I would if you didn't talk like a fucking paranoid mental patient." I rinsed the toothbrush immediately under the full-blast tap water, just for something to do. She was giving me that look again. The kind that could make you admit to anything: even if you'd done nothing.

"You left her number in your dresser."

"Spying on me, I take it? There's a surprise."

"Well, I'm sorry for being curious about what goes on in this relationship."

"So that's what we're calling it now?"

"Don't try to be clever, it doesn't suit you."

Her eyes scrolled down to where the strand of toothpaste still hung from my face. I quickly wiped it away with the back of my hand, and tried to force a laugh. "That all you've got?" And again, came the nerve-slitting silence. Then, just as I was beginning to think that she was ready to retreat back into whatever hole she'd crawled out of that morning-

"I fucked him, by the way."

"Oh yeah?"

A rather glorious, arms-folded smirk was all I received in response. I hated that smirk. Perhaps at one time I'd loved it, along with many of the once appealing little things about her that to me had slowly turned black and wretched around the edges.

Tempted to respond with something, *anything* much worse, I only managed a slight, flippant laugh as I snatched my shirt from the edge of the bath. The collar was wet and I was certain that she had been responsible. I tried not to flinch at the dampness against my neck as I put it on, feeling her eyes fixed fiercely on me.

"Aren't you bothered?"

"Do I look bothered?"

Of course though, I was. I was bothered by the fact that she'd actually said it, more than anything. She was clearly desperate to drag me into a fight- and she knew I hadn't the time for it. Not that I'd told her where I was meant to be going that afternoon; but she must surely have figured out that I wouldn't have been leaving so well groomed, so late on a Saturday, unless I was going to meet someone.

Calmly watching me as I rinsed my razor, she stood behind me at the mirror and fiddled with her pinned back hair, brushing little strands of it over her eyes with her fingertips. I'd always liked her hair that way. It was how she'd been wearing it on our first night together, nearly five years before. And even after that long, I could still remember the smallest details. Her lips had smelled like French vanilla; and tasted a little bit like cooking fat. And the liner on her left eye had been smudged, though I hadn't bothered to mention it. She still had that green dress, which she'd worn that night – despite the fact that she hadn't been able to fit into it for the past year or so and if she could, it would've made her resemble a blonde-haired seaweed sushi wrap, anyway. But I supposed, it made her sort of mourn the past, helped her remember how much happier we'd been. Though it must have also reminded her just how different we'd become. People can be quite sick, like that.

As she stood back to take a quick glimpse of her new-and-improved reflection, a devious smirk spread across her pink-frosted lips again, and I could tell that she was dying to spill something. I was almost afraid to ask.

Ditching my razor in the sink, I immediately gave in. "...What?"

"You know your friend…" one corner of her top lip crept up, almost snarling at me in pleasure. "What's his name- Dave…?"

"Right…" I laughed, "Here's one for you: Julie."

At that her smile suddenly melted, her face dropping. I grinned in triumph, the first sense of triumph I think I'd had in a long time, while I savoured her annoyance.

"*Her?*"

"What're you getting on your high horse about? Dave's the one with the fucking mutant ball…"

As her mouth only hung open and I waited for her to ask me how exactly I would know how Dave looked naked – and wondering if I might as well make her think that I'd fucked *him*, too – I was sure that she could see through my eyes every little cog turning and every switch flicking in my mind, as I tried desperately to plan my next few moves. Smile sneaking along her lips once more, she shot me another cutting remark.

"I hope you showered after that…"

"Of course I did. I'm not *you*…" I cast her an almost affectionate grin, which she reluctantly returned, letting my comment roll straight from her back to the floor. Sly little insults and our tepid-humoured ridicule had become quite a large part of what made us ourselves, in a way. While we were very aware that whatever it was that we had was strange, we were perhaps too used to it to bother changing. The weirdest thing about it wasn't the sneaking resentment, or that we were jumping into bed with anybody, and probably everybody, else that we could, without even really attempting to hide the fact – the weirdest thing, was that we still slept together. I don't think either of us really knew why. Deep down I'd always suspected that it was because by that point, during the daytimes our one life had become our lives, two separate universes that only crossed, just bumping together and brushing harshly against one another's surfaces. But at night, everything else stopped and that meant that so could we. We could lie there, without having to think about all of the wrongs we'd slowly scarred one other with, without the bitter words, or the bitter silences. We could be together, be part of that one life again, even if we couldn't be awake to see it. And I suspected that if we ever stopped that complacent facade, the last thread of what held our little universes together would snap, letting us soar apart forever. Of course, I had never wanted to test that theory. Just in case. Because although, even watching her at that very moment as she slipped her red sundress down over her naked and subtly freckled shoulders, while her obvious callousness and her audacious beauty among many other things repulsed me and I was sure that I must have in some ways repulsed her too, there was something comforting about keeping her close.

It wasn't that I was lonely, or even afraid of being lonely. Of course in a place like this, there would always be someone else around to fill in the gaps – just nobody quite the same. We'd moved from the highlands and into the city nearly two years before—a mutual decision. She'd claimed that she wanted to move to find better 'opportunities', whatever that had really meant, but myself, I'd just been happy to move closer to real life and to other people, to escape the agonizing silence. Which, by that point, had become a pretty familiar part of our relationship, of course, what had seemed like such a wonderful idea had wound up backfiring on me because, where there were more people, there were of course, more men- that she could always use to fill our little silences.

"You're looking nice..."

Barely glancing at me as she rummaged through the bottles lined up along the shelf, "Thanks..."

"So who is it then, this time?"

"You don't know him," she shrugged, her lips curling into a slight smile, and spritzed a tiny cloud of body spray at her neck – shaking her hair into it as though deliberately trying to look like she were in a shampoo advert. Probably thinking that she looked far more glamorous than she really did.

"I didn't ask if I knew him, just who it is."

"Does it matter?"

Well of course it didn't, really. I mean any chance of me ever running into half of the poor bastards she'd managed to sink her talons into was probably quite slim, but if *she* was always entitled so ask, then I should have been, too.

"Besides…" she laughed, flippantly, looking my slightly-too-flashy outfit up and down, "I should be asking *you* the same thing."

"You don't know her."

Something flickered in her eyes; that a part of me truly hoped might have been fury… or something. As I said before, people can be sick, sometimes. Sick enough to want to cause someone else the worst agony that we possibly can, to somehow soothe our own. Sometimes, people will do the craziest things, just to keep hold of something even crazier. Let themselves be stripped down of everything, to keep from having to give up that one all-consuming thing that they just can't live without. For me, I guess, that one thing was her. That was why—despite the fact that I knew the papers had been sitting in her bottom drawer for nearly a year—I'd never once asked her to let me sign them. As far as I knew, she hadn't even signed them, either – they were just lying there. So, with a sort of bleak and hopeless hope, I was sure that meant that perhaps I was her one, all-consuming thing, too.

"You're right, I don't think I know anyone with such bad taste. So… Is she pretty then?"

"Very."

Actually she wasn't, not very. Not that it would have mattered, anyway, seeing as how really, she was my supervisor. And how we were, in fact, going to be talking finances rather than taking moonlit beach walks, bunched up with four other snooze-inducing colleagues around a table in the local drinking pit for the better part of the afternoon. Of course though, I wasn't about to admit that.

Raising her eyebrows and the tone of her voice by a few notches, "Good to know."

"She's loaded," I blurted it out, somehow unable to put up my verbal floodgate. "Very successful, actually."

"That's a plus; maybe she could buy you a better outfit…"

"You know, some women are more interested in getting me *out* of my clothes than into them…" Probably. I hoped.

"Well if you do bring her back here, she just better not be thinner than me," she smiled deviously and leaned forward to plant a glossy, sticky pink kiss on my cheek. Grabbing her handbag that hung from the door handle, she turned to leave me, probably hoping that I would watch her go: which of course, I did.

"See you later."

I knew that whatever could have happened after we walked out of that door, however perfect her temporary plaything for the day might have been, however many drinks I could attempt to knock back before five in the morning and however easy it would be for us to just forget about that hostile, looming cloud that would always be waiting, we would both end up, as always, back here. I smiled silently at her back as the door closed behind her, remembering that although as long as we were sleeping beneath the same pretentious barrier, I would never really live – living without her, without even her harshest words and her most hostile emotional beatings – I would probably never really sleep again.

WITHIN THE WIND
by
Tori Hill

Pausing to push her unruly dark curls out of her eyes, Lorna sat back on her heels to survey her handiwork. Sweat trickled down her back in the still, humid, afternoon and cuttings littered the ground where she had been working. A cool shower awaited her once these had been dealt with. A large copper-hued dog dozed in the sunshine, one ear twitching occasionally. He opened an eye at the sound of her filling the big brown council bin with garden waste and closed it again after satisfying himself that all was well.

The day had been long and Lorna was now sticky, smears of soil on her hands and face. She stretched and tugged at her damp t-shirt, grimacing as it clung to her. A whine made her turn. The dog was standing, hackles raised and eyes wide.

"Hey. What's up? What's the matter?" His stance, and the low growl emanating from him, caused Lorna to shiver despite the heat. There were no sounds to be heard; no traffic, no neighbours, not even the ubiquitous call of the seagull. The silence hadn't been noticeable before, but now it pressed in on her.

She made for the house, cursing herself for her imagination. Within a few steps the sky darkened and the air became more oppressive. The animal stood his ground, body rigid and head roaming back and forth, still growling. As Lorna reached the kitchen the rumbling growl became a cacophony of barking and she looked back to see him staring wildly at nothing.

"Dart," her voice was sharp and the beast wheeled around and hurtled into the kitchen past her. A thunderous crack resounded in her ears and a flash dazzled her. She slammed the door and sank against it, shaking. The rain came then, battering against the windows and Dart huddled against her, whimpering.

He pushed his head into her shoulder and she reached up to stroke him, a small laugh escaping her. Shaking her head she gently pushed him back and rose to her feet. Sudden rain was a fact of life here, along with the North Sea haar, but not thunderstorms breaking in a matter of seconds. Little wonder Dart had reacted as he did. Lorna made her way to the bathroom but the dog followed in her footsteps right up to the door, "No. You're staying out there, stop being so silly." She closed the door firmly.

A crash from outside was immediately followed by a howl and she flung the door back again.

"What the hell?" Dart was cowering in the corner of the hallway. Striding past him into her bedroom Lorna made for the window. He tried to get in front of her but she dodged the now whining animal to see what caused the commotion.

The trees were flailing, the rain ricocheting from every surface and the roof of the shed lay up against the garden fence. "Shit." Lorna grabbed a coat from her wardrobe.

"Oh don't look at me like that. You can stay inside you big baby. Some guard dog you are, frightened of a wee bit of weather." He positioned himself between her and the door, barking.

"Stop that. You're starting to piss me off."

Dart shot forward and gripped the leg of her jeans in his jaws, pulling her further back into the room. She yanked her leg away but he held on and they wrestled. Snatching herself free, Lorna stopped dead in front of the window.

There were shapes in the rain; figures, moving, twisting. It appeared to Lorna as though there were two giants out there. Their heads were level with the treetops and they were translucent;

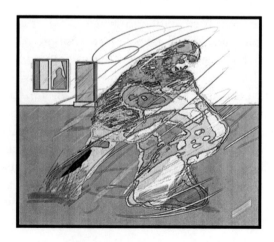

only the rain was giving them an outline. Lorna squeezed her eyes closed and rubbed them. That dog's behaviour was getting to her. She peered through the glass again and could see nothing more than her ruined shed. Optical illusions and canine craziness were no reason to ignore the damage outside. Her neighbours would love her if pieces of shed landed in their garden.

She pressed one hand to her chest and breathed in slowly. She had not even taken her first step when another noise from outside resounded and Dart let out a wail. Wincing, Lorna looked to see what else had joined her shed roof and recoiled from the view. Eyes widening, she steadied herself against the window-frame and her coat fell from her hand.

Two humanoid figures were locked together in a struggle. Large, not men, but more exaggerated, muscular and disproportionate, they tore at one another. They were the rain; melting and coming together with the force of waves in a tempest. Lorna's hands were white-knuckled and her breath came fast. A blow from the larger figure sent the smaller into the trees. A crack heralded a great limb's descent to the ground. It lashed back and the fallen roof splintered. The larger of the two gained the upper-ground, forcing its opponent down, beating and clawing at it. The victim seemed to weaken under the onslaught. The storm raged fiercer, the trees bending double in the gale as the apparent victor roared its triumph.

The creature on the ground radiated pain. Lorna's hand rose to her throat as she watched it contort, water spraying as its tormentor struck it again and again. Rolling to one side to avoid a blow resulted in a kick that sent it sprawling over the grass. As it fought to rise the other lifted the fallen tree limb high and swung it down brutally hard. The creature's ruined body buckled and the ground shook.

It was still moving. Only a little, and with obvious effort, but it was moving. It was heaved up and held in one fist while the other lifted the hefty branch for the finishing blow. Without any thought Lorna flew down the stairs and wrenched the door open, pitching out into the storm. The creature dropped its prey, drew itself up and regarded her. Shivering, soaked to the skin, and heart thudding she met its eyes. Its features seemed to curve into a sneer as it advanced on her, breathing ice on her chilled body. She stumbled backwards to escape the giant, slipping on the slick grass and winding herself as she hit the ground.

As it loomed over her Dart shot from the house, transformed into a snarling, furious beast by the sight of his mistress under threat. He smashed into the monster but within seconds lay broken beneath a tree. Lorna's efforts to regain her breath became sobs, but the creature was turning back towards her. Too late. Dart's sacrifice had given the second being the opportunity to rise up. It threw itself at the aggressor's back and knocked it flat. As it began to slam the other's head into the ground Lorna couldn't look. She pulled herself to her pet and cradled his body, trying not to hear the sickening sounds of battle.

The noise stopped. The wind lessened. The rain still fell hard but the storm had passed. Lorna looked up from her grief to see the smaller creature scrutinising her. The other lay in a heap behind it. It reached out and lifted Dart from her arms, his form suddenly small in its enormous hand. Before she could react it took hold of the other's still body and it was gone. Alone, dizzy and heartsick, Lorna forced herself upright and staggered into her home. She sank behind the door and let the tears come.

In the near-light before dawn she awoke on the kitchen floor, stiff and cold, filthy and bruised. It was impossible; there was no way that it could have happened. She must have suffered some kind of episode. On unsteady legs she bent and gulped water straight from the tap to fix her sandpaper throat and pounding head before surveying the damage to the garden. The storm had left torn trees and her shed in a heap on the ground. She must have blacked out and dreamed it all up. If she had fallen outside it would explain her sorry state. Dart was always nervous in storms, he must be hiding somewhere.

A splash of cold water on her face washed away some of the confusion and Lorna called out for her errant pet at the back door. Silence met her and a cold sweat beaded her forehead. Raising her voice, she called his name again and this time he appeared at the side of the house, bounding towards her. She dropped down to hug him tight and ruffle his fur, eyes filling and tense muscles relaxing. She would have to see a doctor, but right now there was work to be done and a hungry dog dancing around her who would have to be fed. Her smile turned rigid as a shadow in the trees caught her eye and a breeze swept in from nowhere. Then there was nothing but the sun.

WHITE GRANITE
by
Ann Miller

"Doing anything nice for the weekend, Ruth?"

"Oh nothing special; catching up with an old friend for a drink."

The latter bit might make her life sound less boring than usual, but it was a gross overstatement, though you could call it an understatement too. Phyllis wasn't her friend, never mind an old one—except in terms of pushing her mid-seventies. And meeting for a drink? If only that was all. Ruth laughed grimly, hoping Donna wouldn't probe for the details. Donna had lost interest; she was whipping on her jacket, her mind already on getting ready for her new boyfriend's birthday party, which would probably last until at least the early hours of Sunday morning. Kath and Doris would be looking forward to more mundane pastimes, which involved kids, grandkids, painting the hallway, doing the big food shop. Ruth wished their planned activities could all be put into a hat, and she could pick one out for herself—any one. Anything but what she had to face.

"You too," she replied brightly to Donna's exhortation to have a nice time. "Nice weekend, all."

All the way home on the bus she tried to quell her churning stomach, to focus on the streams of rush hour traffic, aggressive honking of horns, people traipsing through the drizzle that had not let up all day and was now turning into rain—driving against the bus window and forming puddles in the gutter. Not a gleam of sun pushed through the greyness. The bus was pulling into Union Street, opening up to let in a queue of bedraggled passengers. She smirked. What would Phyllis say? That this was all pretty quaint—just the way Dad described, only was it always so—well, *grey*? The bus shut its door and lurched forward; so did Ruth's stomach as reality hit her. Phyllis was here. Lurking in her hotel room, perhaps looking out onto these rain-soaked streets—

172

not *these* ones, but it was all the same. She was here in Aberdeen, waiting for Ruth.

At least, thought Ruth, as she raked through her wardrobe, Phyllis hadn't asked if she could stay here. It must have sunk in, that after the divorce, being made redundant and having to take a lower-paid job—all in the space of a year—Ruth had moved to a pokey tenement flat. She wasn't sure if Phyllis knew what a tenement was—despite Dad no doubt having told her about growing up in one—but she must have had a sense that it was at the opposite end of the pole from the home she and Dad had shared for the past thirty years in the suburbs of Toronto, Canada.

Ruth had been there four times over the past few years. The last time—and it would be the last—she'd hardly left Dad's side in hospital. But on the previous visits, she'd sometimes wondered—briefly, not allowing her mind to dwell on it—what life might have been for her. If they, she and Mum and Dad, had all gone off to live there together. But then, would Dad have chosen to emigrate if he and Mum hadn't split? Or was that why they'd split, because he'd hankered after a new life in a new land and Mum hadn't? Would he have come back if he hadn't met Phyllis?

She knew Dad had talked about all this with Phyllis over the years. On Ruth's visits Phyllis had weaselled bits into conversations, and then there was the horrible scene on Dad's death bed when she'd let rip and come out with things that Ruth would never entirely manage to block out of her consciousness, things blurted out in a time of extreme stress—that was the excuse. All forgiven now, all made up for in nice cosy phone conversations—so Phyllis had probably convinced herself ever since, and so Ruth had let her believe. What was the point of doing otherwise? But she'd never reckoned on ever having to see Phyllis again.

She shrugged into the best her wardrobe could come up with. The phone rang at six on the dot.

"Hi…. is that you, Ruth? Oh, how *nice*! How are you?"
Was the North American twang really so cloying, or just when Phyllis spoke it?

173

"Hi Phyllis. Yes, fine. Got here all right?" Too much to hope she hadn't, that the coach was stuck in the Highlands somewhere.

"Sure. Late last night. Too late to call you, I knew you had to get up and out early to work. But yes, I'm really *here*. I can hardly believe it, even now. Here in Aberdeen…"

Ruth wasn't sure if she'd just imagined the slight drop in Phyllis' tone. She was tempted to ask how Phyllis liked it, let her talk on, but that would just be delaying the inevitable. "Still on for seven tonight? I'd better get out to the bus."

"Oh, aren't you taking a taxi, on a night like this, dear?"

Taxi? With whose money? Anyway, the rain had reduced to drizzle by the time she got off the bus and walked the last block to the hotel. She glanced around self-consciously as the doorman ushered her through the lobby towards the dining room. It wasn't the Ritz, but still way out of her league. She scanned the dining room nervously. Tables were pulled together to form blocks, milled around by people who looked as if they were part of groups. Her horror at Phyllis's announcement that she was coming to Scotland had been slightly alleviated by the fact that she was coming with a tour. She'd chosen one carefully, she'd explained to Ruth, one that took in a lot of the places that 'meant so much to your dad.' Aberdeen was almost the final stop, and only a brief one. But while the others in the party were moving on to spend the last few days in Edinburgh, or Glasgow, or both—Ruth couldn't quite remember—Phyllis had arranged to stop here for the weekend before going to join the group for the flight home. How could she skimp on Aberdeen, she'd said—the Aberdeen of Dad's constant reminiscences, where he'd been born and raised?

Perhaps Phyllis' party had changed the itinerary and decided to stay the weekend after all, she thought hopefully. That would make it easier. No, there was Phyllis, alone at a table set for two, already getting up eagerly.

"Ruth! So nice to see you! Thank you so much for coming."

Had she any choice? Ruth submitted to the embrace, the kiss on the cheek, returning it civilly. She had to be civilised. Whatever had passed between them, it would have been cruel—yes cruel to Dad's memory too—to refuse this meeting. She would push the death bed scene, which had threatened to blow up vividly at the first sight of Phyllis, to the back of her mind.

"What will you have to drink, dear? Remember, this is my treat."

"That's very kind, thanks. A glass of red wine would be nice."

If it went on like this, she'd be knackered - if things kept coming up that she had to push to the back of her mind. Like the last 'treat' Phyllis had sent her, at Christmas, six months after Dad died. A cheque for £50. That in itself would have been appreciated—a treat in the true sense, something to help her buy some clothes, maybe—but for Phyllis' note on the accompanying card. "Your Dad would have wanted to see you all right." All right? She'd just lost her job, her home, as well as Dad. She'd hated herself for wondering if Dad had even made a will, why he hadn't thought of her, why Phyllis and her kids and grandkids from her first marriage were the only ones enjoying his inheritance.

She felt her face grow hot. Horrible to think about money, to let even a twinge of resentment creep in and entwine itself with grief. Grief not only over losing him, but over watching him lose himself—slowly, gradually—to the Alzheimer's. And grief, not just over losing him forever but for all the lost years before that.

Pity you only started coming to see him when he got ill…

"Are you all right, dear? Hard day at work?"

Did Canadians make false teeth bigger than here, or was it just Phyllis' particular set? She forced a smile back, met, for half a second, Phyllis' eyes—cold grey behind silver-framed glasses.

"No, I'm fine. Just not used to wine. So how's your tour gone so far?"

"Wonderful."

Bonnie Scotland had lived up to Phyllis' expectations, it seemed. They'd started off in the borders, in Robbie Burns' country, seen his cottage and all the memorabilia. It couldn't have been a better beginning, said Phyllis, because of what Robbie

Burns had meant to Dad. She'd even told the tour guide about how Dad had been chairman of his local Burns club back home. More Scottish than Scottish, the emigrants to Canada were, or so the guide had commented. Then they'd travelled up the west coast to Oban, taken a day trip to Mull and Iona, where the rain and the midges had been pretty bad. They could hardly see anything out of the coach window for the rain, and once they stepped outside for two minutes, those insects...

Well, she had insisted on coming in summer. The guidebooks, or possibly Dad at one time, must have mentioned midges.

"Oh, your Dad did talk about the midges," Phyllis said, as if reading her thoughts. "But still, I can see why he loved the west Highlands. He used to talk about the camping holidays with you by Loch Lomond..."

Ruth nodded. Had Dad also mentioned his and Mum's rows that had almost spoiled those holidays? But she knew he'd loved that area. She'd seen the pictures in the albums from before her own time—Dad and Mum posing happily together amidst hill and moor in their hiking gear.

"We only saw Loch Lomond from the bus, really. Then we went to Inverness and had a trip around the Loch...didn't spot Nessie, though!"

The picture postcard Scotland. It obviously hadn't disappointed. Phyllis was picking uncertainly at a piece of her 'seafood medley.' She'd ordered it because 'you have to sample a fish dish in Aberdeen, don't you?' Suddenly she put down her fork and gazed off into the distance, her eyes misting over.

Please, please, don't let her start getting weepy.

"You know what was the very best bit, though, Ruth? The saddest, but the best? We went to a ceilidh, which was booked for us, one night."

It sounded as if they'd laid it on thick for a bunch of tourists, made a kind of Burns' Night-in-July-cum Scottish theme night rather than just an ordinary ceilidh. Poetry recitations, piping in of the haggis, pipes and drums, lots of swirling kilts and some sword dancing, as well as the usual jigs and reels.

"They had us up, talked us through the Eightsome reel and Gay Gordon," Phyllis half laughed, half choked. "I could just have been right there with him...he looked so swish in his kilt..."

He had. Ruth had seen an enlarged photo of him, proudly displayed on their living room wall. She'd been surprised, never having known until she'd started visiting that he'd taken up this hobby—no, more of a passion—of keeping the Scottish tradition after he'd gone to Canada. Well, how would she have known, when he'd never written or phoned, when he'd only sent her a birthday or Christmas card now and then if he remembered.

He thought your mum didn't want the contact. But **you** *could have written, tried getting in contact when you got older...*

"You know..."

Ruth had learned to dread Phyllis' thoughtful pauses.

Why do you think he ever left his country, when he loved it so? Because he wasn't happy at home.

'I always wonder why he never came back here, when he loved it so? I mean, for a visit?"

Ruth took a gulp of wine, pushed her plate aside.

"Had enough, dear? Me too. I'm not so keen on fish, really. Better than haggis, I must admit. I had to try it, though, for you dad. Anyway, he often said he'd love to take me back, for a visit. Just a visit. He was very happy where he was—settled, never regretted coming to Canada; it was his home as much as here. But he'd love to have shown me his other home. I guess we just never got round to it. There was always something—the house, my kids...you know."

Ruth nodded. Could Dad have also been avoiding the baggage he'd left behind?

"But I should have encouraged him, tried to get it together for us to come, before it was too late, before he couldn't any more. It would have meant so much." Phyllis, head sunk into her chest, fished for a tissue in her sleeve and wiped her eyes. Ruth felt a twinge of sympathy. She spoke gently.

"We never know when it's going to be too late," she held her breath. Would the vitriol follow tears, as it had done before? But Phyllis smiled at her, almost warmly.

"We don't, do we?"

"And he was so happy remembering. He talked so much about it when I was over visiting."

That's all you'd know. I had all the struggle of caring for him.

Phyllis nodded. "Yes, they meant a lot to him too, those memories. Especially in the last few years, when he started to wander..."

If you'd been come over more often, I might not have had to put him in a home, after he started to wander outside...

"His mind, I mean. He'd talk about back home in Scotland, like it was yesterday. Especially Aberdeen. Well, I suppose he would, it was his birth-place, where he grew up and, well, everything...you—you know what I mean." A flush had spread over Phyllis' face.

"So have you managed to see a bit of Aberdeen yet?" Ruth asked quickly.

"Oh, yes. We had a tour on an open-topped bus this morning." Ruth sat back, able to relax as Phyllis got stuck into describing the itinerary. "We went down Union Street, then up past that big statue of Robbie Burns, and past that one of the Braveheart guy, and saw the theatre—His Majesty's, is it? Then through Old Aberdeen—all those nice cobbles and old buildings. And the beach— oh, beautiful! We got off there, wished we could have gone right down to the sea, but it started to rain so we went in for a coffee. Then down to that nice little old fishing village, what do you call it? Fittee, that's right. Through the harbour and we stopped for lunch at that gorgeous park with the tropical gardens. We went to the other park too, with the rose garden. And back into town. We finished where we started, at—let me get it right—Mar-ee-shall…"

"Marischal College."

"Yes. A great time."

Was it Phyllis' sadness over Dad, or today's relentlessly drizzly weather? Or was it just Ruth's imagination that made her think that it had, in reality, been less than great for Phyllis, that although Scotland in general had lived up to Dad's reminiscences and her dreams, somehow Aberdeen had let her down?

"There's lots in Edinburgh," she said. "And Glasgow, even. Dad went there now and again, to visit his aunties…."

"Oh, I'll catch some of them before the flight home. But you know, it's Aberdeen that's important. The Granite City. I didn't realise it was called that. I mean, I thought it was just your Dad called it that."

"Mmm." The waiter was clearing up their plates. She'd almost got through this evening, thought Ruth, but what about the weekend looming ahead?

Phyllis sighed. "He always said the granite was grey, but it got whiter, the nearer you got to the centre of town."

"Oh yes," Ruth smiled. "He said it was pure white right in the centre of town." During her visits, almost every conversation had come around to the white granite. She'd contested it mildly at first, but quickly given up and gone along with his happy if flawed memory of a white granite-centred city.

Phyllis reached a hand across the table, laid it on Ruth's. Ruth resisted the impulse to draw her hand away.

"I'd love it, Ruth, if you'd show me some of that white granite."

"Show you? But…"

"Oh, I know it doesn't really exist. But maybe you could, well, show me around a bit? I know I've seen all the main stuff, but it would mean a lot more to see it with you. Your dad's beloved hometown. With his beloved daughter."

His beloved daughter came at last. Not before time!

There was no sarcasm now. Only pleading. Ruth shrugged and murmured: "Okay."

"Thank you. Thank you so much Ruth." She squeezed Ruth's hand, pursed her lips. "And Ruth…" her voice was almost a whisper as she leaned over the table.

"I want us to find somewhere, together Somewhere to scatter his ashes."

Phyllis looked shattered. Her shoulders were hunched over as they sat eating lunch in the art gallery café. No wonder; after what she'd been carrying around all morning in the small backpack that she must have bought for the purpose, as it wasn't her style. Ruth had tried to help, offered to take a turn at carrying, but Phyllis had snapped at the offer.

"He's still mine!"

She'd hastily apologised. *I'm just a bit raw, dear.* But the old Phyllis was still there, Ruth warned herself. Lurking underneath the cosy, peace-making widow/stepmother was the Phyllis whose long-simmering resentment had erupted so cruelly. Along with— Ruth had to admit—her own.

They hadn't found a place yet. *A place that your dad loved, a place where he could happily sleep forever.* Phyllis would decide; Ruth knew that her own job was to be the guide, to present the choices. All morning she'd played that role. They'd taken buses, roamed the streets. Ruth had watched and waited for the decision to be made, for the spot to be chosen. It hadn't been. Not the old tenement site, long since rebuilt, where Dad had been born and spent his childhood and youth. Ruth had furtively eyed Phyllis as they'd stood there, Phyllis staring up at the fourth-floor window of the tenement that stood now. Was she trying to conjure up a picture of Dad as he was in those days—being nursed, playing with his sisters, living his life behind walls that had long since been torn down? Ruth had waited until Phyllis silently turned and started walking away. It was the same at the site where Dad's school used to be, now a run-down housing estate; the same at the refurbished office block where Dad used to work for a firm that no longer existed.

Except for the odd glance, passers by, rushing about their own business, paid them little attention as they lingered and stared. More curious looks might be attracted if Phyllis decided that this was the place to fulfil their mission. Where would she scatter them anyway? On a pavement, still puddled with last night's downpour? Over an iron railing that fenced off a plush office lawn, or the narrow strip of ground in front of a block of flats?

Old Aberdeen and the parks, explored more on foot than the bus excursion had allowed, seemed better options. The rain abated, and Phyllis seemed to enjoy trundling about these areas, was especially taken with the Snow Chapel. Ruth was sure Phyllis would choose a corner here, among the worn grey stones beneath which other beloved remains had been laid. "But your Dad never told me about this place," Phyllis had remarked. The parks fared the same. No tree, no rose bush or flower- bed was singled out for Dad's eternal rest.

Would Phyllis be up to any more tramping about? Her heavy burden aside, Phyllis had done more walking in one morning, Ruth guessed, than on the entire tour, or even possibly in her whole life, given the way North Americans jumped into cars for the shortest journey. She looked exhausted, but was resolutely munching through her fish pie. Ruth had to admire her tenacity. Apart from the haggis and fish she'd endured, she said she'd eaten porridge for breakfast every day of the trip. *Your Dad said his mother used to make it—lots of it, nice and solid so she could serve it up for dinner as well, if they were short of anything else.*

Phyllis finally put down her fork, a quarter of the pie left. "I know it's been a long tiring morning for you, Ruth, but…would you mind taking me to the beach? Your Dad loved the sea."

He had. She knew as well as Phyllis about how the whole family—his parents and sisters and he—had spent entire summer Sundays on the beach, rain or shine. And in the early days she and Dad and Mum had carried on the tradition. They'd trooped down carrying a big flask, picnic basket, deck chairs and rain gear should it be needed. Mum had sat with her knitting, as his Mum had done, and Dad with his newspaper, though Dad hadn't sat for long; he'd rolled up his trousers and joined Ruth in the water, or building sand castles. Sometimes he'd taken her by the hand and they'd gone for long walks along the sand, often as far as the old fishing village, where they watched the trawlers sailing out of the harbour. They both could have stood there and watched forever.

"Your Dad said the beach was crowded in his day on a Sunday. Everyone came up for their holidays by the sea. They didn't travel abroad much in those days."

He made up for that, Ruth stopped herself from saying. They were sitting on a bench, though Phyllis seemed much revived. The sun had swept away the gloom, the tide was far out, leaving a wide expanse of beach, and the waves lapped gently. People, though perhaps not the droves of them as in Dad's day, were taking advantage; children, joggers, dog-walkers and a few brave swimmers. Ruth found her own spirits lifting. She would come here more often, she decided—take off her shoes and feel the sand as she used to, hike along to Footdee and watch the boats that had once so excited her and Dad. There was one sailing out now, but not a trawler.

"Look, "she pointed out to Phyllis. "The Shetland boat."

"Oh, wonderful!" Phyllis held up her hand to shade her eyes. They watched the vessel as it ploughed along on its journey, watched until it disappeared; sat staring at the empty horizon. Only the ripple of sea gulls' keening and children's playful shouting broke the silence.

Phyllis was drawing her cardigan about her. The sky was clouding over and a breeze was getting up.

"You know, it always amazed me that your dad came to Canada by boat. All that way."

"I suppose people did back then. Plane travel wasn't so common."

"Plus a long train journey once he'd landed. Imagine. What a journey!"

"Mmm," Ruth shifted, opened her mouth to suggest heading back to town, having a coffee, looking for somewhere for dinner, but Phyllis mused on.

"And finding yourself in a strange country. Okay, English-speaking, but still strange. And a whole ocean away from home. Everything familiar left behind."

Not to mention every*one*. Ruth bit her lip. Phyllis was good at wrecking her moments. First, her last moments with Dad, and now, the reliving of an intimacy with him that had been all too rare—their shared excitement for things of the sea.

"He never told me how he'd felt then. Talked about everything with me, your dad did, but not how he felt. Just got on with things. Best way, I guess."

It was. Dad had the right idea. That's what she'd try and do now. And she had only tonight and tomorrow to get through. Phyllis was planning to head off on a Sunday evening train to join her party in Edinburgh. That should leave enough time for a stroll along the old railway line. Ruth had hit upon the idea this afternoon. There were plenty of benches, and views out over the river. Deeside had been another of Dad's favourite haunts.

"Shall we make a move, dear? Look at those clouds! It does change quickly here. Hope it doesn't go all grey before we get back into town. I'm still hoping to catch a glimpse of that famous white granite."

They both laughed. Phyllis heaved her pack onto her shoulders.

They still hadn't found a place to scatter the ashes.

Phyllis waved as Ruth came into the hotel lounge. Just as well they'd arranged to meet here first instead of the bus stop. Ruth shook out her jacket and draped it on the back of a chair.

"My, you're drenched. It's come back with a vengeance, hasn't it?" Phyllis cast an anxious eye at the window. "Do you think it'll ease off?"

"It might. I think it's turned to hail. We could wait a while, get the next bus."

They sipped coffee, listened for the fierce battering to ease. Today's forecast hadn't boded well. Ruth glanced at Phyllis' flimsy jacket, laid beside her on the sofa. It would have been easy being dismissive of the elements from the comfort of her luxury coach, fortified by group camaraderie and the novelty of being in Scotland. Sloshing along the railway line, shivering on public transport in sodden clothes, was different. She should have made contingency plans, but what else was there to do on a day like this? And even if the weather had been better, they'd explored Aberdeen to its limits, exhausted it, and Phyllis had lost her enthusiasm. Her excitement at being in Aberdeen had begun to wane as soon as she'd arrived. Not that Phyllis had said or even hinted at this. Ruth just knew.

She settled back, gritted herself to spend the long morning and afternoon sitting here, listening to Phyllis wallowing in Dad's memories—memories of his beloved city that had somehow not lived up to the image he had built for her.

"Would I find a set of these in Edinburgh or Glasgow, do you think?"

"Er...what?" Ruth, stared dumbly as Phyllis pointed down at the table.

"Coasters, like these with nice Scottish scenes, for Tracey and Jim."

"Oh. Sure. There's plenty of shops there." Shops. Why hadn't she thought of that? There were plenty of shops here too.

Phyllis prattled on. Not about Dad, or Aberdeen, but about the presents she needed to get for everyone. Kids, their spouses, grandkids, siblings nephews and nieces, friends—they'd all be expecting a souvenir from Bonnie Scotland. She'd meant to get most of them here—tokens of the Granite City—but of course she'd had other things to do here—other things on her mind, hadn't she? At that point she sighed deeply, closed her eyes. Ruth was afraid the light relief was over, the reminiscences about to be dragged up and mulled over yet again.

"If it clears up just a bit we could nip out to the shops here."

Phyllis opened her eyes, shook her shoulders. "Goodness, that third coffee hasn't done the trick. Set my tongue lively, but not much else."

"It's up to you. I think we're in for a day of that, anyway." She nodded at the window. Rain and hailstones had kept up an alternate, steady pounding for the past hour or more.

"Oh, you don't mind, Ruth? I mean, you've brought a picnic and everything, haven't you…"

"Couldn't have had it in this. Don't worry, honest."

"Oh, thank good…thank *you*, Ruth."

Ruth had never thought of Phyllis as elderly, especially when Dad was alive. She'd been twelve years his junior. But now, huddled on the sofa, relief and gratitude etched on her face, she could be taken for at least eighty. An old lady who'd lost her husband of some thirty-five years. A big loss, even if she'd plenty of other folk in her life.

Soon Phyllis would suggest going to the dining room for lunch. That would pass the time. She would let any conversation wash over her, as she'd become practised in doing over the past two days.

"Actually, Ruth, I…I hope you don't mind something else, either. You've been so kind, and I'm afraid I've wasted your time today…"

"It's okay."

Both of us so careful, so intent on not re-offending, Ruth mused as she sipped the dregs of her coffee. When she glanced up, Phyllis had straightened herself, was sitting bolt upright, eyes fixed on Ruth. For a second, Ruth met the steel-grey stare. Phyllis's lips parted, the large teeth forming a smile as she quickly looked away and started fiddling in her bag.

"I…I was thinking I might take an earlier train. There's one in about an hour. I've only to collect my case from the lock-up, then call a taxi. And I want to give you this…"

It was a small, cylindrical shortbread tin, pictured with a West Highland terrier amidst a sea of heather. Phyllis had apologised that it was it was the only suitable container—once emptied of the shortbread, of course—she could find at the hotel's small gift counter. But Dad would have forgiven the tackiness; it had been bought in his city. She hoped Ruth would soon find a better place for the contents, and that Ruth wasn't upset about it only being half of them.

You see, I began to think—I started thinking yesterday, while we were going around Aberdeen. Some of him belongs back home, after all. I mean his other home, our home Maybe in the garden where he grew his corn-on-the-cob, or by the lake where we used to go in summer...

Ruth set the tin beside her on the bench, downed the last of the sandwiches and took another sip from the bottle of Merlot red that she'd brought to share with Phyllis on the picnic. Not strictly legal to drink in a public place within the city, but a shelter on the beach promenade was hardly riddled with the public on a day like this. It was a stark contrast to yesterday. The tide was in, leaving no beach. Black waves crashed against the wall, the spray-- mixed with driving rain-- splashing her cheeks.

She couldn't face going home, yet, couldn't face having to find a corner for him until she found a better home.

But half of him still belongs here. You find a home, Ruth—a resting place, even if it's in a bit of that white granite.

Home. Resting place. What would Dad have wanted? To be stuck forever in a church yard, a flower-bed, a piece of old white granite—even if such existed?
She picked up the tin, got up and walked over to the wall; held out her face to the elements. Dad had liked days like this the best. She opened the lid.

Yesterday, it would have been unthinkable, in the calm, mild stillness. He would have sunk gently to the bottom, perhaps been embedded there before he could help it. Today he'd be blown and tossed like the boats he used to spend hours watching--carried way out—who knew where?

She stretched her arm over the wall and threw him as far as she could.

"Good-bye, Dad," she called, and turned away.

JOCK THE RIPPER
by
Sue Baker

The young man sat in his car, hunched over the steering wheel. The knuckles of his left hand were white and in his other hand he held the remains of a cigarette between the tips of two fingers. His expressionless eyes were constantly scanning the car park of the 24hour supermarket. He was continuously searching for that perfect target.

That day's local news paper, the *Evening Express,* with the headline 'Grampian Police still Mystified over Jock,' lay open on the front seat. His smirk showed his objective was to be one step ahead of the police. The infamous Jack the Ripper never got caught. He was going to be just like him. Maybe better.

It had been the papers who had given him the nick name. *Well deserved!* he thought. He relished it. It made people afraid to go out, making Aberdeen fear him. With each kill he got closer to the man. He experimented with each execution. Each one got better and more creative. The realisation in their eyes as they suddenly knew they were going to die.

His driver's window was open, letting the smoke from his cigarette filter out. Odour from the car's exhausts as they passed took its place. It was good to get the smell of fresh fumes around him, instead of the constant stench of rotting fish.

He threw the remains of the stub through the window and watched as the red from the tip slowly faded.

Reaching over to the passenger's seat he picked up the cigarette packet, putting his fingers inside only to find its contents gone. Crushing it, he threw it on the floor to join the rest of the discarded packets, crushed iron brew cans and wrappers from Tunnock's wafers.

Watching the bright lights that illuminated the shop windows, he could see the workforce going about their business. He sat rigid as he saw a member of staff talking to a shopper scanning shopping over the self service checkout, while the staff member started to pack her bags. Rummaging through her large bag the customer pulled out something small then started feeding the mechanical beastie. Placing the bags into the waiting trolley, the two women continued to talk. Turning around the customer waved to the cashier as she made her way to the exit.

His watchful eyes scanned the rest of the shop and the near deserted car park. His breathing became rapid when he realised she was unaccompanied. A leer came slowly to his mouth, he bit his bottom lip. Now was the time to let his imagination start to work and try to outdo his hero. His right hand slowly edged its way down to his coat pocket. He could feel the hardness of the object and it reassured him. It had been over a week since the last. He needed to feel the force of the blade as it entered the soft flesh, feeling the warm blood as it trickled over his hand. There was nothing like it. He could still hear her scream with fear as he gently traced his knife over her lily white flesh. He had to outdo himself this time. He just had to!

Carefully watching as the young woman walked across the tarmac to the cars, her white cardigan making it easier for Jock to follow her through the shadows. Scanning his eyes rapidly once more over the cars, making sure no one was hiding and watching. The sweat started dribbling down his face. He could feel a cold trickle down his back causing his own flesh to stick to his thin black tee-shirt.

His heart beat faster as he watched her getting closer to the cars. A tight knot came to his gut, hoping it was the isolated vehicle.

It was!

No light reflected anywhere around.

He could sense the kill!

He could feel the kill!

With one hand, he smoothly pulled the door handle. Cautiously pushing it open, he looked around. Stepping out into the muggy summer evening he felt his long black, imitation leather coat fall against his ankles. His collar turned up, hiding his oily hair, he watched the woman. Closing the door quietly he scrutinized her every step. At the rear of the car she bent over and flipped open the boot. His heart raced as he anticipated what was about to happen. He was certain she could hear its heavy beating over the short distance on that quiet night. His hand edged to his coat pocket feeling the solid object that rested there. Fingers found their way inside and wrapped firmly around the handle. Gulls overhead called out for him to continue. A loud hum of his own blood sounded in his ears as it pulsated through his veins. His mind raced with excitement at the things he was about to do. A Smile returned. His step quickened as her bags slowly went into the boot. Stopping abruptly he caught sight of a figure leaving the car. A figure was that of a tall and burly man.

Catching his breath at how close he had been. He had been too preoccupied with the woman to notice the still figure in the car, his shape hidden in the shadows. The papers called him *Jock the Ripper* for a reason. Up to now he had been cautious, the way his famous name sake had been in London. One thing they had in common, they took no chances.

Don't get caught, just like *Jack!*
Moving backwards he retraced his steps and stood beside his car. He placed his forehead on the metal roof. The coolness gave him a moment's liberation from the anguish of failure.

Groaning, his stomach dropped. His hands shook, he had been so close. All he wanted was a kill. He had become sloppy, forgetting to look deep inside each shadow for witnesses.

The sound of the boot slamming echoed over the still night, then the car doors. As the car's engine turned over a loud noise came from the exhaust, making it sound like the engine of an army tank. Turning his head slightly he watched as she pulled away. Pressing the button on his watch; illuminating the numbers reading 2.35.

"Might as well abort this fruitless exercise," mumbling to himself. "No self respecting woman would be out alone at this time." He wasn't interested in just respectable women. Any woman would do.

He decided to travel the 17miles to Aberdeen and drive around; he would get more luck there. He needed to fulfil his hunger. Rubbing his forehead he closed his eyes and said a silent prayer to *Jack*.

Pulling open the door he looked around, deep into the dark. A movement caught his eye. She was standing at her car. The overhead light broken. He couldn't see if she was alone, she was too far away.

"Thank you," he whispered, his eyes looking heaven-ward. Getting into his car he drove slowly around shining his head lights into the interior.

She was alone!

She hadn't noticed as he parked a few spaces away. He cut the engine and slowly got out of his car, trying not to let his door slam. He edged his way towards the woman. She leaned against the roof of her car with her left hand to her ear. Her voice was low and she was nodding to whoever was on the other end of her mobile phone. The motion caused her long blond hair to sway as it hung loosely down her back. Her long scarlet cardigan, which stopped at her ankles, hid her legs as the movement of her stepping from one foot to the other swayed her coat.

She was tall for a woman, plus a little broader than the average female. Something alerted him, shouting at him that something wasn't right, but he ignored it. He continued. The need to kill overpowered him. He should walk away, leave it.

Sliding his hand into his coat pocket, his fingers wrapped firmly around the handle of the blade. His steady soft footsteps brought him ever closer to his prey. Taking the knife out of his pocket he hung his hand by his side.

Quickening his pace as the smell of her perfume caught on the night's summer breeze, fluttering like a butterfly in his direction.

Just as he was a few feet away his arm slowly came back ready to strike. As it swung, aiming for his mark, the woman turned quickly. He froze in mid-swing looking into her face with horror. It was the ugliest woman he had ever seen. It would be an honour to dismember this object, put her and the world out of its misery.

Dark facial hair surrounded the mouth. They were both standing transfixed looking at one another.

The last thing Jock saw was the sausage like fingers, dressed with bulky rings, coming at him with the speed and the feel of an express train. Easily finding their mark, all he could do was stand there transfixed. He was unable to move until the taste of blood become fresh in his mouth. The clatter of the knife, as it bounced on the tarmac, echoed loudly over the still night. Falling to his knees, Jock looked up at his assailant with puzzlement. The last thing he heard was a deep gruff voice saying the words:

"Playtime's over!"

A BIRTHDAY SURPRISE
By
Ian Beattie

The balloon bobbed and weaved in the air in front of him, taunting him with smooth tight rubber, reflecting the sun. A long piece of white string was holding on to the balloon keeping it anchored. The balloon bounced and swooned like a small puppy pulling at a lead, hearing the call of the wind and the air. The boy held the badge in his hand. The salty pin unsheathed and glinting, eyed the balloon hungrily. He didn't like that Marcus got all the attention, it was all about Marcus. Every day it was Marcus did that, Marcus did this, Marcus got another gold star for something he'd done. What a teacher's pet, but he'd get his own back. Now was the perfect time. The thing about Marcus was that everyone swooned over him and he got way with so many things. Things that *he* never got away with, *he* always got caught and then got the tanning his father thought was fairly deserved. Just once he could take the wind out of his sails so that little Marcus would see what it's like for the rest of his pals.

The boy looked around the room, thinking and *planning* what he would do. Marcus's birthday would be one that he would not forget. It was Marcus's sixth one and mum and dad were spending a lot on him. At least that's what he thought he had overheard when he was in the kitchen yesterday once they had sat down to tea. Ever since his younger brother was born it was as if he no longer existed. Some days it was as if he was invisible, some days it was as if he really *was invisible*. With a bit of luck it would make him think twice about the way he looked down on people and especially him. Even though he was his older brother it was a constant struggle to get anyone to notice him. He was the quiet one of the two and most of the adults just left him to it. Marcus on the other hand, he was a livewire and a total chatterbox, you could never get him to shut up. He didn't talk about anything in particular but just *talked*.

Everyone was outside in the sun, playing games and laughing but *he* didn't feel like joining them. Gran and granddad had come all the way from Edinburgh to visit and were staying over. This meant that *he* got kicked out of his room for a few days and had to spend it sleeping in the same room as Marcus. Little Marcus and his friends were outside playing cops and robbers or cowboys and Indians and making a racket doing it too. Gran had fallen asleep about an hour ago on one of the sun loungers in the back garden. Granddad was busy talking with dad about cars or football. It was all they seemed to talk about. Mum was in the kitchen, just next door, washing the dishes in the sink by the sound of things. Yes this was the time, now or never the boy thought.

First he would hide all the presents in places even all the adults wouldn't think of. It would be fun to see them all searching for Marcus's presents. The candles and cake would be a bit more of a problem but the garage had plenty of places to get rid if it, and there was always the bin. The balloon that had stared him in the face for the last ten minutes was his first bit of fun though, then he'd burst the rest. He would have to wait until mum had gone back outside. She was too near now and the sound of balloons being popped tended to make a noise that made everyone sit up. He sat in the corner seat in the dining room and waited. He would wait until all the people outside were so noisy that he could do it without worrying. Then he'd blame someone else, just like Marcus did. He decided that he was going to say that Peter did it as Peter and Marcus had fallen out over who had the best collection of football stickers. Marcus being Marcus said he had and then a scrap ensued, Peter came off worst though and had said to him that he was 'going to get it'. He had the perfect cover and the opportunity, all he had to do was do it.

A few moments later the sound from the kitchen stopped and he could hear footsteps coming in his direction. Quickly he hid under the large dining room table and sat very, very still. Mum had passed through and not seen him. Phew! What a relief. He crept from under the table and looked out the window from just behind the curtains. He took the pin in his right hand and set to his task, before long all the balloons had gone. Just then his dad walked in and caught him, right in the middle of everything.

"Jonathan, what do you think you're doing?" he demanded.

The boy froze a look of fear in his eye. Boy was he gonna get it now.

I AM MORAL
by
Mark W Duncan

The rain had just started. It complemented the chill of the night perfectly. A perfectly shit night. Rebecca Morrison pulled her hood tight, as much a disguise as for warmth. Union Street was crowded. She kept her eyes downcast, avoiding all the night-time revellers. She made her way down the street. Reaching into her pocket she pulled out the change, which jingled merrily with every movement. Twenty-four pence was all that was left from the  eighty pounds she took from her mum's purse three days before. The first three nights of living on the streets had been spent in comfort and warmth. Two B&B's and a Travelodge. Now she had no money.

Several shirts stumbled past her. One drunkenly barged into her. "Watch where you're going you dickhead."

The group hurried off, ignoring the solitary girl and her insult. A shrill beep came from her jacket pocket. Pulling the phone out she pressed a button. The screen lit up. Forty-six missed calls, the last of which was from home.

Her mobile had hardly stopped ringing since the second day she had run away from home. Every so often it was punctuated by a text message. This would teach her bitch of a mother. It was her fault that her fifteen year old daughter was wandering the streets of Aberdeen. How could she move in that prick and not even think to ask her? Now there was no chance of Dad moving back home.

She threw the phone back into the pocket and continued walking, past Union Terrace Gardens. Laughter and voices haunted the dark depths of the park. On a whim she walked nameless streets and drab buildings to the only landmark she knew for sure. The rearing heights of the college provided some comfort. It was only a couple of months ago that her dad had accompanied her there for an introductory interview. Mum would never have done that. She was always too busy with him. Bitch.

Her empty stomach gave an angry rumble of protest, a painful reminder. It had been almost a day since she had eaten properly. It was seriously cold tonight. Better find somewhere to bed down for the night. No more warm beds. Sleeping rough was never going to be easy. She found herself walking past a large roundabout. The name made her laugh. Mounthooly. Strange name for a roundabout. Up another nameless street. A school on the left and numberless businesses closed for the night.

Maybe calling home wasn't the worst idea she had ever had, a warm bed, food. No, running home to Mum would teach her nothing. She was going to rough it even if just for a few more days.

The voice startled her, reviving her from reflection.

"Sorry, I don't mean to bother you. Are you alright?"

Rebecca looked up from out of her hood, pulling lank damp blonde hair from her face. Before her a suited man holding a large golfing umbrella stood. He smiled reassuringly. His balding head had become shiny from the rain and streetlights.

"Oh, I don't mean to startle you. I just saw you walking alone. The pubs are that way," he indicated the lifeless lights of the city centre. "Unless you're heading home—or are lost."

Trying to sound confident she said: "I'm on my way home". She failed.

"Uh huh, where is it you live?" His smile broadened and his English accent took on a posh twang. He reminded her of Mr Thompson, the history teacher. "I'm not some kind of perv or anything like that. Tell me to mind my own business if you like it's just I have a daughter about your age. I would hate to think that she was wandering the streets alone. My name is John. Look if you're heading home that's fine, I'll let you go your own way. I was just trying to help."

He made to leave.

Rebecca studied him, he seemed harmless enough. Don't talk to strangers had been drilled into her head since she could remember but what harm was there talking to him. She wasn't a kid anymore.

"I..." she was unsure what to say. "I just need a place to stay tonight..." The rain began to fall with force, smashing against the umbrella. "It's...Maybe you could lend me some money to get some food and a room tonight. If you give me your address I will send you the money back."

The words sounded stupid to her, let alone what John must have thought. Homeless people or junkies tried that kind of false promise. She was neither, but she was desperate.

"It's OK; you don't have to tell me anything you don't want to. Sarah, my daughter, I'm lucky if I get two words from her. I can do better than lend you money. There's a hostel run by some charity or other that take young girls in, no questions asked. Hot food and a warm bed for a few days. Give you time to think? I read an article about it in the newspaper last week. My car's parked behind that building, I could drop you off?"

He moved forward slightly, raising the umbrella higher so it offered protection to them both.

It sounded like a perfect solution though the niggling, rational voice of doubt screamed protests.

"Why you doing this?"

He sighed slightly and shook his head. "Just trying to do the Christian thing I suppose, and I hope that if someone saw my daughter out on a night like this they would offer her help. Come on you'll catch your death."

"Well..."

"My car's parked just round the back of there; I could have you dropped off in less than fifteen minutes. What harm?"

"Well OK, just so you know I have my mobile, so any funny business and I'll call the police."

He smiled again – the previous look of anticipation was now replaced with one of his ever-ready smiles.

"You're right to be cautious. You never told me your name? It's OK to be cautious, sensible. A lot of freaks out and about these days."

He swept an arm, indicating they should begin walking to his car.

"Rebecca."

"Beg your pardon?"

"My name, it's Rebecca."

"Oh yes…" he hesitated. "It's a pleasure to meet you Rebecca. The car is just round the back of here."

The building was lifeless, darkened windows reflected the sullen night. They passed a sign. The building was a funeral home. Showpiece gravestones lined the large windows. Morbid spectators to the machinations of the living world. Something caught Rebecca's eye. The sign they passed, at the bottom bravely emblazoned the words: 'Proprietor – James Wilson and Sons'. One final test perhaps for the Good Samaritan.

"Is this your shop?"

"What? Oh uh… yes. I've spent years building this company up."

Keep pushing. Something seemed wrong. Was it her imagination or was he becoming more distracted?

"You must be really busy running the place. Is it just you or do you have help with it?"

"No, no, just me. My wife keeps complaining she never sees enough of me, Josh, she says, sometimes I wonder if you should have married the job and not me."

"You said your name was John" Run.

Rebecca began turning to run. Her hand rose from her pocket, mobile phone held tight.

John or Josh moved quickly for a man his size. The umbrella fell to the ground. The phone fell from her grasp. Fat arms entrapped her. Quickly he pulled her round the side of the building. Her attempted scream died as a meaty hand was clasped over her mouth. The false sense of tenderness now completely forgotten.

She tried to bite the hand. The vice like grip intensified. A tear fell from her eye mixing in with the rain that fell. Her free hands clawed his, but to little avail.

A black limo stretched across the otherwise empty car park. She was bundled towards the vehicle. Home. The place she ran from was the one place she would trade anything to be at.

The door opened and another suited man stepped out and spoke.

"We didn't think you would get anyone. She is quite young."

"Just the way you like them Sid. Help me get her in the car. Be careful though she's feisty. She scratched my hand. It's pissing with blood."

Together they roughly forced her into the car. The hand was released from her mouth as she fell to the floor of the limo. She screamed. A stinging blow delivered from a seated third man cut off the sound. A fourth sat watching. A smile on his wrinkled face.

"Who's first?" His speech was slow and slightly slurred.

The third man who had struck her began unfastening his belt. "I'm first."

The awful realisation dawned on the mute Rebecca. She closed her eyes. In her mind she was at home. Her mother cooking in the kitchen and her father at the piano, as they were in better times.

Something pressed against her mouth. Clamping her mouth and eyes shut she turned her head. Was that the scent of spaghetti bolognaise wafting from the kitchen? The unmistakable cold of a blade was pressed against her cheek forcing her to face forward. Her father began his recital of Moonlight Sonata. Somewhere, perhaps from the TV, grotesque laughter polluted the otherwise perfect scene.

The rain fell with a fury. The cold granite building resisted the rage and stood in defiance. A figure lurked in the corner, shadows concealing him from the world. A bare hand rested on the wall. Black and grey, the world matched his life, at least in the night-time anyway. No lights here, just the numb colourless abyss. The prelude to what was coming next. Emotion had no function anymore. Just base animal instincts. Anger. Hate. They were present like a faithful dog and would serve him well. They never left. It was beyond simple anger or hate now. A primal urge had taken over, one that could only be numbed with retribution.

From an innocent plastic shopping bag he pulled out a leather mask. Formally a sex aid, now where a zip had covered the mouth, the leather had been cut away in stages. Like the grates of a drain the gaps grew in size symmetrically along the face. Smaller at the front getting larger as they spread towards the ears. Almost a shark's smile, it allowed easy breathing while still concealing the face. He put the mask on and walked from the shadows. The leather of his trench coat quickly became soaked. The limo sitting in the empty car park soon came into view. Faint sounds filtered through the night from the vehicle. The blanked out driver's windows gave him his first glimpse of himself. His visage was one of terror, like something out of a nightmare. He allowed himself a smile. The first in many months. His trench coat fell open revealing the hard leather beneath. Purchased from an Internet historical company, the armour was like that of a Roman Gladiator. Designed to give the false impression of an Adonis like body. It encumbered him only slightly. From his pocket he pulled out a heavy industrial pair of gloves. The right hand glove had been augmented. Along the inside fingers and palm countless small spikes protruded. Thrusting his hands into the gloves he balled his fists in anticipation. The unmistakeable sound of a scream came from the back of the limo. Now, it was time.

He pulled open the driver's door. The dozing occupant slowly opened an eye. Catching sight of the figure both eyes opened wide in shock.

"What the fu…"

The punch sent him sprawling over the seat. Without concern the masked figure pulled the deadweight from the car. Letting him fall to the ground he gave him a sharp kick to the ribs before placing his hand on the car horn.

The shriek broke through the night. The partition window between driver and seating began to slowly fall downwards. The masked figure removing his hand from the horn and twisted his body just out of view. He waited. A head soon appeared over the retreating glass. The masked figure moved swiftly, he struck out with his fist taking the man in the face. A second strike and he pulled him through the window and threw him to the ground outside, beside the unconscious driver. Straddling the bleeding suited man he rained down blow after savage blow. Left, right, left right. He did not stop, even when he felt his knuckle crack. A noise from behind, he fired one last blow, rolled over the body before coming to his feet. He turned to the source of the sound.

"What the fuck? What's..." The man burst into uncontrollable laughter. "Halloween was last month. What are you supposed to be anyway?" More laughter.

He was intoxicated with drugs. The seriousness of the situation eluding his muddled brain.

"I...am. Moral," the voice was slow, lacking emotion. "I am just a nightmare. Your nightmare."

In two strides Moral closed the distance between them. The heavy metal contraption he wore under his sleeve was used to good effect. With as much force as he could muster Moral backhanded the metal into the face of the man. There was the unmistakable sound of breaking cartilage. He collapsed silently. The blood from the first two victims ran off the leather coat, mixed with the falling rain.

Another scream. Moral moved. He entered the vehicle's seating area. A semi naked girl sat on the floor, her face streaked with tears. Blood trickled from a cut beside her eye.

"Jesus fucking Christ."

The fat suited Josh jumped from his seat, heaving his massive bulk he struggled through the gap to the driver's seat. The window began to rise.

"Hurry up, Hurry up. Please." The window sealed the gap and ended his pleading.

Moral ignored him. His attention focused on the last man. He was naked below the waist. Erect, he held himself before the crying girl. Through drugs or the thrill of the situation he had yet to notice Moral until a hand seized him by the throat, forcing him back into the chair. The impact caused his eyes to bulge. Rebecca screamed, fell backwards and crawled from the limo. Her ankle twisted awkwardly. She continued to crawl away.

Moral brought his right-hand up to his prey. Opening his fist he showed the array of tiny spikes. Moral's eyes dropped.

"No, no please. I ..."

The spiked hand dropped and snatched the erect penis. The man screamed as the numberless spikes pierced him in a grip of iron. Moral began twisting his wrist, like revving the throttle of a motorbike. He twisted until there was nothing but a mass of ripped skin and blood left in his hands. The screams were intense. Moral leaned in close and whispered in his ear. 'The greatest symphony to my ears are your cries.'

He slapped the face of the screaming man, the spikes ripping though his cheek. A monstrous slash opened up, his teeth visible beyond. The screams died. Sitting the man up, Moral secured the seatbelt around his bleeding form.

Only moments had passed. Moral leapt from the limo, moving round to the driver's seat he ripped open the door. Josh sat beyond.

"Looking for these?"

Moral held up the limo keys, shaking them in his hand.

The fat man lashed out, the blade hidden moments before became visible when it struck Moral in the stomach. He spat the words out. 'Fuck you.'

Realisation struck Josh. The leather armour deflected the blade. Moral laughed. It was a cold terrible sound.

Moral heaved the fat man from the limo. He landed on the two bloodied bodies. Scrambling he pulled his massive frame to its feet. They faced each other, framed in the dark; pouring rain falling around them.

Josh pleaded. "What do you want? Money? I can give you as much as you want, just let me go."

Moral remained silent.

"Fuck," he moved the blade from hand to hand. "I know people who could break your fucking legs just as easily as look at you, if you want to get out of here alive let me go."

More silence. Moral watched; his head tilted to the side slightly.

"Please, I won't tell anyone about you."

Moral shook his head. The brief movement forced the fat man to action.

"I'll kill you, you fucking freak."

Josh lunged with the blade. Moral moved to the side, striking out as he moved. He caught him in the face. Josh stumbled past Moral. The fat man again slashed wildly. Missing. They again faced one another. His eyes darted from side to side, scanning for an escape, an escape that Moral now blocked.

Moral's bloody hand reached up to his left elbow. He pushed down. A loud click sounded. The homemade metal contraption unleashed its secret. A foot long blade issued from the sleeve. The steel although dull did not suffer, for it was sharp with lethal intent.

"Oh God, please No."

Moral spoke. Slow. "God? You know nothing of God. I am here to educate you."

Josh charged forward, a high-pitched scream torn from his throat. The blade snaked out and cut the suited figure across his hand. The knife fell. Crouching low Moral sped past the fat man bringing the razor sharp blade across the back of his knees. First one then the other. A howl of pain escaped his lips as the tendons were severed. Josh fell first to his knees then onto his back.

Like a predator sensing the kill Moral pounced and straddled him. The blade, poised waiting across the neck.

"Please. I have a wife and kids. Please. Don't kill me."

"I will not kill you. How many women have you and your associates done this to? I count three. It took me weeks to track you down. I have found you. I have judged you. Your punishment will be to wander this world an empty shell, like the victims you leave in your wake. A lifetime of penance and just a little bit of pain. Penance for the fallen."

Moral reached into his pocket, removing a small bible. He placed it on his chest.

"Get someone to read you this."

He punched the man sending his head snapping back striking the concrete. The blade moved from his neck to his hands. He stabbed and cut repeatedly. Several fingers were severed as each hand was ruthlessly lacerated. He did not stop until satisfied they were useless and beyond repair. Little more than tattered remains. The fat man went between quiet sobbing and cries of anguish.

"You asked me what I want. I will share a secret with you. I want to walk this city and not see evil such as you lurking in every darkened street. Like a parasite you leech of all that is what I love about this place. I will leave a message to the people of Aberdeen. It will no longer be tolerated. The infestation of your kind is over. Aberdeen has Moral."

The whimpering that came from the wounded man finally ceased. Finally silence. The pain taking him to blissful unconsciousness. In a heartbeat Moral used the tip of the blade to pierce the eyes, both were stabbed, they bulged until with a popping sound burst. Fluid seeped from the wounds. They eyelids were ruined. With his free hand Moral pulled each eyelid in turn. They snapped like elastic that had reached the end of its tolerance.

As a last act of punishment Moral forced open Josh's mouth. With a vice like grip he seized the tongue and began cutting through it. The blade made swift progress severing the tongue. Holding it up to the scant light Moral observed it as a butcher might a tender piece of meat. With little thought he threw the remains behind him.

"Judgment is served."

Moral brought forth a small leather pouch. From it he removed a medical clamp. Using it he stemmed the blood flow.

He tied tourniquets around the arms to stop the fat man from bleeding to death.

After a moment's pause, Moral stood. Taking the fat man's mobile from his jacket pocket he turned and walked to the cowering form of the girl, she screamed but could not flee, immobilised by fear and her weak ankle. Placing a finger to the shark smile, he motioned for silence.

She fell quiet.

"Take this and phone the police. Tell them what happened here."

He moved to leave when her quivering voice asked. "Why?"

He threw her a discarded overcoat from one of the occupants of the limo. Snatching it up, she covered her semi-naked shivering form.

"I am Moral and this city deserves better."

He ran, disappearing into the darkness of Aberdeen. A shadow returning home.

SEASONS GREETINGS
by
Phil Scott

"So ye made it have did ye? I might hiv guessed – a drunk aye finds his way hame even if it is jist tae collapse on his ain doorstep. Get up, get up ye drunken bastard ye, get up so's a can pit ye back doon, ye pathetic excuse fir a man.

The bliddy granbairns Xmas money – that's fit ye swiped – the granbairns Xmas. Nae doot the bookies and the bar'll hae it noo. I ken it's no gone on wimmin onywye, we all ken there's nae lead left in your pencil.

Get up ye feckless arsehole – look at ye, jist look at ye. God knows whit wye I got in tow wi you – a waste o'bliddy space. The biddy granbairns Xmas – ye should be ashamed o'yersel but there's nae danger o that – there's nae shame aboot ye. Aye, weel, you can explain to them fit wye they're nae getting ony presents fae us. An if you winna, I will. It's cos yer ganda's a stupid, selfish, alky drunken bastard.

The bliddy state o ye – aw Christ, ye've pished yersel as weel. Oh. That's real classy that – Jesus, maist men manage tae piss their money against the wall, you cannae even manage that. It widna be so bad if it wis yer ain money either – but it's no. ye've pulled some low stunts afore but that takes the biscuit.

An I'm sittin in the hoose bliddy freezing – nae money fir the meter and where are you? Oot pissin it up and chuckin notes at the bookie. Christ, they dinnae need a big windae tae see you comin! Last time ye backed a winner Lester Piggot wis on top o it. Ye useless piece o' shite, I should've left ye bliddy years ago. Aye, but I winnae. Will I whit? I'm bidin tae make sure yer life's a bliddy misery til the day ye die an it canna come quick enough, believe you me.

Aye, an dinna think I've been oot lookin fir ye either – I widna waste my time. I wis on my way tae Roberta's, I jist came back cos I forgot ma fags. Nae chance of hivvin ony eh? Nah, that's right, ye jist snore awa where ye are, ye fat bleezin pig that ye are. Mind you, nae harm in lookin eh?

Nah, nae fags bit.....here, whit's this? Christ, there must be ower a hunner pounds in yer pocket. So, maybe yir nae the worst punter in the world efter a. Aye, weel, this'll dae me n Roberta jist fine. An if I'm nae hame the morn dinna come lookin fir me – I'll be stawlin roon the shops fir the granbairns Xmas. Wi a massive hangover. See you later ye usles article ye."

THE HAGBERRY POT
by
Sandra Smith

The mouldering masonry of Gight Castle crumbled inwards on itself, almost as if it was rotten to the core. A blanket of ivy draped over the disintegrating stone, protecting the secrets of the castle's treacherous history. Standing desolately near the River Ythan, the dark empty ruins exuded an air of sadness. Although not far from the Gordon village of Methlick, the whole area felt remote and forlorn; a magical place lost in its own time. It had been Kate's idea to have a family adventure weekend, and having studied the local area she settled on this particular spot and do some wild camping. She led her family towards the crumbling carcass of castle, stumbling through the thick waves of grass. Enclosed by a wire fence, they climbed over, and Kate spread her hands over the moss riddled stone.

"Feel the history," she sighed, running her fingers over the braille of rock. Kate hoped her enthusiasm would rub off on her kids. She had goaded them into coming along this weekend, persuading them that it would bring the family closer, as lately, all they seemed to do was fight.

Rob peered through a gaping archway into the dark depths of decayed rubble, as he rubbed his hands over the stone walls.

"Yuk! It feels slimy, almost furry. Mum, I can't understand the attraction of a few bits of boulder and decayed branches. Why did you drag us out here?"

"You used to love castle ruins when you were a child."

Snorting, Rob dumped his rucksack onto the grass.

"Eh, hello? That child has long gone. I'll be leaving school next year, remember."

Kate sighed, despair etched on her face. Was it worth it?

It was Kate's fiftieth birthday the following month, and she was consciously aware there was more sand in the bottom of the hour glass than in the top. Both Rob and Jess were now independent teenagers and Kate felt she had lost her whole identity of late but she was now determined to rekindle her life. Tom, her ex-husband, called this her mid-life crisis – Kate called it escaping from the chrysalis and turning into a butterfly.

"Don't get upset, Mum." Jess picked her way over the carpet of rocks and stones. "I like it – it's very gothic. Do you think the castle could be haunted?" Jess sniffed. "And why are we the only ones here? We've been here for at least an hour and haven't seen another soul!"

Kate shivered as she scanned the valley around her. She looked at her daughter, acknowledging the same concern but perhaps they only felt this way after reading the ghostly stories in the guide book; maybe they ought to have waited until after this visit before exploring the castle's history. Suddenly sharp gunshots blasted in the distance and a flurry of feathers scattered through the wild grass in the valley below.

"Not quite alone," Kate replied. "Looks like someone is out shooting grouse - now let's see if we can find the Weeping Stone. Remember; from the guide book? 'Hidden away in the moss-covered dankness lies a Weeping Stone which continuously cries for the torment and troubled past the castle has endured.'

Rob smirked, turning his gaze towards the river.

"What rubbish!" he muttered.

"Well, I want to find it!" Jess snapped.

She studied the ruins, trying to imagine what the castle would have been like in its hey-day. Time had shrivelled any majestic qualities and all that remained was a deformed hulk of stone with empty, black, gaping holes. The castle was a brooding stone creature - a toothless witch.

"I can't believe there is so much history and folklore embroiled in one spot," said Jess. "This castle once belonged to Byron's mother, and the story... remember we read a story in the guide book about a ghostly piper?"

Howling, Rob turned towards Jess, his arms outstretched as he dragged his legs like a ghoulish zombie through the thick gorse.

"One night, during an awful storm, the piper of the castle, heavy with drink, staggered into the cave on the far side of the river, never to be seen again. Some say, on a dark night, the lonely cry of the pipes echo through the land...cree...py! I wonder if we will hear the ghost piper tonight!"

"Oh shut up! Mum!" Jess sighed, dumping her rucksack onto the ground. "That's it. I want to go home! I don't want to camp overnight in this God awful place!"

Kate glared at her teenage son, who flipped his hands up in the air, mockingly.

"Don't worry, little sister, it's only a story, probably invented long ago to keep people away from here, to stop them from trying to steal the Hagberry Pot treasure. Speaking of which, let's go down to the river. I want to see the Hagberry Pot."

Leaping ahead, Rob manoeuvred the kissing gate, and scrambled down the precarious path that led towards the river.

Kate and Jess followed at a more cautious pace. The path twisted down a steep incline, and from time to time, Kate paused, snapping with her camera.

"Look at that weird tree stump!" Jess laughed.

They paused to recover their breath and examined the grotesque stub of decayed tree that looked almost like a creature of nature, its head drooping towards the path, as branches flayed outwards behind it, like abandoned arms.

"Do you think he is the Keeper of the Hagberry Pot?" Jess continued. "The Old Stump Man stands guard; a protector of the lost treasure?"

"Jess, you really should do something with that imagination, but I admit I can see a strange beast like fellow. Even the moss that's foaming from the top of the trunk resembles a mop of hair! I'll take a photograph."

Finally they reached the bottom. It wasn't exactly the best place to camp, Kate thought, examining the boggy ground. She crossed the wooden bridge and decided it would be better to set up the tent on the opposite side of the river. She collapsed onto the grass, exhausted. The sun beat down, scattering beads of light on the water's surface. Kate lay back, resting on her rucksack. The particles of light shimmering on the water reminded her of gold coins – gold coins falling from the sky. A sudden shiver snaked up her spine as she realised this was a borrowed image from childhood. She had been four years old and it was a summer's day. It was difficult to remember the exact details, and Kate drifted back in time, floating on a nostalgic cloud of memory; childish laughter, jam sandwiches, splishing, splashing fun. She truly believed as a four year old that gold coins were falling from the sky onto the pool close to where they had picnicked and she had tried desperately to catch them, but it had only been the sun playing mischievous games of light. Blinking, Kate returned to reality and faced the cold dampness of dark water that stretched before her; a cold, hostile contrast to her sunny memories.

"Maybe we should go home," she muttered, but her fears were not acknowledged for Jess and Rob were standing on the bridge, playing a childish game of pooh sticks. Kate stared at the gloomy water and understood why such spooky tales had been written about it. She felt a chill of menace tapping into her mind. I've too much imagination, she thought, dismissing the dark thoughts blindly; I've read too many ghost stories and watched too many horror films.

The Hagberry Pot was a deep dark pool where the river seemed to bulge and ferment. Many believed it to be bottomless. In contrast to the torrent of rapids on the other side of the bridge, the Hagberry Pot was sluggish and still.

The surrounding land once belonged to the Gordons of Gight, a wild and fearless bunch who were well known for plundering and stealing in the area. Hundreds of years ago, one of the Gordon Lairds hid his stolen treasure in the Hagberry Pot and later sent down a diver to recover the treasure. The poor diver emerged, terrified, claiming that below the dark waters was a gate to hell, with the Devil and his worshippers there to welcome him. Angry that his treasure had not been recovered, the Laird apparently tortured the diver then forced him once more to delve into the pool. His dead body later reappeared on the surface in a froth of swirling bubbles, mutilated and cut to shreds.

211

"Fancy a swim? Perhaps we'll get lucky and find the Laird's treasure!" Rob stripped off his t-shirt.

"No!" Kate yelled. Oh, I'm being stupid, she thought, getting to her feet. It's only a silly story! Kate shrugged, admonishing herself for allowing her irrational fears to dominate.

"There's plenty of time for that later – we have other more important things to do. We need to set up camp! Come on, let's get on!"

The family spent the remainder of day exploring the thick woods, returning to the campsite for an evening feast of sausages and burgers. Indigo clouds swarmed over the skyline and the evening sun gently burnished in the twilight. The fire's flames flickered and glowed, a halo of light surrounded by gloomy shadows. Kate stoked up the fire and a blanket of silence encircled the campers, interrupted only by the occasional spark from the flames, and the lonely skaark call of a jay.

"Anyone fancy a twilight walk?" Kate asked. "I'd like to go back and explore the castle. According to the book, the only way to see the Weeping Stone is in twilight; they say it illuminates."

"I'm not sure," Jess sighed. "It looks kind of creepy."

Rob shrugged, refusing to budge.

"I'm going nowhere. Too tired, but Jess, well, you're such a coward. Frightened you will meet the Ghost Piper?"

Jess frowned and got to her feet. "On second thoughts, I'd rather go with Mum than be left alone with you!"

He watched as they crossed the bridge and began the ascent up the steep path. They disappeared into the knotted branches of the forest. Rob smiled and gazed up at the sapphire sky. He loved summer nights; the sky was a kaleidoscope of tangled blues and gossamer clouds, unlike the flat, solid blackness of winter.

The flames from the camp fire rippled on the inky water; a hypnotic amber snake dance. Sighing, Rob closed his eyes, lulled by the warmth of the smoky heat of the fire. He felt completely drained.

A screeching sound – a sound like the skirl of bagpipes scrambled his mind back to the surface of reality, and he jolted upright, snapping his head in all directions.

"What the…"

From behind him came a low growl, and Rob froze. A second growl and a chilling screech sliced through the air and Rob scrambled to his feet, leaping forwards, terrified. He spun round quickly, peering into the black beyond the fire. Panting with fear, his eyes darted frantically, trying to decipher reality from imagination. Branches like claws surrounded the clearing; mysterious skeletal foliage, but only a tree, he reminded himself, only a tree… a third growl ripped through the silence and startled, Rob pounced backwards, towards the river. Unbalanced, he slipped on the wet boggy ground, tumbling into the Hagberry Pot. His protests were silenced by the water.

He plunged downwards, waving his hands frantically, searching for something to hold onto. His hair meandered upwards from his skull, undulating sea snakes, dancing in the current. The water twisted, transforming into a giant aquatic beast, toying with his body, wringing it, shaking him violently, senselessly, until he opened his mouth to scream. A tidal wave of liquid burst into his lungs and he felt himself going deeper, deeper into blackness.

Thunder clapped, cats screeched, wolves howled, banshees screamed – noises penetrated his mind, peeling away reality. His soul sizzled in hot fat, a torrent of steaming acid rain slashed onto his skin, hell shrilled into his mind - silence. He had reached the pit of the pool.

He became a creature reborn – his soul detached from a lifeless body that floated above him, on the surface of the pot. Torn from the familiar, he explored this water kingdom with no body to embrace. He could still smell, still feel, still see, still think, but there was no material anchor of flesh to support these experiences.

Suddenly he was conscious of flaming red beads of eyes shimmering in the blackness of the swill, surrounding him.

The water curdled around Rob's soul, strangulating and suffocating. A chanting began; a slow, rhythmic growling chant as the water began to boil and sizzle. Shooting upwards from the bottom of the pool, a spectre of phantoms surged towards the surface, dragging Rob's lifeless body down into the dark gloom of the watery universe. The phantoms clamped onto Rob's body, slicing their elongated steely fingernails into his flesh, clawing and ripping his skin. Rob's soul screamed and thrashed in desperation, as he encircled the beasts who had laid claim to his body. Snarling, one phantom paused, glaring with conceited anger, as blood dripped from its snout; it howled.

"What was that noise?"

Kate turned to Jess, and shuddered. They were standing in the gloomy cavern of the Gight castle, as Kate shone her torch onto the walls, hoping they could find the Weeping Stone.

"I'm worried about Rob. Perhaps we'd best head back to the campfire. Besides, it's getting cold."

"Oh, but Mum, I wanted to find the Weeping Stone!"

"Look, it's time to go back! Enough's enough!"

Jess looked at her mum, in exasperation. "Mum, what's your problem? It was your idea we came here, not mine! I'm just getting into the swing of things! Do you really think I wanted to come on this lousy, 'field trip', to try at the end of the day to resuscitate family life? Well, sorry, Mum, but there is one thing missing and that's Dad!"

Kate stared at her daughter and suddenly crumbled, acutely aware of the shift between being needed and needing. She swung her arm out, trying to grasp hold of Jess, reassuringly, but her torch tumbled into the dark grass and stones, and she fell forwards into her daughter's arms.

"I'm sorry, darling, I'm trying my best."

"Mum?"

Kate savagely wiped the tears from her face. Damn it! She was not going to cry tonight! She wanted to be strong for her children, and lately, after the horrible divorce, she felt such a failure.

"I said I'm sorry, darling."

Kate smothered into her daughter's shoulders and sighed.

Behind Kate, a cloud of blackness gathered, as she felt the slow tug of Jess's body pushing her aside.

"Mum, turn around."

Kate felt Jess's nimble fingers guiding her slowly around until she faced away from her daughter.

She gasped!

Wedged between the dark blocks of the stone archway, the Weeping Stone glowed like a beacon in the twilight. The hidden inscription was now emphasised and trickles of tears danced over the crumbling stone, dripping onto the ground below.

"Oh, Jess!" Kate cried, clutching her daughter closer. "The Weeping Stone really does exist! We couldn't see it with the torch light!"

Quickly, Jess unscrewed her water bottle, emptying the contents on the ground.

She stood below the archway, catching the dripping tears of the stone in her bottle.

"What are you doing?"

"I'm capturing the tears. Isn't it amazing?"

Kate looked at her daughter, caught up in the fantasy of this beautiful, eerie place, and smiled. So be it. Everyone should be allowed fantasies.

"What does the inscription say? Can you read it?"

As Jess filled her bottle with tears, she read aloud the words inscribed in stone:

"Cast my tears into the pot,
To dispel the Devil's lot.
Tears from the stone
Will unwind all hell
Tears from the stone
Will undo the spell."

215

A screeching chanter of bagpipes blasted from the river below and Jess jumped backwards into her mother's arms.

"What was that?"

Kate shook her head, unable to comprehend the sound, but it was coming from the direction where they had left Rob!

"We need to get back to Rob!"

Kate searched frantically for her torch amongst the broken stone that scattered the grounds of the castle.

"Where is it? Damn, where's the bloody torch? Found it…..no, it won't work! Oh, hell! Jess, we need to go back to Rob! We'll just have to manage without a torch. Grab onto me and I'll guide you. Everything is going to be okay."

"But I'm frightened, Mum. What's happening? What was that horrible noise? It sounded like bagpipes! Oh, maybe it's the Ghost Piper!"

"Oh, don't be so silly. We are just panicking because it's getting dark, and we are not used to the countryside, remember? There are lots of strange noises that we don't understand. It was probably a bird of prey or something like that. Anyhow, Rob will be wondering where we are! Come on, there's a girl."

The sky was darker now and Kate realised how dangerous it would be to descend the steep path, but she was desperate to get back to her son. The last thing she wanted to do was frighten Jess, but she, too, was scared. Something very weird was going on. She suddenly wished for the strong arms of her ex-husband.

"Jess, keep close and hold onto me…Ahhhh!"

Kate tripped over a gnarled tree root and stumbled, falling onto the path. "Mum!"

Panic-stricken, Jess moved sideways, towards the edge of the trail. The soft ground crumbled beneath her feet and she slipped, sliding down the hillside. She grabbed hold of some tangled foliage growing from the side of the hill, and she hung there swinging like a pendulum in the breeze.

"Mum, help me! I can't hold on! I'm falling!"

Kate struggled onto her hands and knees as she searched about in the semi-darkness for her daughter's hands.

"I'm coming for you, Jess, I'm coming!"

Suddenly, there was a tormented sound of snapping and wrenching and a huge carcass of roots and bark tore away from the ground. Kate screamed, as the deformed hulk of "Stump Man" came to life. Hypnotised with fear, Kate stared at the face of the strange creature. She saw moss covered eyebrows shadowing dark hollows of eyes, and a drooping, gaping cave of a mouth.

The Stump Man lunged forwards, as Kate tried desperately to find her daughter's hands. Stooping over Kate, the strange tree like monster used its arm like branches to grab hold of Jess and uproot her from hillside.

"No!" Kate shrieked, grabbing her daughter's legs. A tug of war began between her and the Stump Man. Jess screamed as she thrashed wildly, desperate to escape from this supernatural being.

The Stump Man swung his head lower, and drew his face close to Jess. She recoiled, disgusted at the vile stench reeking from the Stump Man's mouth.

"The tears will save…" he croaked, and as Jess landed safely on the path, the Stump Man receded back into its original form and stood silently in the darkness of the night.

Kate crawled over to her daughter and held her close. "I have no idea what the hell is going on, Jess, but we need to find Rob and get out of here, now! Are you okay? You're not hurt?"

Jess shook her head. "Mum, I want to go home."

"I know, and so do I, but we need to find Rob first. Come on, be brave."

"What was that? What happened there? I want to go home! Tell me this is a nightmare! Tell me I'm not awake!"

Panting, Kate tried to compose herself. "Jess, I want you to calm down. I wish this was a nightmare, but we both can't be having the same dream! Jess, we need to find Rob. Come on, sweetie, we can do this."

Cautiously, they snaked down the remainder of the path until they became in full view of the Hagberry Pot. The camp fire on the other side of the river lit up the darkness revealing a frozen sheet of ice covering the pot.

"Mum," Jess whispered, "Why is the pool covered in ice? This is not winter. Mum? And that's not Rob on the bridge, is it?"

The lonely figure of the Ghost Piper turned as the bridge creaked beneath him. Kate and Jess grabbed each other as they stared at the grotesque creature staring back at them. Peeling skin flapped from its bones as the Ghost Piper snarled and blew into the blow stick of his bagpipes. Suddenly, he stopped, and the noise became a distorted whining. There was no sign of Rob.

"Where's my son? What have you done to my son?" Kate screamed.

The Ghost Piper sneered and spat a mouthful of maggots from his jaws.

"You want your son? Well, I want him too. I want him to join our legion, and live in the waters forever.

You dared to disturb us! Now, you have to pay the piper. You have lost your son! He belongs to us. He will grow to be like us and become one of us. I claim your son!"

Jess cowered behind her mother, as Kate stepped boldly forward.

"No, Mum, please no! Don't go near him. Don't leave me!"

"Where is he? Where's Rob? Rob! Rob!"

The Ghost Piper flicked his head towards the frozen pool.

"You want him? You think it's that easy? I find you ridiculous, but I also find you amusing. You want your son? He's in the water. He is lost to you forever."

Frantically, Kate scrambled onto the ice.

"You are not taking my son from me!" she cried, tears streaming down her face. The Ghost Piper cackled and lifted the blow pipe to his gaping mouth. He began to blow, pressing the bag with his right elbow. The noise ended abruptly, and when Kate looked up, the Ghost Piper had vanished.

Kate hammered on the frozen pool, smashing her fists on the cold ice. The ice began to crack, a creaking, crackling sound, as shooting fissures quickly disfigured the frozen lake of ice. Kate gasped as she suddenly felt icy water surrounding her.

"Mum!" Jess screamed, as she watched her mother sink beneath the ice.

I am facing death, Kate thought, as wetness bubbled around her. She landed clumsily on what appeared to be an ice shelf, floating below the surface of the pot. Kate tried to hold her breath, aware she would drown if she did not reach the surface, but after several minutes of panic she found, incredibly, she was able to breathe below water. The surface ice reformed above her, snapping together; she was a prisoner, caught below a frozen pool of ice. Gripping the edge of the platform, Kate peered downwards, realising she was on a floating island with many such islands scattered below her. At the bottom of the pot, she could see the savage water creatures tearing her son apart.

"No!" she screamed as she lost her balance.

The ice island wobbled, tilting to one side, and Kate slipped into the water, landing on another island of ice. The red eyes of the water phantoms stared up at her, grey globules of saliva dripping down their snouts.

Kate's tears mingled with the water and her screams were silenced in the liquid hell. Shooting up from the dark stench below were stalagmites of ice and Kate grasped hold of one, trying to recover her balance. What could she do? Suddenly the mass of ice she was on jilted precariously sideways and she lunged forwards into the water. She stretched her hands outwards, trying to find something to grab onto. Her hands slammed onto the needle-sharp, frosted spears below her and she screamed in pain, staring at the stigmatic ruptures of her palms. She was crucified to the ice. Beads of blood silently dripped downwards into the open mouths of the phantoms, and they began to scramble upwards, leaping and pouncing on all fours, intent on their prey.

Their sharp, elongated finger nails acted like crampons slicing onto the ice islands below Kate, and she realised her fate was sealed. Kate closed her eyes, awaiting the snarling Devil's Army to unleash on her.

Above surface, Jess screamed, and clambered onto the frozen water.

"Mum! No! Come back! Rob! Mum!"

Her thuds on the ice were met by silence, until exhausted, the rhythm of her beats began to slow down, and she eventually stopped. Jess melted her face into her hands, stumbling back to the river bank.

"I'm sorry, Mum. I don't know what to do."

She collapsed onto the grass, paralysed with resignation. Then suddenly, Jess remembered. The Stump Man!

"The tears will save, of course!"

Jess grabbed her water bottle and with shaking fingers, unscrewed it.

She screamed as she spurted the Weeping Stone's tears onto the frozen pool. She babbled the words from the inscription as she sprayed the ice with tears.

"Cast my tears into the pot…" she cried, "to dispel the Devil's lot."

Jess squeezed the last drops of tears from her water bottle.

"Tears from the stone will unwind all hell… tears from the stone will undo the spell!" The ice began to thaw.

The water below the melting ice began to spin into a vortex, rising in a spiral above the Hagberry Pot. Howling and screeching flung from the twisting coil, a storming debris of sounds.

"Mum! Rob!" Jess screamed. Finally, there was silence.

Jess shivered. On the other side of the pool, a burning fire raged. The flames devoured the camp site, reducing everything to ash.

There was no sign of her family.

"Mum? Rob?"

Jess collapsed onto her hands and knees and peered into the pot. The ice had finally melted. Jess dipped her hand into the pool, trying to assure herself the spell had broken. Her hand felt hot and sticky. Confused, she pulled her hand from the liquid and held it in front of her face. Her hand was crimson. Blood trickled down the white stem of her arm.

"Oh my God! Mum!" Jess sobbed. She retched, overcome by revulsion. Suddenly she felt her breath shoot from her lungs as she was lassoed tightly by the warped arms of Stump Man. Branches whipped around her and she was lifted into the air, hovering in a cradle of dead foliage over the pool of blood. Jess could hardly breathe. She stared up at the misshapen face of Stump Man, whose dead eyes drilled into her. He swung her sideways towards the bridge. Standing on the bridge was the Ghost Piper.

The Ghost Piper blew into his blow pipe, shattering the silence with a tortured whine.

Finally, he stopped and glared down at Jess.

"When will you ever learn? This is our domain, and how dare you assume you can invade it. Did you honestly believe it would be so easy to escape from Satan's grip? Can the blind now see? No?"

Jess tried to breath but it was becoming harder and harder. The Stump Man tightened his hold on her and she could not move.

The piper snarled and leaned over the edge of the bridge.

"My precious child, you were truly convinced it would be so simple to undo our curse. You thought it was all but a silly game, but you have no idea! The Weeping Stone cries? The tears will save? Nothing but an inscription of lies, my dear. Once more, another pathetic mortal is fooled by a stone.

And Stump Man? Well done for your observation. He is, indeed, the Keeper of the Pot. He only rescued you to lure you down to the water.

This evening has been grand entertainment; a little aperitif to whet the appetite. Oh, and I thank you for bringing the tears to the pot. You have been such a useful tool. The tears have turned the water to blood, as you can see, and now the spell can never be unbroken. The tears will save? They will save our Kingdom of Hell!"

The Ghost Piper cackled as woodlice streamed across his skull. He flicked his head, irritated, spraying the insects across the pool.

"Say goodbye to this world, child, for soon you shall join your beloved family in the pool. Do not cry, my dearest, for the best has yet to come. Why insist on clinging onto your flesh and blood? Why let the soul be harnessed when it can be free to join my legions of the deep! The body is merely a robe, to be discarded.

Do not be upset, for soon you shall join your mother and brother for hell eternity. I now have my Queen, and my Prince of Darkness and you shall be my Princess."

Jess tried to shake her head, but she felt herself drowning into blackness, unable to catch a breath. The piper howled and nodded at the Stump Man.

"Release her. Throw her in and let the feast begin."

The Stump Man untangled his knotted branches and Jess tumbled into the pot.

The piper lifted his blow pipe to his jaws.

"Welcome to Hell!"

As the Ghost Piper played an eerie lament, the Hagberry Pot began to bubble. The party had only just begun.

Other Titles from Cauliay Publishing

From The Holocaust to the Highlands By Walter Kress
Michael By Sandra Rowell
Child Of The Storm By Douglas Davidson
Poets Centre Stage *Vols 1&2* Various Poets
The Fire House By Michael William Molden
To Save My Father's Soul By Michael William Molden
The Upside Down Social World By Jennifer Morrison
Love, Cry And Wonder Why By Bernard Briggs
Buildings in a House of Fire By Graham Tiler
Revolutionaries By Jack Blade
The Haunted North *Paranormal tales* By Graeme Milne
Kilts, Confetti & Conspiracy By Bill Shackleton
Tatterdemalion By Ray Succre
The Strawberry Garden By Michael William Molden
Amphisbaena By Ray Succre
Underway, Looking Aft By Amy Shouse

Lightning Source UK Ltd.
Milton Keynes UK
02 February 2010
149433UK00001B/58/P